PRAISE FOR

The Trick

"As I flipped the pages, I was reminded of the best magic of all: love's ability to turn our greatest disappointments into our biggest blessings."

—*First for Women* magazine

"*The Trick* is a lyrical, uplifting, and funny story that will tug at all of your heartstrings. A true miracle from the first to the last page."
—Armando Lucas Correa, bestselling author of *The German Girl*

"Emanuel Bergmann is a formidable writer and he has meticulously weaved the story with two great characters. You will enjoy this brilliantly written debut novel no matter what your mood and age are."

—*The Washington Book Review*

"Haunting."

—*The New York Post*

"Bergmann's novel, a pleasing blend of Sara Gruen's *Water for Elephants* and Jonathan Safran Foer's *Everything Is Illuminated*, puts magic back into everyday life."

—*Booklist*

"Sweet, funny, magical."

—*Kirkus Reviews*

"The twin stories of Max and the octogenarian born Moshe Goldenhirsch in Prague will mesmerize readers as they move ever closer to the finale. While Max hunts down his quarry, I was envisioning the fortune-telling machine at the heart of the Tom Hanks film *Big*, but the images Bergmann creates are eerier and more devastating in his exceptional work."

—*Library Journal* (Editor's Pick)

"Bergmann's storytelling is a feat of magic in and of itself."

—RT Book Reviews

"A poignant story about one's true worth."

—Historical Novel Society

"By turns sentimental and quirky, *The Trick* has much to love, most notably a charming intergenerational friendship between a boy who clings to his magical thinking and a disillusioned old grouch. . . . Bergmann packs in enough magic and miracles to leave the reader under his spell."

—*Shelf Awareness*

"A lovely story . . . A tale for those who continue to look for magic in the world."

—*New York Journal of Books*

"The tragedy of the past weaves together with humor, love, and a belief in the impossible in *The Trick*."

—*BookPage*

"A wonderful, inspiring book. Don't miss it."

—*The Jerusalem Post*

"If you liked the book *A Man Called Ove*, then you'll like this book also. The whole book is beautifully written."

—David Halpern, Barnes & Noble, Akron, OH

"It brought me to tears and it was such a powerful and magical story. An emotional, amazing, and magical read. I cannot wait to recommend this to my customers."

—Toni Ness, Barnes & Noble, Grand Rapids, MI

"There was a lump in my throat and a tear in my eye as I came to the climax of this most endearing story. This debut is well worth reading, [over and over] again."

—Lynn Price, Barnes & Noble

"Bergmann manages to develop a character the reader can find both mesmerizing and menacing."

—Watermark Books & Café

"The aliveness of this novel is charged by its characters' simple quest to find the end, the proper end, to their own stories. I found myself reading increasingly quickly to get to the end, and since finishing have found the book hard to shake. To me, that's all you can ask in a novel."

—Steve Shapiro, bookseller

"This book grabbed my attention from the very first sentence. The writing is beyond anything I have ever read before. I felt as if the author was sitting in the same room with me, quietly telling me this tale."

—January Gray, librarian

THE TRICK

THE TRICK

A NOVEL

EMANUEL BERGMANN

ATRIA PAPERBACK

NEW YORK LONDON TORONTO SYDNEY NEW DELHI

Library of Congress Cataloging-in-Publication Data

Names: Bergmann, Emanuel, 1972- author.
Title: The trick : a novel / Emanuel Bergmann.
Other titles: Trick. English
Description: First Atria Books hardcover edition. | New York : Atria Books, 2017.
Identifiers: LCCN 2016050065 (print) | LCCN 2016058088 (ebook) |
    ISBN 9781501155826 (hardback) | ISBN 9781501155840 (eBook)
Subjects: LCSH: Magicians—Fiction. | Boys—Fiction. | BISAC: FICTION /
    Historical. | FICTION / Literary. | FICTION / General.
Classification: LCC PT2702.E4628 T7513 2017 (print) | LCC PT2702.E4628
    (ebook) | DDC 833/.92—dc23
LC record available at https://lccn.loc.gov/2016050065

ISBN 978-1-5011-5582-6
ISBN 978-1-5011-5583-3 (pbk)
ISBN 978-1-5011-5584-0 (ebook)

THE TRICK

THE WAY THINGS
OUGHT TO BE

In the early days of the twentieth century, in the city of Prague, lived a man named Laibl Goldenhirsch. He was a rabbi, an unassuming teacher who sought to understand the mysteries that surround us all. A daunting task, but he pursued it with heart and soul. He spent countless hours brooding over the Torah, the Talmud, the Tanakh, and other riveting reads. After years of learning and teaching, he slowly began to understand the way things are, but more importantly, the way they ought to be. There seemed to be some discrepancies between the shining glory of creation and the often baffling and rainy world in which we humans are forced to spend our lives. His students valued him, at least the ones who weren't fools. His words could light up the darkness like a candle.

He lived with his wife, Rifka, in a tiny apartment in a ramshackle tenement building near the banks of the Vltava River.

Their home consisted of only one room. They didn't own much. A kitchen table, a woodburning stove, a sink, and, of course, a bed that creaked rhythmically during each Sabbath night, as it was written and decreed.

Between the floors of their building was a miracle of modernity, an indoor toilet. To their daily annoyance, they had to share it with their upstairs neighbor, Moshe the Locksmith, a noisy man, an oaf, who fought frequently and loudly with his unpleasant wife.

Rabbi Goldenhirsch lived in a time of great renewal, but for the most part he remained blissfully untouched by the momentous changes around him. Just a few years earlier, the gas lamps on the streets had been replaced by electric ones, which had people divided. Was it the work of Satan or was it socialism? Also, steel tracks had been laid by the banks of the river, and soon the carriages that used to rattle up and down the roads made way for a tram, its metal wheels screeching and emitting sparks of fire.

This is what it looked like, the everyday magic of a new age.

Laibl Goldenhirsch had little use for it. Trams or no trams, life was hard. He went about his daily work in much the same way that the Jews of Europe had done for centuries and would presumably do for centuries to come. He didn't ask for much, and as a result, he didn't receive much either.

His face was narrow and pale; he had a black beard. His eyes were deep and dark, and he peered out at the world with a certain amount of distrust. At night, after the hardships of the day, the rabbi rested his head on a pillow next to his beloved wife, Rifka, a strong and beautiful woman with rough hands, gentle eyes, and flowing auburn hair, and he imagined that he could see the stars above the ceiling. His eyes wandered far into the heavens, then turned like a leaf in the breeze and looked back down to earth, this tiny spark in the universe. As exhausting as life could be, there was—behind the thin veil of the ordinary—a brilliance that mystified and exhilarated him. "The simple act of living," he liked to say, "and living well, is in itself a prayer."

Lately, however, he couldn't sleep. Night after night, he would lie in bed and stare into the darkness. In this new age of man-made wonders, was there no more room for real miracles? Rabbi Goldenhirsch was in need of one.

There was something missing in his life: a son. He spent his days teaching the sons of other men—idiots, the lot of them—and when he looked at them, he imagined that one day he would look into the face of his own child. So far, his prayers went un-answered. The sun rose for others, but not for Laibl and Rifka. Many a night, the rabbi toiled away on top of his wife, but it was fruitless. And so the bed creaked less and less.

※

The new century was still young when a war broke out. This was, in and of itself, nothing remarkable. Wars were always breaking out, like the flu. But this war was unlike others, even though Rabbi Goldenhirsch and his wife failed to notice it at first. This was the Great War. It would soon leave millions dead in its wake. It was no flu, it was the plague. His students asked him to explain what was going on, and for the first time in his life, he was confronted with something beyond his reach. Until now, he could simply blame God and His mysterious ways, but this new war was anything but divine. The rabbi was perplexed. He stood in front of his class, his mouth hanging open, stuttering helplessly. He knew the plain facts, of course. Archduke Franz Ferdinand had been assassinated in Sarajevo at the hands of a coward. But Sarajevo was far away from the center of the civilized world, deep in the Balkans: what did it matter if someone was shot there? The goyim were always shooting at one another. Was one archduke less really such a tragedy? He knew, of course, that human life was immeasurably precious, that each violent death was an act of blasphemy and so forth, and he understood why the emperor of Austria-Hungary—to whom he and the citizens of Prague had sworn their allegiance—was upset. But really, why should this concern him?

But it did, greatly. Within a few months, agitation spread through the streets of Prague. Old men paced around the cafés, shaking their fists and waving newspapers around. Everyone tried to make sense of the latest developments on the front. Women anxiously gathered at Wenceslas Square, trading information about their sons, husbands, brothers, and fathers, who had eagerly joined the war effort. Very few realized that most of their men would never return. Those who were too young to fight studied the lists of the wounded and fallen, published every day, like the results of a soccer match. How many of ours? How many of theirs? The young were anxious to fight, and they would soon get the chance. The war raged on for many years and, in the process, became less and less choosy: it devoured all.

Even the Jews.

And so it happened that, one sunny day, Laibl Goldenhirsch was conscripted into Emperor Franz Joseph's army. When Rifka came home from the market, she burst into tears. Her spindly-legged husband was standing uneasily in front of their only mirror, dressed—somewhat unusually—in a uniform. He seemed confused as he held out his bayonet.

"What do I do with this?" he asked her.

"You stick it in a Russian," Rifka replied, fighting against tears, but in vain. She hid her face and turned away.

And so, Laibl Goldenhirsch marched off to a war he still didn't understand.

Rifka had to survive without her husband. Which, as it turned out, was remarkably easy. She realized that he really was rather useless around the house. She missed him anyway. Never before in her life had she missed something so useless with so much fervor.

Almost every day, Rifka left the city and went into the woods outside of Prague, carrying two buckets full of coal, which she traded for butter and bread at nearby farms. Better to be cold than hungry.

When summer approached and the days grew warmer, her endeavor became more difficult. She had to find other things to take to the country, and on the way back, she hid the butter under her skirt. Danger was everywhere. More than once, there was nothing left by the time she came home, especially when there was partisan fighting and she had to hide in the woods until it was over. Nothing left but a warm trail of molten butter running down her thighs.

One evening in September, as she came home, she found Moshe the Locksmith from upstairs sitting on the staircase. He wore a ragged soldier's uniform, and he was weeping. It was odd to see this giant of a man crying, his heavy bulk wavering, his head bobbing up and down. Deep and sorrowful sobs emerged from his body. When she went up to him and asked him what was wrong, he told her that he had just returned from the front, on furlough, but no sooner had he entered his apartment than his wife had told him it was over between them. He hadn't heard from her in a while. No letters, nothing, he said between sobs. Rifka felt sorry for him. She had never cared much for the Locksmith's wife, and she wasn't terribly surprised that the cow had left the pasture.

She took him into her arms and comforted him. The butter was still sticking to her leg.

※

One bright Wednesday morning, Laibl Goldenhirsch returned from the front. He was limping, but otherwise in the best of spirits. Rifka was sewing a shirt when the door opened, and looked up to see his gaunt shape leaning against the doorframe. So bony! So thin! She dropped her needle and thread and flung herself into his weak arms. He held her, as best he could, and tears of joy streamed down her face.

"Good news," said Laibl, holding up his bayonet. "The Russian was quicker—he stuck me first. They put me in a field hospital."

Laibl's injuries were hardly dramatic. He showed Rifka a scar on his thigh. His commanding officer, he said, had spoken up for him, and he didn't have to go back to the front. He was allowed to recuperate at a sanitarium in Karlovy Vary. He had a limp, but Laibl was now officially a wounded veteran. He sat down. Rifka gave him bread and asked him to tell her about the war. But his smile froze, and he seemed to be looking straight through her. Taking her hands in his, he gently kissed her fingertips. She searched in his eyes and found nothing but darkness. He shook his head. They made an unspoken pact to not talk about the front.

Three weeks later, after years of war, peace finally came. The war to end all wars had ended, and people were celebrating in the streets. Peace, peace at last, only without the glorious victory that had been promised. At least the nightmare was over. The survivors drank and sang, happy to be alive. People were bellowing and dancing, a few windows were broken, why not? Despite all that, there was a tangible feeling of shame, a deep sense of exhaustion. The people of Europe had grown tired of fighting and dying. Revolutions had broken out in Russia and Germany. The czar and his family were slaughtered. The emperor of Germany went on vacation, opting not to return. The Kingdom of Bohemia became the Republic of Czechoslovakia. Good news, all in all. But not as good as the news that Rifka had for Laibl Goldenhirsch:

"I am pregnant."

Rifka's husband was stunned. He could hardly believe it. How was this possible? All right, the bed had creaked for the first few nights after his return, but wasn't it too early for the pregnancy to show? Rifka's belly had already grown slightly larger underneath her dress.

Laibl was pacing up and down, his black overcoat flapping about like the wings of an agitated pigeon. And as Rifka looked out the window, she suddenly had an idea. What was it that the goyim believed? What was it that their alleged Virgin Mary had said to Joseph?

"It's a miracle," Rifka exclaimed.

"A what?" said Laibl.

"God has worked a miracle for us." As she said this, she cast her eyes downward in what she hoped was an appropriately virtuous manner. She managed to make her lips and hands tremble ever so slightly, because she seemed to remember that miracles were generally accompanied by trembling.

"A miracle?" the Rabbi asked. He was baffled. As a rabbi, he was something of an expert on the subject of miracles. And this one seemed suspicious.

"*Oy gevalt!*" he said.

"Look around you," Rifka said. "God makes everything happen. Everything! Why wouldn't he make a miracle happen for us? Surely he must know how much you wanted a son."

She felt certain that it would be a son. She walked over to Laibl and put her head on his shoulder. She whispered sweetly into his ear. "God has granted your wish."

Rabbi Goldenhirsch was still distrustful of the miracle. Also, his stomach was unwell.

"It was an immaculate conception," said Rifka.

"Nonsense," said the rabbi. "Every conception is maculate. This one especially. Who is the father?"

"The father is God," said Rifka stubbornly. "I was visited by an angel."

The rabbi threw his hands up in the air and began pacing once more. As night fell, he was no closer to solving this mystery. He decided he needed a break. The growling in his stomach was getting thunderous.

"I'll be right back," he said. After removing the large toilet key from the hook by the door, he stormed out of the apartment, slamming the door behind him. He went up the staircase, where the miracle of modernity awaited him.

It was occupied.

He waited patiently, more or less, bouncing on the balls of his feet. A few minutes later, he was seized by restlessness. He knocked. He heard a gruff voice from inside, and some rustling. Finally, after what seemed like an eternity in the dark and cold staircase, the door opened.

His noisy oaf of an upstairs neighbor, Moshe the Locksmith, came out, grumbling something incoherent, perhaps a greeting, then quickly averted his eyes to the floor as he furtively hurried past the rabbi. He was a large man, clumsy in movement and mind, too big for his own body, his arms and legs barely covered in torn rags. Like a golem. The rabbi looked after him.

A thought occurred to him. "Moshe!" he called.

"Yes?"

The Locksmith stared at the rabbi. There had always been a strain of animosity between the two men. The rabbi considered the Locksmith a lowlife idiot, and the Locksmith thought of the rabbi as an arrogant fool. Laibl Goldenhirsch looked into Moshe's eyes, hoping to detect something, anything, a strain of guilt, perhaps.

"I meant to ask you something," the rabbi cautiously began.

Moshe simply nodded and continued to glare. If he felt any guilt, he certainly didn't show it.

"It's about . . ." Laibl didn't get any farther. His words ran out like water on sand.

"Yes?"

Another attempt: "It's about a lock."

"What about it?"

"I can't get it to open," the rabbi explained. "My key, I stick it in and wriggle, but . . ." He fell silent. Then he gathered his thoughts and said, "Nothing is happening."

"Must be the wrong key," said the Locksmith with the arrogance of an experienced tradesman talking to an amateur.

Laibl Goldenhirsch was left standing in the gloom of the staircase.

Suddenly, he heard Moshe call out to him from above, "Rabbi? Are you still there?"

"Yes," he said.

Silence. Then, after a few seconds, he could hear Moshe's voice. It was quavering. "Forgive me," said the Locksmith, barely audibly, as if his words had been swallowed by the darkness.

"For what?"

Another pause. Rabbi Goldenhirsch heard a single, desperate sob echo through the staircase.

"I miss her," Moshe said. Then he trampled up the last few wooden steps and fled to his apartment, banging the door shut.

The rabbi was puzzled.

Glancing out the round window above the staircase, he observed the nearby snow-covered roofs glistening in the moonlight. The sight was so beautiful it bordered on the miraculous. A thought occurred to him: The truth of a miracle is measured by faith alone.

He saw a cloud drifting toward the pale brightness of the moon. The rabbi was thinking: if the cloud managed to hide the moon completely, he would take it as a sign from God. He would accept the birth as a miracle.

He watched, spellbound, as the cloud slowly floated across the night sky.

Then it covered the moon. For a moment, the rabbi stood in complete darkness, as if the world were yet unformed.

When the cloud moved on, the milky moonlight engulfed his face. Suddenly, his anxiety left him. He stood there, trembling in the cold, his feelings like the bottomless sea. Waves of gratitude and love rose to the surface and drove salty tears down his cheeks.

He took a deep breath and opened the toilet door. He went inside, closed the door, unbuttoned his trousers, lifted his overcoat, sat down, pressed his eyes shut, and chose to believe. Every child is a gift, and he decided to accept it as such. Why look a gift horse in the mouth?

THE END OF IT ALL

In the early days of the twenty-first century, in the City of Angels, lived a boy named Max Cohn. About three weeks before his eleventh birthday, his parents took him to a sushi place on Ventura Boulevard and told him they were getting a divorce. They didn't come out with it right away. For most of the evening, they pretended everything was normal. But Max had a suspicion that something was wrong. They were just too nice to him. He pretty much knew what was coming, right from the start. His best friend in school, Joey Shapiro, had the same thing happen to him a couple of months ago, making Joey something of a tragic hero in class, the object of much admiration and pity. Joey had tasted the bittersweet nectar of tragedy, and he was one step closer to adulthood than the rest of them.

Joey had given Max a piece of sage advice: "They'll take you out to dinner. And they'll ask you what you want to eat."

He leaned in closer and whispered, "I made a mistake and said pizza."

"So?" Max asked, thinking, What's wrong with pizza?

"So we went to Mickey's Pizza Palace."

Ah, Mickey's Pizza Palace! Max knew it well. A fast food chain for the very young. The pizzas were gigantic, and the place had lots of video games and other fun stuff. This is where he was hoping to celebrate the momentous occasion of his birthday.

"Yeah, so?"

"I ordered a medium pepperoni with extra cheese."

"So? Go on!"

"Then they told me that there were getting divorced. And all I could do was sit there with my pizza. . . ."

At that point in the narrative, Joey made a weird choking noise and averted his head. "As long as I live, I'll never eat pizza again," he said.

This came as a shock to Max. Parents divorce, sure, whatever, but he'd always assumed that pizza was one of those things in life you could count on.

At first, Max had taken comfort in the fact that his own parents would never do anything like that to him. They loved him, they loved each other, they loved Bruno the Bunny—a charming animal who mostly sat in his cage and wiggled his pink nose—and that was that. Or so he thought. But then he began to notice small details that weren't immediately apparent, hints of a larger picture. Mom wiping her eyes, her eye shadow smeared as if she'd been crying. Dad staying away from home a lot, having to "work late," even on the weekends. Or sleeping on the downstairs sofa, with the TV on, which Max was totally forbidden to do. Doors that had previously been open were now shut. Something was wrong, he could sense it.

One day, when he came home from school and left his bicycle on the front lawn, he found both Mom and Dad sitting rigidly on the sofa, giving him fake smiles.

"How about going out for dinner?" Dad said. His voice was too cheerful. Too loud. Alarm bells went off in Max's head. "You choose," Dad said.

"What do you mean?" Max said.

"Where would you like to eat?"

Max thought for a moment. And then he said, "How about sushi?"

His parents looked at him in bewilderment.

"Are you sure, honey?" Mom asked.

"Yeah," Max said. He figured, so what if he never ate raw fish again in his life.

They went out for sushi. Max had tuna, swordfish, and sea urchin eggs, even though Dad said that sea urchin wasn't kosher. Max ate it anyway, and it was so gross, he almost puked, and when his parents suddenly held hands and told him that they both loved him very much and that nothing would change for him, he turned red, fought against tears, and started shivering. His mouth was full of fish cum or whatever it was, and in his head, he kept repeating to himself, At least there'll still be pizza.

Up until this point, Max's life had been fairly normal. Max was a standard-issue ten-year-old, lanky, with pale skin and unruly red hair. He wore a pair of glasses that his mom had fixed with electrical tape after Dad had sat on them one day. He lived with his family in a one-story house in Atwater Village. His dad was a "music-licensing attorney," whatever that meant, and his mom owned a small boutique on Glendale Boulevard, where she sold Asian furniture and various knickknacks. His family also had the usual assortment of aunts, uncles, and cousins, the worst of which probably were Uncle Bernie and Aunt Heidi, who were always bickering. And then there was Grandma, a difficult, high-strung woman who lived on the other side of the mountains, somewhere in the wilderness of the San Fernando Valley, in a far-away place called Encino.

The news of Max's parents' impending divorce spread through his class like a wildfire. Joey Shapiro gave him a sympathetic hug, and the girls started looking at him differently. Even Myriam Hyung, with whom he'd had hardly any contact so far, found a few kind words to say.

"Sorry about your folks."

Yada yada, he thought. But realizing she was only a girl, not capable of really understanding, and not wanting to be completely dismissive of her feeble attempt at human kindness, he graciously accepted her condolences and replied, "Yeah, whatever."

Today he was a man. Your parents' divorce, Max realized, is your true bar mitzvah. It is a rite of passage separating boys from men. He began to realize how many of his classmates came from what Rabbi Hannah Grossman called "broken families."

At first, being from a broken family was awesome. Nothing changed much in the beginning, except that Mom now slept alone in the master bedroom and Dad had to make do on the foldout couch in the living room, which was annoying. Because that's where the TV set was, which Max had always regarded as his personal property. Now Dad took over, watching sports all the time. But there were advantages. Max relished playing the role of martyr. He was showered in an amount of attention and comic books previously unknown to man. His mom bought him the latest issue of *Spider-Man* as well as several *Batman* trade paperback collections. Used to be that Max had to choose: Marvel vs. DC. Dad always said that life is about the choices we make. Which, as it turned out, was a load of crap. You could, in fact, have everything—that's what being an adult meant. Without a doubt, his parents' separation was the best thing that had ever happened to his comic book collection.

But deep down, he was worried. He had a secret. He knew why his parents wanted a divorce: it was his fault. Sure, according to Mom, they had to split because Dad had not been able to keep his hands off that "slut of a yoga instructor." But Max knew the truth.

It had happened a few weeks before the fateful sushi night. Max had once again been forced to clean out the bunny cage. Mom had repeatedly pointed out to him that he was the one who had wanted the damn rabbit in the first place. Therefore, bunny duty fell entirely on him. But this time, he asked Dad to do it. Just this once. Pretty please, with sugar on top. Max wanted to go to the movies with Joey Shapiro. And Dad said no. This led to an argument; then Max lost his patience and grumbled at Dad, and Dad defended his point even more bitterly.

So instead of enjoying popcorn and ice cream in an air-conditioned movie theater, Max had to clean out bunny poo. So unfair! When he finally, with much protest, brought out the trash bag, Dad stood by the door and glared disapprovingly at him. "Watch your tone," he said. "That's not how this works, young man. One more peep from you, and we'll give up Bruno for adoption."

Max threw the trash out, like he was supposed to, but he could feel torrents of rage roiling inside him. Give up Bruno! How mean!

Then he saw a penny by the trash bin and remembered Grandma saying that if you find a penny, you can pick it up, close your eyes, and make a wish. You mustn't tell anyone what you wished for. And it'll come true.

He picked up the penny, squeezed his eyes shut as hard as he could, and wished that Dad was gone. Just like that. When he opened his fist, the penny was still in his hand. He heard the distant rumble of thunder in the San Gabriel Mountains. It would rain soon. Max suddenly felt bad. He looked around and immediately squelched his thought, but it was too late. Someone—God, maybe?—must have heard him thinking. A terrible chain of events was set in motion.

For the first few weeks, Max thought he'd gotten away with it. Until the night at the sushi place. That's when Max knew that he had cursed his family. Except the bunny, who seemed okay.

Initially, Max tried not to think about his part in this tragedy too much. Instead, he enjoyed the bounty that came with his parents' divorce. His mom started giving him plenty of gifts, presumably to outdo Dad.

"I'll get you anything you want for your birthday," Mom would say to him, in an attempt to purchase his feelings. Max was easily purchased.

"Anything?"

Every toy was proof that his parents still loved him. But the proof was fleeting. There was no more certainty in his life. Everything began to change, and Max didn't particularly appreciate change. Turned out it wasn't all that cool to come from a broken family. Au contraire, he realized there were consequences! There was a lesson to be learned, a lesson that his heroes—Spider-Man and Joey Shapiro—had learned the hard way.

※

Telling their son was one of the hardest things Harry and Deborah Cohn had ever done. Harry in particular dreaded that moment, since he usually tried to avoid confrontation. Deborah not so much. Though officially a Buddhist, she seemed to thrive on conflict. Harry always joked that she was a "Raging Buddhist," but she didn't find that funny. In fact, she found very little about her husband funny these days. Seeing him mope around the house, with that guilty look on his face! Traits that she used to find endearing were now nauseating to her. She could hardly wait for him to get out.

But, of course, there was Max. They even considered staying

married for his sake. Or rather, Harry considered it. Deborah didn't.

"I want you out," she said firmly. She said it not just because she wanted to punish Harry, although that was certainly a factor. No, she said it because his affair had left her deeply wounded. She needed to be rid of him, and couldn't stand to look at him anymore. It was like tearing off a Band-Aid. You did it quickly.

"But what about Max?" Harry whined.

"Max," Deborah replied, "is better off without you."

And so it went. They tried to remain civil to each other, but almost every discussion ended in a heated argument.

"How are we going to tell him?" Harry asked Joey's mother when she stopped by their house one afternoon to pick up her son.

"Try to make it as easy on him as you can," said Mrs. Shapiro, who had some experience in these matters. "And do it on neutral ground, such as a restaurant."

Deborah nodded and typed some notes into her phone.

One sunny morning not long afterward, Deborah took the freeway to Woodland Hills. The law firm of Gutierrez & Partners was on the third floor of a vast glass monstrosity of an office building, a monument to bad taste. The inside wasn't any better. The waiting room was adorned with a painting of dogs playing poker. Who buys crap like that? Deborah wondered. Divorce attorneys, evidently. Then she was called into his office.

Mr. Gutierrez, the senior partner, stood up and shook her

hand limply. He was an unnaturally cheerful man, given the nature of his profession, a smiling, paunchy, and jolly executioner of love.

"What can I do for you?"

She explained the situation, and he listened, nodding silently. After some back-and-forth, Harry and Deborah had decided on an "uncontested divorce." Deborah had found the term online. It simply meant that they weren't going to court over their belongings, or to fight over custody. Mr. Gutierrez seemed a tad disappointed to hear that, having looked forward to many billable hours.

He explained that an uncontested divorce was simplicity itself. Deborah would file the papers and then they would be sent over to Harry, so he could look them over. Provided that both parties agreed on the terms, the petition would then be sent over to the LA Superior Court, where a judge would review it. If everything was deemed acceptable, both parties would sign the divorce decree and that would be that. They could be divorced within a matter of weeks and their life together would finally be over.

The wedding had been way more complicated, Deborah thought.

One thing was obvious to Harry and Deborah: they didn't want to subject Max to prolonged court battles. They didn't want him to have to choose between one parent and the other. They agreed on how to proceed once Harry moved out, which was taking way too long, in Deborah's opinion. They decided that Deborah would have Max during the week, and Harry would keep him from Friday to Sunday. He would pick him up and drop him off at school, so that there'd be as little contact between Harry and Deborah as humanly possible.

These were trying days for them all. Harry started drinking again, and Deborah took up smoking, a habit that she thought she'd kicked. Both began having difficulties in their respective careers. Deborah began missing meetings with wholesalers and suppliers, despite her frantic use of modern technology, and Harry simply showed up to the office a little bit too late every day, frequently hungover. His coworkers were reasonably forgiving, at least for a while. Harry soon realized that getting divorced bought you a lot of points at the water cooler. The women in the office began doting on him. But he found it hard to concentrate, and his performance was beginning to suffer.

Both Deborah and Harry felt as if their lives were slipping through their fingers like sand.

THE MIRACLE

Lying on the bed in their small apartment, Rifka Golden-hirsch cursed the world. She cursed herself and her husband, but most of all, she cursed the angel who had gotten her pregnant. Her husband Laibl remained at her side, holding her hand like a fool.

"There, there," he said, patting her hand in a misguided attempt to comfort her.

Rifka's legs were propped up on two rickety chairs. There was a pot of water boiling on the stove, clean towels were lying beside the bed, and Magda the Midwife was stationed between her legs, eagerly awaiting the outcome.

Rifka had grown up in the country, in a small village near Plzeň. As a young girl, she had sometimes watched as the cows were calving, a seemingly agonizing procedure that took several days and was accompanied by loud and indignant mooing.

Now she understood how they must have felt. And her useless schmuck of a husband was sitting next to her, condescendingly patting her hand.

Magda looked up at her and said, "I can see the head."

Rifka moaned.

"Push," Magda said.

"What does it look like I'm doing?"

Magda was a young *goyta*, a gentile, who lived just outside Josefov. She was said to be one of the best midwives in the city, which meant that most of the children she helped to deliver actually lived. Rabbi Goldenhirsch had assiduously put aside a few coins each month to be able to afford her services when the time came. And now the time had come. The days were getting warmer, and summer would see a new child. Magda dabbed at Rifka's forehead with a clean handkerchief; Laibl petted her hand. Her child took its own sweet time to come out.

But finally, it did.

Magda held the baby by the legs, cut the umbilical cord with a hot kitchen knife, and smacked its *tuches*.

The baby started crying, a sharp scream piercing the thick and sweaty stillness of the room. Magda wiped it off with the warm towels, careful not to burn or blemish it. Then she handed the child to its mother. "A boy," she said. "Strong as an ox."

Rifka took the child in her arms, looked at it, and fell in love. This was the most beautiful thing she had ever seen.

"What should we call him?" said Rifka, out of breath, exhausted but at peace with the world.

"How about Moshe?" said Laibl with a hint of sarcasm.

"Moshe?" asked his wife. "Why Moshe, of all things?"

"What, you don't like 'Moshe'?" answered the rabbi. "It's a fine name. Don't you think?"

"Like the Locksmith?" she asked suspiciously.

"Like the prophet," Laibl replied. "Moses." There was a strange and determined gleam in the rabbi's eyes, and Rifka felt it better to relent.

And so it came to pass that the boy was named Moshe Goldenhirsch. Even though his father would occasionally question his lineage, especially after one too many glasses of pilsner, he was, all in all, happy to have a child. He tried telling himself that he didn't care who the father was, and he thanked God every night for the miracle.

Moshe Goldenhirsch turned out to be a small and sickly child. Not long after his painful birth, life seemed to drain from his body. He lay in his crib next to the stove, his skin as pale as wax, and he hardly moved, making pitiful gurgling sounds.

Rifka sat by his crib and sang him a song:

> *Far above in the distant sky*
> *The wind carried a lonely cry*
> *Far above, where eagles fly*

Her singing did nothing to better Moshe's health. Eventually, Rifka became so worried that she left Josefov in the middle of the night to fetch a doctor. Her husband stayed behind with the child. He had told her about the doctor, a man named Ginsky.

Rifka ran all the way from Josefov across to the other side of the Vltava River, then up the hill to the castle. The night air was wet and cold, and she was drenched in icy sweat by the time she reached her destination. The sidewalks were covered with red and yellow leaves, and with chestnuts that had fallen from the trees. At last, she found the doctor's house, near the Hrad Castle. She could see the many turrets looming in the night sky, and felt the gargoyles of St. Vitus Cathedral glaring down at her. The doctor lived in a splendid art-nouveau mansion. She banged on the door, and after a few minutes a disheveled maid answered. Her face was flushed and she was straightening her underskirt with her left hand. Her eyes gazed coldly up and down the sweaty, bedraggled woman.

"Dr. Ginsky," Rifka uttered.

"He has already retired," said the maid curtly.

"My husband sent me." Rifka pointed out that her husband wasn't just anyone, he was the rabbi of the Staronová Synagogue.

"A Jew?" asked the maid with some amazement.

"He said to tell the doctor that he helped him once." And then she added, pleadingly, "Please. My child is dying."

Her words moved the maid's heart. "Come in," she whispered. "Wait here." She pulled Rifka into the villa's foyer, closed the door, and then hurried upstairs.

Rifka looked around the entrance hall. What luxury! A tall, wooden clock was ticking ominously. Expensive furs and hats hung on a coatrack, and mahogany walking sticks protruded from an umbrella stand. Dr. Ginsky, small and pudgy, came hurriedly down the carpet-covered staircase. He was dressed in a nightshirt, which he nervously struggled to adjust. His face was red, his glasses foggy, and the few hairs remaining around his mostly bald pate were sticking straight up. It occurred to Rifka for the first time that maybe she had interrupted the doctor and the maid during some important business.

She looked at him imploringly and held out her hand.

Ginsky stared at her. "I'm afraid," he said, "I cannot shake your hand, since you are a member of the Mosaic tribe." He looked at the floor, embarrassed.

"I understand," said Rifka and nodded. She did not want to do anything that might incur his displeasure. After an awkward moment, she dropped her outstretched hand and nervously wiped it on her wet skirt.

"To what do I owe the pleasure of your unannounced visit?" the doctor asked.

"My child is ill."

"And I am the only medical practitioner in all of Prague?" he asked.

"My husband said I should go to you. Only you."

"And why me, pray tell?"

"We . . ." She paused, then she swallowed hard. "We have no money," she finally said and averted her eyes.

"Of course," said the doctor.

"My husband is a teacher. Truly, we have not much."

"And what is the name of your husband?"

"Goldenhirsch. Laibl Goldenhirsch."

The doctor stood there with his mouth open, and for a moment did not move. Then he removed his glasses, wiped them on his nightshirt, and said, "Why didn't you say so in the first place?"

Rifka had never sat in an automobile before. Had she not been so frantic about her son's health, she probably would have enjoyed the experience. As it was, it struck her as rather uncomfortable. Her *tuches* felt every bump of the cobbled street. The motor emitted foul-smelling steam and chugged along slowly. When Dr. Ginsky's automobile finally reached the tenement building by the Vltava, they had difficulties finding a place to park it. Rifka was convinced that these so-called cars would never catch on.

She proceeded to lead the doctor up the stairs. He was huffing and puffing, and after only one floor, he was out of breath. By the time they reached the door to their apartment, Rifka worried that the doctor's heart might fail. She knocked and Laibl let them in, holding the sickly child in his arms. Rifka was touched, not just by how weak her boy looked, but also by the obvious tenderness with which Laibl held him. She had never seen her husband so attached to the child. *His* child, she reminded herself.

Laibl had tears in his eyes. Rifka gently took the baby from him.

Dr. Ginsky entered the room and looked around disdainfully. Then he and Laibl faced each other. Suddenly they both seemed to stand much straighter. Then they saluted.

"At ease," said Dr. Ginsky.

"Colonel," said the rabbi.

Much to Rifka's surprise, the two men embraced. They remained that way much longer than she thought seemly. Something unspoken passed between them.

Then Dr. Ginsky turned to the child. He felt his forehead, looked inside his mouth, and measured his temperature. The baby's condition was not too serious. A fever due to influenza. Many a child and many a man had succumbed to the Spanish flu after the war. But Moshe was to live. Rifka prepared a hot water bottle while Dr. Ginsky administered medicine to the child. Laibl offered the man a few coins, but the doctor indignantly refused. Soon, the baby fell asleep in his crib.

When Laibl and Dr. Ginsky bade each other farewell, they hugged again, and kissed each other on the cheek, the way men do. But Rifka was not stupid, and from the way they looked at each other, she understood, with perfect clarity, what had gone on between her husband and the doctor.

Laibl held the door open for Dr. Ginsky, and he remained there for a while after the doctor had left, staring into the darkness.

"Laibl?" Rifka then asked.

He slowly turned around. "Yes?"

She looked at him, and all her strength seemed to drain from her body. Her lips were trembling.

"What happened at the front?" she asked in a quiet voice.

Laibl walked over and sat down beside her. He took her hand and they both stared at the coarse wooden floor.

"If you don't ask me about the front," Laibl said finally, "then I won't ask you about the miracle."

HIS GREATEST TRICKS

When Max Cohn came home from school on Tuesday afternoon, there was a moving van in front of the house. Max was immediately alarmed. A moving van? Already? He went inside. Boxes were everywhere. The furniture was in disarray. Bruno the Bunny sat in his cage in a corner of the living room, looking frazzled. His ears were shaking. The movers were two large men. One of them wore jeans and a Shakira T-shirt; the other—in an apparent nod to tradition—was dressed in denim overalls and a checkered shirt.

"*Buenos días,*" said the man in the Shakira T-shirt, nodding at him. He was holding a box filled with papers and file folders.

"Hey," said Max. He noticed that his voice was trembling. "Where are my parents?" he asked.

"*¿Qué?*" said the man in the Shakira T-shirt.

"*Los padres,*" said Max. "Mom *y* Dad."

The man looked around helplessly and shrugged. Max stared at the box he was holding. Those papers and files probably belonged to Dad. Papers and files were part of his job. Like the Batmobile was for Batman.

The guy in the overalls approached him, carrying two boxes, also full of papers.

"In the bedroom," he said.

"What are you doing?" Max demanded, his voice growing shriller.

"We're getting the boxes out," said the man in the overalls. He had a thick accent.

"Put them down!" Max demanded. He looked up to see Dad emerge from the bedroom carrying a box as well. His hair was unkempt, he obviously hadn't shaved, his shirt was buttoned incorrectly, and his eyes had a glazed look. Totally alarming. The only other time Max had been so disturbed by his father's appearance was when, at age three, he had decided to lick the back porch clean with his tongue. Halfway through, his father had come running out, naked, to snatch him off the porch. There's nothing creepier than seeing your own father naked. Dad had rushed toward him, his penis dangling back and forth. It was a body part Max had never paid much attention to before. What is that thing? he thought in bewilderment. It can't be good.

Which is exactly what went through his mind right now:

It can't be good.

His father looked as if he had woken up from a deep sleep. As if he had gone through life in a haze and only now saw the light.

"Dad!" Max yelled and ran toward him. "There're movers everywhere!"

Dad took Max outside. He put the box down and they sat on the front steps. The stones were warm from the sun. Max heard the voices of the neighborhood kids playing. In the distance, he could see the cloud-covered peaks of the mountains.

For a while, neither of them spoke. Max and his dad simply sat there and stared off into the distance.

"We talked about this," Dad finally said.

"About what?"

"About today. About me leaving."

"You said Thursday."

"Tuesday," Dad corrected him. "I said Tuesday."

Max suddenly felt cold, despite the sun. He couldn't shake the feeling that Dad was trying to sneak out on him while he was still in school. He was gripped by the fear that he might never see his dad again, that as soon as he walked away, his dad might forget all about him. He wanted to cry, but he fought against it. What would become of him?

"Max," Dad said. "Nothing's going to change."

Max knew this was a lie. One of the bitter lessons of life was that everything changes. Both Spider-Man and Batman had lost their loved ones, causing them to wear spandex outfits and spend their nights fighting crime instead of watching reruns on TV like every other normal person.

Dad moved to hug him, but Max drew away. Then he had an idea: since it was his fault that Dad was leaving, maybe he was also the one who could undo it. He pressed his eyes shut and tried to will Dad to stay. He was sorry about wishing him gone. He would clean the bunny cage every day for the rest of his life.

Dad got up. "I still love you," he said.

"Dad!" Max said, panicked. "Stay here! I'll clean the bunny cage. Forever. You'll never have to do it again, ever!"

"I'm sorry," Dad said. Apparently, Max's thought wasn't powerful enough. Dad tried again to take him in his arms, but Max got frustrated and started punching him. Dad let go. Max ran up the steps to the house. He didn't get very far. Stumbling over one of the moving boxes, he fell flat on his face. The contents of the box spilled out over the front lawn.

"Max, are you all right?" Dad said.

Max sat up. "I'm fine," he said, pouting.

His knee was scraped, but he wasn't paying attention to that. He was staring at something lying on the lawn.

It was a flat, round, black, shiny thing that peeked out of a cardboard cover. Max knew what it was. Dad had told him about it. An item from the stone age, from before he was born. Something called a "record." He was immediately drawn to the album cover—the photograph of a middle-aged man dressed in a turban and a flowing, silver toga. He had thick, horn-rimmed glasses and seemed to be concentrating really hard on something. In his left hand was a magician's wand, and in his right hand a cute white bunny. There was something odd about the way he held his left arm, but Max couldn't tell what it was. Part of the toga was draped over it, covering the arm almost entirely. Never before had Max Cohn seen such splendor. This man, Max knew, was the very epitome of elegance and sophistication. A silver toga! Holy cow! This man was cooler than even James Bond. Feeling like an archaeologist who had discovered a great treasure from a long-vanished civilization, Max removed the black disc entirely from its sleeve. The title was written in bold, yellow letters in the middle of the disc:

ZABBATINI: HIS GREATEST TRICKS

THE EAGLE
AND THE LAMB

Moshe Goldenhirsch remained a sickly child. No wonder his mother constantly doted on him, calling him "my little miracle." It dismayed her greatly that Moshe was always coughing and sniffling. He was always the first to catch a cold and the last to overcome it. Rifka was kept so busy by her son's health that she neglected her own body. Something was eating her up from the inside, but she was too busy to pay attention to it. She lived only for Moshe.

He was often quiet and withdrawn. Much like his father, Rifka often thought. Moshe would spend hours on the banks of the Vltava River, sitting in the sun, skipping stones or simply lying in the grass staring at clouds that in his daydreams took on the shapes of castles and knights. Because he was young, time had no meaning for him. His life had not yet assumed a shape, and he had no fear in his heart, not yet. The world outside was gray and dreary, but his inner world was magnificent. A line in the wall became a road, on which his namesake Moses led the Israelites to freedom; the breath of a horse in the cold winter night became a dragon's fire. Days would go by without his uttering a single word to his parents. This was not for lack of love, not at all; it was simply that he was far away, even when he was sitting at the kitchen table with them. Moshe stared into oblivion, his movements became slow and mechanical, and he drifted off. "I've lost you," his mother would say with a sad smile.

☀

When Moshe was eight years old, he and his father came home one evening to find Rifka leaning over the old stove, as if exhausted. Clay shards were on the floor; potatoes were scattered. She was breathing heavily, and there was sweat on her face.

"Are you all right?" Laibl asked, concerned.

She nodded. "I'm fine," she said. "All is well." She took a deep breath, then bent down to pick up the shards.

Moshe eyed her suspiciously. He knew she was lying, he could feel it. All was not well. The world had cracks: there were things that were hidden from sight and truths that were unspoken. He looked to his father for comfort. Laibl gazed at his wife, who seemed to be in great pain. He held out his hand to help her, but she swatted it away angrily.

"Maybe," Laibl said helplessly, "you should see a doctor?"

"Maybe *you* should see a doctor," Rifka replied with some sarcasm.

Moshe knew that Dr. Ginsky had saved his own life, soon after he was born. Since then, he had become the family physician, and Laibl had started to complain of many ailments, which required him to visit the doctor frequently.

Rifka took a broom and swept the remaining shards into a dustpan. They sat down to a dinner of steamed potatoes and cottage cheese with fresh herbs. Moshe observed his mother and was inexplicably scared. She had seemed to him a much larger woman, but in the last few months she had grown disturbingly thin.

Rifka was shivering.

"Is everything all right?" Laibl asked.

Rifka stifled a sob and shook her head. Laibl pushed the chair away so forcefully that it fell over. He rushed over to his wife's side and held her tightly. Moshe thought it must hurt to be held like this. But Rifka did not resist. Laibl led her to the bed and helped her lie down.

"Oh God," Rifka cried out.

"What's the matter?" Laibl asked.

"Nothing," Rifka said, and suppressed a moan. It looked as if she was fighting a battle inside her body.

"Moshe!" said Laibl. "Fetch Doctor Ginsky."

"No!" Rifka said with surprising sharpness.

She threw her arms around her husband and pulled him close to her. Her face was covered in sweat.

"Do you remember," she whispered, "when you asked me to marry you?"

He nodded. "In a field. You were lying in a field. Like you are now."

"Do you still love me?" she asked.

"Yes," he said.

And she believed him.

∿

When winter came, her health deteriorated rapidly. She grew weaker and weaker, and her once-full body seemed to vanish. She had difficulties getting up in the morning. Often, she was nauseous, and would throw up in a metal bucket that Moshe had placed by the bed. When she was done, Moshe would carry the bucket down to the river, empty it out, and wash it carefully. Initially, he did this once or twice a day, but then he ran to the water more and more frequently. He didn't complain. He wished he could do more, he wished he had magic powers to heal his mother. But nothing he did made her better. And the worse she got, the angrier she became. Feeling the end drawing near, she resented her husband and son for living. As the days grew shorter, so did her own remaining time. She would stare blankly out the window, her mind clouded. Her son would live to see another spring. But she would not.

Eventually she became so weak that she could no longer get up from her bed. Against her wishes, Laibl called Dr. Ginsky. Rifka eyed him with great suspicion as he entered. The doctor did everything he could to help, but it wasn't much.

Laibl suffered as well. It was as if he himself were dying, and not Rifka. For many years she had been the center of his existence: she was his heart. Life without her was unthinkable.

He became haggard, perhaps out of solidarity with his diminishing spouse. He barely slept. Whenever Rifka coughed, Laibl would leap up, wide awake, and ask her what she needed. He was haunted by guilt. He had not been faithful to his family or his principles. He had sinned in the eyes of the Lord, and now his wife was being taken from him. He spent much of his time praying, but his prayers went unanswered.

Dr. Ginsky came over more frequently, to prescribe different medicines. He was a good doctor: he cared for all his patients, even the ones of the Mosaic tribe, and he understood full well that his contribution to their well-being lay not only in the realm of the body, but also in that of the soul. He talked to Rifka, he told her jokes, he informed her about what was going on outside her four walls: Lenin was dead, Turkey had ended the caliphate, and the Cinema Lucerna was showing a new picture by Lubitsch. The world of the living would go on, with or without Rifka Goldenhirsch. Dr. Ginsky made her laugh in a way that Laibl never had. In the face of death, Rifka became surprisingly fond of her husband's lover. He took her seriously and told her of the momentous political changes in Europe. He told her of a man called Hitler, who was leading a new movement in Germany, and who promised to wrest Prague away from the Slavs and the Bolsheviks and restore its freedom. Ginsky was quite fond of this odd little fellow, particularly of his views on the Jewish question. This always led to a somewhat awkward silence in the Goldenhirsch household. Dr. Ginsky was convinced that the Jews—with the notable exception of those present—were to blame for the lost war and the end of the monarchy. It was the Jews who had nearly succeeded in poisoning Europe and who were working tirelessly to bring about communism.

Ginsky was an enigma to Rifka, a riddle she would not be able to solve in the little time she had left in this world. He was wise and compassionate, gentle and understanding, an excellent doctor and a good man, and yet, his political views were absurd. Ginsky was kind to her and her family, but unkind to the Jews.

"Forgive me, my dear Mrs. Goldenhirsch," he said. "I meant no offense."

"None was taken," she replied, and smiled demurely, as became a woman on the verge of death.

"But I fear that the Jew . . ." he went on.

And Rifka said, "Spare me, doctor."

"Present company excluded, of course . . ."

"Of course."

"But surely you must know that the international Jewry . . ."

Rifka coughed pointedly, and Ginsky took her pulse and her temperature, forgetting all about the international Jewry for the time being. She was constantly amazed at how small and gentle his fingers were. She thought of them caressing her husband.

"Your fever has receded," he announced, as if expecting applause.

Rifka nodded, and he continued talking about art, music, and the theater, about the world of the goyim. Rifka listened with fascination, grateful that this small, odd man was bringing the world to her just as she was about to leave it. Her husband looked on as they talked, and a hint of jealousy glinted in his eyes.

Young Moshe, meanwhile, was in a state of near panic. The

thought of losing his mother was worse than that of his own death. He refused to believe his eyes, and kept telling himself that everything would be all right, that she would recover. Deep down, he knew this was a lie. He could not understand how a good and loving God could take her from him. He offered his own life in her place, he offered himself as a sacrifice, like the ram for Isaac. But God would not listen. God wanted Rifka. All that remained for Laibl and Moshe was a world of despair.

One other person was greatly affected by Rifka's illness: the other Moshe, the Locksmith from upstairs. He, too, visited Rifka frequently, and soon his visits became an excessive burden on her. Was it asking too much to die in peace? Why was everyone around her all the time? Why must her deathbed be as crowded as a train station platform?

She instructed her husband to let no one in anymore, no one except Dr. Ginsky. One night, the Locksmith came to the apartment, drunk, rapping against the door and calling Rifka's name. Laibl went out to talk to him. Muffled sounds wafted into the small apartment. Rifka told Moshe to go see what was going on.

Moshe ran outside and saw the bear of a Locksmith holding Laibl in a headlock, spanking his behind. Laibl's face was bright red with pain and indignation. "Let go of me!" he yelled, "you *klutz*, you *mieskeit*!"

"I want to see her!" roared the Locksmith.

"Out of the question!"

"I love her!" the Locksmith yelled. Other apartment doors opened and the neighbors looked on with great interest.

"Kish mir in tuches!" yelled Laibl.

The Locksmith continued to spank the rabbi. Laibl howled like an animal. Moshe tried to tear the men apart, but it was useless. He felt like a fly trying to move a rock. Eventually, he heard a voice:

"Stop it," said Rifka weakly. She was leaning against the doorframe, a pale imitation of her former self.

"Rifka," said the Locksmith, releasing his grip on the rabbi. Laibl fell to the floor.

The Locksmith approached Rifka, and for a moment Moshe thought he was going to break his mother in half. But he stopped in front of her and raised his large, paw-like hands. They were shaking. Then, very gently, he touched her cheek with one hand, as if she were made of porcelain and he was afraid to break her.

"Let go of my wife," cried the rabbi.

Rifka looked at the Locksmith and said, "He's right. You have to let go of me."

"But . . ." stammered the Locksmith. He withdrew his hands.

She took his large fingers into her hands and gently stroked them. "Let go of me," she repeated.

Suddenly, a deep sob emerged from the Locksmith's colossal body. He fell down on his knees in front of her and pressed his head against her body.

"Don't go," he said.

"Do I look like I want to?"

After a few more sobs, the Locksmith calmed down. He looked at her with unending sadness. Then he got up and went back upstairs. Shivering, Rifka drew her nightgown closer. She turned to Laibl and Moshe, who had watched the scene in silence.

"Can we go to bed now, please?" she asked.

"Yes, dear," said the rabbi.

"Why must he be such a noisy oaf?" Rifka asked.

"Also, he takes a lot of time on the toilet," her husband opined, but Rifka shot him a menacing look, and he shut up.

☀

Death came on a winter morning. Rifka woke up from an uneasy sleep feeling cold, and asked for a hot water bottle. Moshe prepared one for her, but she remained cold. She asked for more blankets, but still the cold wouldn't leave her. It was the chill of death.

"Moshe . . ." she said weakly.

"Yes?"

"Where is my husband?"

"He's not here," said Moshe. "He's out drinking with the goyim, where they don't keep kosher. At U Fleků."

"I am dying and he drinks?" Rifka said indignantly.

"Yes," Moshe replied, somewhat ashamed. "He went with the Locksmith."

For a moment, Rifka seemed puzzled. Then she said to Moshe, "Hold my hand."

He did.

Then, Rifka said, "Hold me. I'm so cold."

Moshe climbed up into his mother's bed. He pressed his small body against hers and wrapped his arms around her.

"One day soon," Rifka said, "you will be a man. And you will have a wife, and she will be safe and warm in your arms." Rifka stared at the wall, the paint peeling off, and it irked her that the last thing she should see was this ugly wall.

She closed her eyes, and heard her son crying softly.

"I've lost you," Moshe said.

"Sing me a song," Rifka said.

And Moshe started singing the song that she had sung for him when he was a baby in his crib:

> *Far above in the distant sky*
> *The wind carried a lonely cry*
> *Far above, where eagles fly*

Rifka's heart rose when she heard the familiar melody. She tried singing along, but all she could muster was a whisper.

> *A sorrowful and lonely sound*
> *Why do I have to die?*
> *Cried a lamb, tightly bound*

She knew the song well. As a child, she had always thought that she was an eagle, not a lamb. Now she knew better. All of mankind was the lamb.

Far above in the distant sky
Far above, where eagles fly

Moshe's voice grew stronger and more confident. Rifka felt a surge of motherly pride. This was her son, her life, her gift to the world. His fingers clutched hers. She could feel the warmth of his body, and it was the only thing she still felt. Then she saw her husband standing in the doorway, looking much as he had upon returning from the Great War nine years ago. Drunk now and smelling of schnapps, he approached her bed, saying nothing, as Moshe continued to sing:

Why can't I fly through the sky?
Why, oh Lord, why?
Like an eagle in the sky

By the time Moshe had finished, his mother was no longer breathing.

THE SWEET LIFE

Max carefully pushed the record back into its sleeve and turned it around. On the back, he saw the list of the "greatest tricks" that the man in the silver toga had to offer: THE WONDERS OF THE FAKIR, Max read, MAGICAL NUMBERS, TOAD MAGIC, and, all the way at the bottom: THE SPELL OF ETERNAL LOVE. Apparently, the whole point of the record was to explain magic spells to the listener, for "the amazement of family and friends . . . and to change your life!" It was just what he needed. The wheels started turning inside Max's head. Eternal love?

"Can I keep this?" he asked his dad.

"Sure," Harry Cohn said with a sigh. He continued gathering up the items that had fallen out of the box and were scattered over the front lawn.

A short while later, the movers finished loading the last box. The moment of departure had arrived.

When Dad gave him a final hug, Max was already cooking up his plan.

"Bye, Dad," he mumbled.

"Okay . . ." Dad said weakly. "I'll be in touch." He looked at his son with helpless desperation. He felt there were a million things to say. Waves of words and feelings ebbed and flowed through his heart. He opened his mouth, but then closed it again. The waves receded. He was at a loss, and simply waved at Max.

Max didn't wave back.

⁂

"So Dad finally moved out," Max said to Joey Shapiro the next day in school. "Took him long enough."

"Yeah," Joey said.

"About time," Max added.

They were standing in line in the student cafeteria, food trays in hand.

Max got chicken teriyaki dippers and cornbread. Joey had a salad.

"I'm trying to cut out carbs," Joey said. Max nodded, even though he wasn't sure what that meant.

They took their trays outside and sat down at a table at the edge of the schoolyard. Behind them, they could see the rolling hills of Silver Lake.

Max told Joey about his find, the mysterious record. "There are magic spells on it, by a guy named Zabbatini," he said.

"If you play it, the spells are supposed to . . ." He cleared his throat.

"What?"

"I don't know. Something's supposed to happen. Magic, whatever."

"And how are you planning to play this record?" Joey asked.

"No idea," Max said with a shrug. "I'll ask Mom." But first, he had to do some more research.

※

Who was the Great Zabbatini? Where had this record actually come from? Max decided to ask Dad this weekend. His father was staying at Grandma's house in Encino while searching for a new place. This was bad news for Max, because it meant that whenever he wanted to see Dad, he had to put up with Grandma. And Grandma was really annoying. Apparently, some bad stuff had happened to her when she was young, in "the Old Country." As a child, she had been rescued from "the Camps." Ever since then, she considered life highly precarious, a privilege that might be revoked at any moment. She managed to slip that information into almost any conversation. The worst of the Camps was a place she called "the Suitcase Factory." She was always itching to tell her tale of the Suitcase Factory, but no one in the family wanted to hear it anymore. Especially not Max.

"When they sent me to the Suitcase Factory . . ." she began telling him one Saturday afternoon, after making Max some lemonade.

"Grandma!" Max called out, rolling his eyes. "I'm trying to watch *Scooby-Doo*!"

She shot him a dirty look. "I survived the Camps for this?" she asked.

Max, too, had survived a camp, Camp Isaiah in Redondo Beach, where he had been forced to go on hikes and listen to counselors play Cat Stevens on the guitar. "Matzo ball soup for the soul," they called it.

Grandma had made it clear that the Camps were even more unpleasant. They were "Death Camps," which, as it turned out, had absolutely nothing to do with the Death Star in *Star Wars*. "They brought us there to be killed," she said simply and wiped a stain off the counter. This information, Max felt, cast a cold chill on an otherwise perfectly pleasant summer day.

"In the Suitcase Factory as well?"

"Especially the Suitcase Factory."

He was sitting in Grandma's fastidiously clean kitchen, at her Formica table, his feet barely touching the linoleum, drinking lemonade and staring out into her garden at a lemon tree, from which the lemonade came, watching its leaves sway ever so slightly in the summer breeze.

Max stared into his glass. A lemon seed was drifting to the surface.

Grandma sat across from him, seemingly frozen.

"Grandma?" he asked.

She didn't respond. His hand reached out to her, and even though she was sitting right at the other side of the table, she seemed to be in another world. Max realized for the first time that people had wounds you couldn't see.

꜀ⅰ꜀

Her second husband, Herman, aka "Grandpa," had died some years ago. His death was an event that had barely registered with Max, who didn't fully realize that the dead stay that way. Grandpa had suffered from dementia, and hadn't played a very important part in Max's life. He had merely been an extra to Max, not a leading actor. He hadn't even been his real grandpa. Max remembered the funeral only vaguely. He had dim memories of a distant and somewhat unpleasant day at temple—aren't they all, though?—that ended with a large crate being lowered into the ground. Afterward, there was boring food and countless adults pinching him on the cheek.

Grandpa's death, however, brought about a remarkable change in Grandma. She bought new, gold-rimmed glasses, started dyeing her beehive blue, and took to wearing brightly colored jogging outfits, even though she never jogged. She began attending Mexican cooking classes and subjected her family to forays into the art of tofu tamales and kosher enchiladas. Also, she had affairs—a phrase Max was beginning to understand all too clearly—with some of the men she met at the temple's senior citizens' activities program. Apparently, these activities included Grandma peeling out of her athletic suit and doing the nasty with some decrepit geezer.

Now that Dad was living with her, the atmosphere was even

weirder. Grandma's formerly ordered and structured environment was now cluttered with Dad's trail of papers, files, and pens. Two worlds collided. Max had never liked Grandma's house. There was something stuffy about it. Dad being there only made it worse.

When Max visited his father that weekend, they went out for Thai food with Grandma, Uncle Bernie, and Aunt Heidi. Grandma didn't like Aunt Heidi and always called her "the shiksa." Uncle Bernie and Aunt Heidi had brought their bratty kids with them, Max's cousins Esther, Mike, and Lucas. Everyone always assumed that Max would be eager to talk to and play with other kids, but nothing could have been further from the truth. Other kids, his pudgy cousins in particular, were stupid, and Max tried to keep their interactions to a minimum, like neighboring nations trying to avoid a war.

Pattaya Bay was a small, run-down restaurant in a strip mall on Victory Boulevard in Burbank. Its walls were adorned with panorama wallpaper depicting tropical beaches, and plastic plants stood before the windows. On the left side as you entered was a giant fish tank, with only one fish inside, an eight-year old pacu named Bhumibol, a large, monstrous, and somewhat sad-looking creature. Max often thought that Bhumibol must be very lonely, all alone in his fish tank. Above Bhumibol's tank, next to the karaoke machine, were framed portraits of the king and queen of Thailand. As it turned out, the king was also named Bhumibol. The fish reminded Max of a king in exile.

"Is there any shrimp paste in this curry?" Aunt Heidi asked the waitress, pointing at the menu.

The waitress smiled and nodded.

"Shrimp paste," Aunt Heidi declared indignantly.

"Yes," said the waitress.

"Shrimp paste is bad," Uncle Bernie explained. "No shrimp paste."

Bernie, Dad's older brother, was an odd man, oddly shaped and oddly proud of it. Whenever he came home, he would immediately disrobe, much to the dismay of Aunt Heidi, and lounge about in a silk kimono, his ample belly sticking out, before grabbing a beer from the fridge.

"Yes," said the waitress. "Shrimp paste bad."

"No," said Aunt Heidi. "Bad."

"Yes," said the waitress. "No."

She turned around and left, seeming to have no idea what Aunt Heidi was talking about. Like most people, Max thought. He looked at his dad. It seemed like a good time to pose the question that had been on his mind.

"Dad," Max began, "about this record I found . . ."

"Yes . . ." Dad said, and took a sip of water.

"Where did it come from?"

Dad told him that the Great Zabbatini had been a somewhat popular stage magician when he was a boy.

"He was often on the radio," Uncle Bernie interjected. In the seventies, when Bernie and Harry were young boys, he had made the switch to television, more or less successfully.

Dad nodded. "We used to see him on *The Tonight Show.*"

"He could predict the future. He was a mind reader," added Uncle Bernie.

"A *ganef*," Grandma said. She turned to Max and pointed her chopsticks at him. "Your father and your uncle were crazy about this man. Harry even wanted him to come to his bar mitzvah."

"What happened?" Max asked.

"What, I'm going to ask some schmuck to come to my boy's bar mitzvah? What am I, an idiot?"

"I wrote him a letter," Dad said with a melancholic air. "But Zabbatini never came."

"Your grandfather, God rest his soul, bought him a record instead. That stupid thing. Money out the window."

She took a sip of her Thai iced tea. Then she shook her head and said, "This is awful. Just like in the Camps."

"They had Thai iced tea?" Max asked.

"No," Grandma said. "You see, when they sent me to the Suitcase Factory . . ."

"Not again!" Dad said, rolling his eyes.

Everyone moaned dramatically. Moaning at Grandma was one of the few family activities everyone could agree upon.

"Did you ever listen to it?" Max asked Grandma. "The record, I mean."

"I should listen to this *crap*?" She shook her head and cleared her throat.

The waitress came with the food. Aunt Heidi, a convert to Judaism and therefore much more observant than the rest of the family, reiterated her desire that there be no shrimp paste. She continued questioning the waitress on each individual ingredient. With an impatient gesture, Uncle Bernie put a stop to the interrogation. His wife didn't need to know that he occasionally indulged in a shrimp or two, sometimes even a prawn, behind her back. If she didn't know it, then neither did God.

Grandma was annoyed because the shiksa was, once again, making a scene. And, as always, she took it out on her eldest son.

"Sit up straight," she said to Uncle Bernie. "You're thirty-nine years old and still slouching? For this I survived the Camps?"

Bernie sighed, shrugged, and slouched even more.

"What was on the record?" Max asked, trying to steer the conversation back to more important things.

"Zabbatini gave instructions about the spells, explaining them step by step. And if you followed the instructions to a T, you could do magic," Dad said and winked at Max.

"Really?" Max asked excitedly.

"No," Grandma said. "It's all nonsense."

Max looked imploringly at his father. "Dad?"

Dad said nothing. He simply gave a resigned shrug. Aunt Heidi called the waitress over to complain that there was shrimp paste in her curry.

She could definitely taste it.

※

The weekend was agonizing. Dad and Grandma were always getting into arguments. On top of that, Max had to sleep in Grandpa's old study, a den in the back of the house overlooking a concrete patio and a sad-looking, empty swimming pool that was only used by raccoons who would rummage around the garbage can at night and then wash their finds in the few drops of stale water at the bottom. Grandpa's study had fake wood paneling and an oil painting of an old man with a beard, whose eyes seemed to follow Max's every movement. Also, Max didn't like the bed he was sleeping in. He knew that Grandpa had died in it.

"I found him in the morning," Grandma had told Max once with tears in her eyes. They had slept in separate beds for years, on account of Grandpa's snoring. "His heart had given up the struggle," Grandma continued. "His bowels, too. Typical of your grandfather, making a mess like that."

Max was totally creeped out that he had to sleep in a bed where a man had shat and died. He couldn't wait to get home to Mom's house in Atwater Village, back to civilization. He had his own room there, his trusted bunny, and, of course, his comic book collection.

The most annoying thing about Grandma was that everyone she talked about was dead. She seemed to spend more time with the dead than with the living, and constantly told boring stories about long-lost relatives who had been killed in the war. It was confusing—she didn't seem to realize that Max had never met his extinguished family. None of those people were alive anymore. They didn't even have graves. They had become stories told by a lonely old woman, and once she left this world, all of them would be forgotten, fading out over time, as if they'd never existed. To Max, Grandma had always been old—he couldn't imagine that she had been young once, a girl named Rosl Feldmann, with dreams and fears and a future. But that future was far behind her now.

Every once in a while, Grandma showed him her albums

of faded black-and-white photographs, but he only glanced at them. There was, however, one picture he remembered quite vividly, the reproduction of an old photograph that he had found in a history book on World War II. It was a grainy, black-and-white picture showing a pile of human bodies, all naked and white, lying in disarray on top of each other. There must have been forty or fifty dead people, Max figured. They looked odd, like twisted puppets. A man in a uniform was standing in front of the pile like a proud hunter, leaning on his rifle. The picture was a snapshot that the officer had sent to his family. There was an inscription, in German, which Grandma had once translated for Max:

"My darling. Kiss the children for me. Love to all. Living the sweet life."

Max was impatient to get back to his own sweet life. Not just because Grandma's house was over-the-top weird, but because he knew that in his room, Zabbatini's magic awaited him.

ALL THAT REMAINS

Rifka Goldenhirsch was buried in a small plot in the Old Jewish Cemetery by the Staronová Synagogue. Moshe was inconsolable, crying throughout the ceremony, and it was so cold that the tears froze on his cheeks. Laibl held him close, and they clung to each other for comfort, though there wasn't much to be had. And then they said Kaddish, the prayer for the dead:

"May there be abundant peace from heaven, and life, for us and for all Israel. Amen."

It was all over within a few minutes. The mourners left the cemetery, moving quickly, and Moshe could scarcely hear their feet touching the frozen ground. A few minutes later, when everyone had gone and only Rifka Goldenhirsch was left—alone underneath the cold earth—the Locksmith came, sneaking into the cemetery like a beaten dog. He placed a stone on her grave. He, too, had ice on his cheeks.

After the funeral, they went to Zilberman's, a kosher restaurant on the Pařížská, known among culinary connoisseurs as "the terror of Prague." The food was awful and the service awful, and each visit there bordered on masochism. Moshe didn't mind. He couldn't eat anyway. Laibl and the others sat around in gloomy silence at an old wooden table. There was nothing to say. A life had ended, the world was poorer for it, and there were no words for that. The room was filled with cigarette smoke, wafting past the yellowing windowpanes. Laibl was drunk. He was drunk most of the time lately. In fact, Moshe was a bit tipsy as well.

The night before the funeral, Laibl had poured Moshe his first shot of schnapps, and the clear liquid had burned Moshe's throat. But it didn't seem to bother his father: he drank the schnapps as if it were water. Alcohol had become his constant companion.

※

Moshe carried the loss of his mother within him like a stone in his heart. The days following her death were a blur. He barely slept, he couldn't concentrate, and he saw everything around him as if through a veil. It took several months for him to become a little more sociable again. And it was hard work. He played with the other children and pretended to be merry, as if there still was laughter left in this world.

But the earth kept turning. Winter became spring, spring became summer, and then, fall came. Moshe was nine years old. His days were hazy. He got up, ate, brushed his teeth and went to the toilet in the stairwell. He got dressed and met his friends on the street, so they could walk to shul together. He went to the Staronová Synagogue, where his father was the rabbi.

Laibl Goldenhirsch was very proud of the synagogue and its history, considering himself the guardian of a great treasure. The treasure, however, was cold, dark, and crumbling. It had oddly shaped, deep-set windows, and its inside walls were blackened with the soot of thousands of candles. It always smelled funny.

During the day, when Laibl taught, his senses were sharp, and he was even-tempered. But in the evenings, when he took to the bottle, he unleashed his grief and anger over Rifka's death onto Moshe. When he was drunk, all the injustices in the world would roil up inside him and come thundering down on Moshe, who was helpless before his father's sudden rages.

Until Rifka's death, the relationship between father and son had been harmonious, but despair took its toll. Laibl became increasingly unpredictable. At times he was as sweet as honey; at others, he became bitter like maror, the disgusting herbs he and his son had to gulp down during Passover, in commemoration of the hard times the Jews had in ancient Egypt. When Laibl came home from the inn at night, Moshe never knew whether his father would be tearful or angry. Sometimes he took Moshe into his arms; other times, he would beat him. He was usually too drunk to seriously hurt him, but that was beside the point. It wasn't the pain that hurt Moshe. He felt himself drawing away from his father, a little more with each passing day.

Laibl, too, could feel the increasing distance between them, and it bothered him. His son was the only thing he had left in this world. But the child seemed to him like a ship, drifting off toward the horizon.

One fall afternoon, in a rare display of paternal affection, Moshe's father took him up the creaking steps into the synagogue's attic. Moshe stood there waiting, amid the gloom and dust of the centuries.

"This is where Rabbi Löw kept the remains of the golem," Laibl said.

His eyes were clear, and his breath didn't smell. He hadn't been drinking today, not yet.

"The what?" Moshe asked.

Laibl motioned for his son to sit, and he sat down as well on the wooden floor beside him to recount the story of the golem, a mythical homunculus made of clay, created by the famed Rabbi Löw to protect the Jews of Prague. A dumb creature that longed to be human.

"'Your eyes beheld my unformed substance,'" Laibl said.

"What?"

"Didn't you pay attention in my class?" asked Laibl with mock reproach.

"Is that from the Torah?" asked Moshe. It seemed a reasonable guess.

Laibl nodded. It dismayed him that his son showed not the least bit of interest in the mysteries of the Tanakh. The knowledge of the ages dripped off the boy's thick head like water from a rock. "Psalms 139:16," he said.

Moshe nodded, and suppressed a yawn. He felt uncomfortable in this dark attic. Outside, the sun was shining. There probably wouldn't be too many more sunny days this year. He longed to be outdoors with his friends, playing, pretending to be alive.

Laibl got up and walked over to a large, wooden crate, covered with coarse cloth. With a theatrical gesture, he removed the cloth.

It was above all this gesture that would remain imprinted upon Moshe's memory: the tiny bow his father gave, stretching out his arms to reach for the hemline, straightening his sleeves, then gently yet firmly touching the cloth and pulling it off in one swift motion, the sheet making a sound like thunder, followed by a rising cloud of dust that sparkled in the thin beams of sunlight like a thousand tiny diamonds.

Though Laibl didn't know it, the memory of this gesture would have a profound and lasting influence over the crooked course of Moshe's life. With sudden fascination, Moshe looked at the wooden box. Laibl carefully pried it open.

"What do you see?" he asked his son.

Moshe came closer, raised himself up on his toes, and gazed into the darkness inside the crate.

"Nothing."

"Nothing, really?"

Moshe looked once more. In the darkness, he could barely make out a few clay shards at the bottom of the crate.

"'Your eyes beheld my unformed substance,'" Laibl said again. "'All my days were written in Your book when as yet there was none of them.'" He paused, then added, "They kept the golem in this crate. And these pieces of clay are all that remains."

Moshe nodded.

Laibl said, "Remember that the Hebrew word for 'substance' is *galemi*."

Again, Moshe nodded.

"One day, in the year 5340, Rabbi Löw and two of his assistants went to the bank of the Vltava River. In those days, rabbis were paid better and could afford help. At the river, the three of them measured out a man. They drew his face in the wet earth, his arms and legs. And then Rabbi Löw circled the Golem seven times, and when he was done, the shape lit up as red as fire. A vapor arose, and the golem grew hair, and a beard, and fingernails."

Laibl took his son's hand in his. With a dreamy look on his face, he said, "'And God created man in His own image, in the image of God He created him.'"

Moshe stared at him with fascination.

Laibl smiled and said, "And the Golem opened his eyes and peered out in amazement." He cleared his throat.

Moshe leaned against the box, lifted himself up on his toes one more time, and looked inside again, this time much longer.

"Now what do you see?" asked Laibl.

"Everything," said Moshe.

ETERNAL LOVE

Max carefully opened the garage door and peered into the darkness. This was where his parents kept all their old, discarded stuff. When he was five years old, he had stumbled upon a lizard in here. The encounter had been as troubling for the lizard as it had been for Max, but Max couldn't have known that. The lizard was perched on a broken mirror, a creature from the age of dinosaurs, staring at Max. The two looked into each other's eyes, like gunfighters in a Western movie, and then the lizard turned around and scrambled away. Ever since then, the garage had been a place of dark mystery to Max. It frightened him a little bit, but like all things mysterious, it also exuded a certain fascination. The furniture in the corners was covered with white sheets. The place was full of boxes, containing God knows what. The garage called out to him, challenged him to unearth its secrets. With death-defying daring, Max took a step inside. He had to find it.

That morning, Max had shown his mom the record: "This is Dad's," he explained. "I found it when he moved out."

Mom seemed unimpressed by that momentous revelation. "So?" she said, stubbing out her cigarette in the ashtray.

"This—was—Dad's—record!" Max emphasized every word, as if explaining the world to an idiot. Ever since Dad moved out, Mom had changed, and not for the better. She was either rushing around the house, feverishly cleaning, or simply sitting there staring at nothing. Both displeased Max, and he was determined to do something about the current state of things.

To accomplish that, he needed an archaic device that his parents called a "record player." Mom had told him that it was probably in the garage, behind Grandma's old sofa. Although he didn't find it there, at least he didn't stumble upon any more members of the animal kingdom. Still, he was nervous. Rummaging through several boxes, he found many interesting treasures: broken picture frames, old action figures, ashtrays, yellowing papers. Relics of family life. A small sliver of sunlight fell through the crack above the garage door as Max continued his quest. Nothing could deter him, not even his fear of lizards. He looked into every box and crawled under every piece of furniture.

Then he found it. In an old cardboard box with the words BOX BROS written on it, buried under blouses and—gross!—several of Mom's old bras. The record player was a large, bulky thing, with a round surface right in the middle, and something that looked like a thin robot-arm. A silver sliver by the side read DYNAVOX DL-420.

Max carefully carried the record player into the house and set it on the kitchen counter.

His mom seemed surprised. "Look at that old thing," she said. Her voice had an odd quality to it that he couldn't quite define. She was wearing yellow rubber gloves that went up to her elbows, and an apron. She had been cleaning all day, vigorously scrubbing every surface. It was as if she was trying to get rid of a bad smell. She threw her sponge into a bucket filled with soapy water. Then she cautiously approached the record player. "Your father and I used to listen to music on that," she said.

Max was annoyed. Lately, she had started to call Dad "your father." It made him a stranger.

Mom helped Max dust off the record player. She asked him if this was what he wanted for his eleventh birthday, which was coming up in two weeks.

"No way!" Max insisted. "I want a real gift."

The record player had a switch to turn it on, and a knob to adjust volume. It was hard to believe people ever used anything like this. He carried it into his room. He wanted to be alone during the crucial phase of the experiment.

His mom looked on with some bemusement. Then she turned, got the sponge from the bucket, and threw herself frantically into the housework with renewed vigor.

At last, everything was prepared. Max had closed the door to his room, taken the record out of his closet, and drawn the curtains. He plugged the player in and turned it on. Then he carefully took the record from its sleeve and put it on the player. The turntable was spinning. So far, so good. Very carefully, he sat the needle down on the record. He heard a crackling noise. And suddenly, Zabbatini's voice filled the room. The man spoke with a thick accent that Max couldn't place. He sounded a little bit like his grandma and a little bit like Dracula from one of the old movies.

"Ladies and gentlemen, boys and girls. Here speaks to you the Great Zabbatini. . . ."

It worked! Max felt like an explorer encountering an exotic civilization. "On this record you will find very powerful magic to make better your life, or your money back." Max closed his eyes. "My magic can everything make," Zabbatini continued. "Is it money that you want? Strongness of the body? Or the mind? Happiness? Or eternal love?"

At that point, Max opened his eyes again. Zabbatini said the word *love* with a long, drawn-out *o*. It sounded like "eternaaal loooove."

Max became impatient. He consulted the record sleeve to find out where the love spell was supposed to be. It was the last one. All right. Max raised the needle and carefully put it back down, more toward the end of the record. Zabbatini was talking about some other spell, but finally, Max heard:

"The next magic is maybe the mightiest magic in the big world, yes? Is love magic."

It wasn't easy to make out what the Great Zabbatini was saying. As the man rambled on, his accent seemed to become thicker, his grasp of the finer points of the English language ever more tenuous. But this much was clear: The spell was designed to make someone fall in love with you. "With this magic," Zabbatini explained, "two people will become forever more closer together."

If the spell worked, Dad would move back in, Mom would finally stop her infernal cleaning, and the divorce would be called off. Everything would be cool again. Max had to listen carefully—he didn't want to miss anything. No easy feat, given the magician's accent. Max learned that for the spell to work, he would need a candle, which he hadn't been aware of. All right. No problem. He stopped the record and hurried off to the kitchen.

Mom was standing in front of the fridge, pondering what to do with the brussels sprouts she had so carelessly bought.

"They were on sale at Ralphs," she said. "You like them, don't you?"

Max shrugged. When he was small, he had tasted the stuff once, and immediately felt like puking. No, he didn't particularly like brussels sprouts. It occurred to him that other moms seemed to know what their children liked. Sometimes he felt like a stranger in this house.

"I need a candle," he said.

"What for?"

"Nothing."

He hunted through the cabinets until he found an IKEA tea light and some matches. Then he rushed off to his room. Hopefully, Dad would be back home soon, and that would be the end of brussels sprouts.

"Be careful!" Mom called. "Don't burn anything."

Max banged the door shut and set the tea candle on his desk next to the record player. After lighting the candle, he turned the record player back on.

"And now," the Great Zabbatini boomed, "comes the spell. The spell of eternaaaaal loooooove!"

Max listened attentively. Maybe he should take notes, like in school? He fished around in his desk until he found a notepad and a ballpoint pen.

"The spell of eternaaaaal loooooove!" Zabbatini reiterated.

Max held the pen in his hand. He was ready. The candle was flickering. Hardly any daylight penetrated the drawn curtains. Even Bruno the Bunny, who was nibbling on a carrot in his cage on the other side of the room, seemed to listen up. His ears were perky.

"The spell of eternaaaaal loooooove!"

Yes, Max thought. I know. Got it. Moving on.

"The spell of eternaaaaal loooooove!"

Weird, he thought. Why is nothing happening? What's going on?

"The spell of eternaaaaal loooooove!"

Max stared at the record player. Almost imperceptibly, the needle jumped back every time it reached a certain spot. Max turned the record player off, then on again. And again, the needle jumped. Max tried putting placing it right after the jumping-off spot.

"Istgahe Ghatar Kojast!" said the voice suddenly. "Thaaaank you, my ladies and gentlemen, boys and girls," said the Great Zabbatini. "And now, good night!"

He'd missed it. He must have skipped the entire spell. Max tried a few other places to put the needle down, but it was like a squirrelly little animal. It jumped too early, it jumped too late, it shivered and shook, but the one thing it didn't do was play the spell. Hard to believe that people back then would willingly deal with such a dumb device.

He took the record off the turntable and examined it carefully in the light of his desk lamp.

The record had a scratch. The spell of eternal love was ruined.

∿

That night at dinner, Max was pouty and withdrawn. His mom tried to cheer him up, but Max just sat there, moping, sticking his fork in the brussels sprouts and mashed potatoes, and wallowing in misery. It was as if all color had drained from his life. Max used to imagine that before he was born, the world existed only in black and white. He knew this because old movies on TV were usually in black and white. Until about the age of six, Max had been convinced that it was his birth that had brought color into the world. And once there was color, everything became much more joyful. But now, as he sat in the glare of the overhead lights in the dining room, it was all back to the old black-and-white-days. Everything around him seemed joyless.

"Everything okay?" Mom asked.

No, he wanted to snap. How could things be okay? Where's Dad?

Instead he sullenly said, "Yeah." Resting his head on his hand, he made a mashed-potato castle with his fork.

"That's not true," Deborah said, gazing at her son. She knew he was hiding something from her. Over the last few days, Max had slipped into a deepening funk and was becoming unbearable. He had difficulties sleeping and was always late for school.

Deborah had grown worried. At first she'd thought that Max had handled everything surprisingly well. Even when Harry moved out, it hadn't seemed to bother Max too much. There were even times when Deborah had felt proud she was protecting her son from the influence of his wayward father.

"Have you been talking to your dad?" she asked.

Max nodded.

"What did he say about me?"

"Nothing," Max replied moodily.

Deborah knew that wasn't true, and suspected that Harry was trying to turn her own son against her. She lit a cigarette. Before the breakup, she had tried to keep her smoking habit a secret from Max, and had only smoked outside, not wanting to be a bad example. But she was no longer able to resist the lure of tobacco, nor could she pretend to be something she wasn't, a whole person. She was wounded, and she didn't care who saw it. This, she felt, was a time of truth. No more lies.

She blew the smoke toward the ceiling. Maybe his behavior is just a delayed reaction, she thought. Max didn't understand how good his life with her was. For days now, he had been dismissive of her. Either that, or full of sarcasm. As if all this were her fault!

She felt like a failure as a mother.

☀

The next day at school, Max had difficulties concentrating. His best friend, Joey Shapiro, seemed worried.

"What's wrong with you, dude?"

Joey and Max were sitting with Myriam Hyung at a table in the school cafeteria.

Max simply shrugged and said, "No idea."

He didn't want to talk about his problems, and he especially didn't want to talk about that stupid record. He didn't want to talk about anything. What's the point? he thought to himself.

But at Joey's insistence, he finally confessed. He told him that he'd played the record to cast the spell of eternal love, but that the record was scratched.

"What, you think you're going to play a record and your dad will come back?" Joey asked. He started sniggering. Joey was half a year older than Max, which meant that Joey knew everything and Max knew nothing.

"That's so stupid," Joey said. "Grow up. This'll never work."

"Shut up," said Myriam.

"But it's stupid," Joey insisted.

"You're stupid," Myriam said.

Max thought it was nice of Myriam to come to his aid. But he was afraid that Joey was right. Maybe he was just stupid.

※

Recently, Deborah had become cautious and quiet around her son, especially when he was in a mood like this. Sometimes, she thought, it was just like living with his father.

She remembered, quite vividly, the day she realized she was going to have a child. She had missed her period and was frantic. They were both much too young to start a family. They went to a Rite-Aid to buy a pregnancy test. If the little plastic thing was blue, you were all right.

But it was red. She was deeply shocked, and Harry took her out for beer. Lots of beer.

"How could this happen?" she said.

"Sex," he replied.

"I know *that*. Maybe the condom broke?"

"I thought you were on the pill," Harry replied.

And so it went. After some back-and-forth, they had decided on an abortion, a difficult choice that they both weren't exactly thrilled about. They had driven to Planned Parenthood in downtown LA, but they didn't get any farther than the parking lot. The car engine was still idling: Deborah threw Harry a mischievous glance, and Harry put the car in reverse. They took off like two getaway drivers after a robbery.

And now, all these years later, the end product of an ill-advised drunken romp that had led Deborah into Harry's bed sat across from her, looking sullen and refusing to eat his dinner.

The phone rang. Deborah went to pick it up. Max heard her talking in a low voice. When she came back, he asked her who it was.

"Eat your food," she said.

"Who was on the phone?"

She sighed and said, "Mr. Gutierrez."

Max knew who that was. Her divorce lawyer. "What did he want?"

"It's none of your business."

"Yes, it is," he replied.

"Nothing will change for you," she said with a forced smile. It was a phrase he'd heard before.

And then, more gently, Deborah added, "Just some paperwork I have to sign. I have to stop by his office next week."

Just some paperwork! Max thought contemptuously. He felt panic rising within him and was having trouble breathing. "I hate you!" he shouted.

Within seconds, Deborah and Max were engaged in battle. She screamed at him, and he screamed at her. He told her that he wished she were dead.

"Oh yeah?" she shot back. "Me too! I should have had that abortion—then I wouldn't have to deal with any of this!"

Bravely swallowing the tears rising up inside him, Max got up and stormed out of the room, slamming his bedroom door shut.

For a long time, he lay on his bed staring at the Spider-Man poster tacked to the ceiling.

Then he opened his closet. He took out the record and gazed pensively at the cover. In a moment of sudden clarity, he realized what he needed to do.

He had to find this magician.

Only the Great Zabbatini could save his family.

SECRETS

When Moshe Goldenhirsch was fifteen years old, he came home from shul and was surprised to find the Locksmith standing in the staircase, perfectly still.

"What do you want?" Moshe asked suspiciously. His father had warned him repeatedly that the man was not to be trusted.

"I wanted to see you," said the Locksmith.

"Why?"

"There's something I want to show you. Come with me."

Moshe was dubious at first, but curiosity won out. He went inside and put his leather bag down, then went back into the hallway where the Locksmith was waiting for him, standing in front of the door. He smelled of beer, and was swaying a little.

To Moshe's surprise, the Locksmith held out his hand. After a moment's hesitation, Moshe took it. He was surprised how well their two hands fit. As soon as Moshe touched him, the Locksmith seemed to stand a little straighter. They went outside. It was a bright day in June.

"Where are we going?" Moshe asked.

"Everywhere," the Locksmith said with an air of mystery. And then, seeing that Moshe looked concerned, he added, "Don't worry."

For reasons he couldn't explain, Moshe believed him. From Josefov, they walked south toward Vyšehrad, where the Locksmith had his shop. It was a dusty old room, near a bypass road, where carriages and the occasional automobile would rattle past, spitting exhaust. The windows were gray with soot and smoke. Moshe was fascinated by the different locks and mechanisms, gleaming in the dull afternoon light. The Locksmith packed a few of them in his bag and said, "Let's go."

For hours, they walked through Prague. The lumbering man showed Moshe the various types of locks he had installed in doors throughout the city. Big locks, small locks, simple locks, ornate locks. Moshe was fascinated.

"Every lock," the man said to Moshe, "is a riddle cast in iron."

They were going at a brisk pace, uphill and downhill, but neither seemed to be out of breath. Every few blocks, they would stop by a beer hall, where the Locksmith would drink a black lager or two, and Moshe would sit there quietly, watching him get more and more drunk. Just like his father. He found it odd that grown-ups were so dependent on alcohol.

Finally, they went back to their tenement building in Josefov. The Locksmith opened the front door and they both went up the stairs. He ruffled Moshe's hair with surprising tenderness: "You're a good kid," he said.

Moshe was unsure what to say. The Locksmith's eyes darted to the floor. He held his coarse workman's cap in his thick fingers, kneading it.

He looks, Moshe thought, like a knight from an old story, about to proclaim his love to a maiden.

"Would you," said the Locksmith tentatively, "like to go to the circus?"

Moshe nodded hesitantly. He'd never been to a circus before. It wasn't the kind of place his father would take him to, but at the same time, he was curious, and he could feel his heart pounding. Still, he was somewhat suspicious, as he always was when grown-ups were too friendly.

"Yes," said the Locksmith. "Let's go to the circus, you and I." He attempted a smile. "Soon."

※

Since Rifka's death, Laibl was searching for redemption, not only at the bottom of a glass, but also in the pages of the Torah. Neither supplied him the answers he sought. He was stumbling, both externally and internally. But he was determined to make his son a better version of himself. If he had his way, Moshe would be a scholar, like himself. But Moshe didn't dream of it, and he showed no discernible talent for scholarly wisdom.

Whenever he made a mistake in Hebrew school, if he wrote

the wrong letter on the blackboard, Laibl, always the stern teacher, would reach for his ruler.

"Which hand?" he would ask.

Moshe usually held out his left, since he used it less often than the other one. Then Laibl would bring the ruler down on his outstretched tender palm. The pain would shoot through Moshe's hand and arm, spreading through his body like liquid fire, invading body and soul and bringing tears to his eyes.

※

One afternoon, Moshe came home from school with an aching hand to find the Locksmith sitting on the stairs in front of their apartment, grinning. Moshe put his leather schoolbag down and looked at him expectantly. The Locksmith held up two large, colorful rectangular pieces of paper. "Do you know what these are?" he asked.

Moshe shook his head.

"Come here," the Locksmith said. Moshe approached him and the Locksmith handed him a piece of paper.

It said: *The ZAUBER-ZIRKUS. Come and be amazed! Tonight: The Amazing Half-Moon Man! An evening of magic and mystery!*

It wasn't an ordinary circus, the Locksmith explained, where one had to fear stepping in camel droppings and the like. No, the Zauber-Zirkus was a "magical revue," with only a few acrobats, animals, and clowns to support the main act, the "Half-Moon Man." This type of show, Moshe learned, was all the rage in Europe these days.

"Have you ever heard of Harry Houdini?" asked the Locksmith.

Moshe silently shook his head.

"Houdini was the greatest magician who ever lived. He was an escape artist. He could escape from anything. Even," the Locksmith added with a smirk, "the law." He grinned. "He could free himself from any lock," said the Locksmith with professional admiration. "He understood that each seal is meant to be broken. That's the kind of guy he was."

"Was?" Moshe asked.

"Yes," the Locksmith replied. "There was one thing he couldn't escape from."

Moshe nodded. He understood. "Like Mama," he said.

A wistful look appeared on the Locksmith's face. He averted his eyes. Then he explained that the director of this particular circus—the ringmaster and main attraction—was a famous magician. A baron and veteran of the Great War!

The streets were wet. Gray clouds loomed over their heads, waiting to unload their wrath.

The air was crisp and smelled of the coming rain. The sky was the color of a dull blade. To Moshe, everything appeared in shades of gray and dark brown.

Everything, that is, except the tent where the show was to take place. A ragged army tent that had been sewn up and adorned with yellow stars, it glowed with bright colors, and the shine of its lanterns was reflected in the puddles along the street.

What if there's a fire? Moshe suddenly thought. For a moment, he was gripped by an inexplicable feeling of anxiety. Not unusual for Moshe Goldenhirsch, particularly considering that he was doing something forbidden, or at least something that his father had no idea about. Bad enough. He forced himself to calm his breathing. But there was so much to gawk at! The gypsy wagons parked in a circle behind the tent, the red carpet leading up a few improvised wooden steps to the main entrance, the smell of wet sawdust. A swarm of people were shuffling inside: most of them appeared to be working-class, in ragged clothes and stained shirts, but there were also a few bourgeois, with fine hats, scarves, canes, and the occasional pince-nez.

Moshe and the Locksmith entered the tent, appearing out of place among the throng of gentiles who were giving them hostile looks. The two took their seats, high up in the back of the bleachers, far away from the arena. The Locksmith was not a rich man, and he could only afford the least expensive seats. Enchantment had its price.

Moshe was enraptured by what he saw. Above the artists' entrance was a balcony, and on that balcony sat a four-man orchestra, playing popular waltzes. When the audience was more or less seated, and whispering excitedly to each other, the orchestra played a fanfare. A red curtain was pushed aside, and then *he* stepped out.

The tall man walked up to the footlights with calm, measured steps.

"Good evening, *mesdames et messieurs*," he said in a sonorous voice. "I bid you all welcome." He made a grandiose, inviting gesture with his arms, took off his top hat, and bowed. Despite his ample stomach, he seemed youthful and elegant. He was dressed in a black frock coat with a red sash, and his blond hair was slicked back with brilliantine. He wore white cotton gloves, and was leaning on an impressive black cane with a silver handle. But more than anything, Moshe was fascinated by the man's face. The left half appeared completely normal. But the right side was covered by a brass mask, in the shape of a half-moon. Moshe was transfixed by his every gesture. There was something about this man, about the entire spectacle, that touched him on a level that no one, least of all the Locksmith, was able to understånd.

This, here before him right now, was Moshe's future.

"Meine Damen und Herren," purred the man, "welcome to the show of shows. Trust nothing you see. Believe nothing you hear. Your eyes and ears will lie to you. Everything here is real. But nothing is true." And then he said, with a bow, "They call me the Half-Moon Man."

The crowd started to murmur.

The magician stretched out his arms, and two yellow canaries suddenly appeared. The birds chirped and fluttered, then shot up to the top of the tent, their wings flapping. The audience was stunned into silence. A few of the girls gasped, then giggled. Then, a smat‐tering of applause. The Half-Moon Man was still bowing, a mysterious half smile on his half face. The applause swelled like a wave. The Half-Moon Man rose from his bow. This, Moshe realized, was the crucial moment. When the Half-Moon Man had first bowed, the audience and he had been strangers. But then he released the birds, and from that moment on, they were his accomplices. They were his friends, his lovers, his adoring public. Suddenly, Moshe wanted to have an adoring public of his own.

He leaned over to the Locksmith. "Why is he wearing the mask?" he asked.

The Locksmith shrugged. "I heard that he was wounded in the Great War."

Moshe looked at him quizzically.

"The enemy," the Locksmith went on, "used chemicals against us. Terrible new weapons. If you were caught in a cloud of chemical gas, your flesh would melt."

"But a gas is nothing but a smell," whispered Moshe.

"It's much more than that." The Locksmith leaned in closer and hissed, "I saw some of the victims. Their skin and muscle were . . ." He fell silent and shook his head, as if trying to rid himself of an unpleasant dream. Then he put a smile on his face. "Let's just watch the show, shall we?"

"Is that what happened to the Half-Moon Man?"

The Locksmith patted Moshe's arm. "Just watch," he said, and leaned back.

The show was dazzling, in part because the Half-Moon Man was accompanied by a beautiful young assistant with long black hair. He introduced her as Princess Aryana from Persia. After some lion taming and acrobatics, the Princess slipped into a trunk, a large overseas suitcase, which had been previously standing off to one side of the arena. The Half-Moon Man closed the lid, grasped the silver knob of his cane, and with a quick flourish pulled a sword out of the wooden staff. Holding it up so that the audience could see it gleaming in the foot-lights, he took out a silk ribbon and cut it in half, proving that the blade was sharp. Then he adjusted his cape and assumed a fencer's stance. An instant later, he lunged forward and plunged the thin, sharp saber right into the suitcase. The audience gasped. Several of the ladies nearly fainted. But the Half-Moon Man calmed the audience with a condescending smile and a dismissive wave of his hands. He went around and opened the trunk.

There was nothing inside.

No blood. No princess. Nothing. All Moshe could see was the lining. He was stunned. Then the Half-Moon Man closed the trunk once more, shut his eyes, and mumbled something. Maybe a prayer, Moshe thought. When he opened the lid again, the young woman stepped out, unharmed. Moshe was dizzy with excitement and applauded more loudly than anyone else in the audience. He must have drawn the young woman's attention, for suddenly he felt as if her eyes were touching him in the dark. He turned a bright red and stopped applauding.

What a world we live in, he thought. Where beautiful women emerge from luggage.

Princess Aryana was not only proficient at appearing and disappearing, she also seemed to be an expert at quick costume changes. Every time she showed up, she was wearing something new, and each gown was, to Moshe's eyes, more ornate and beautiful than the last one, embellished with brocade, then feathers, then sequins.

The Half-Moon Man made rabbits appear and pigeons disappear; he made cards and coins move about magically. Moshe had never seen anything like this before, and became suddenly aware that his father had been right all along: The miracles of the Torah, the mysteries of the Kabala—it was all true.

After an exhausting two hours of mind-boggling magic and miracles came the coup de grâce.

"And now, ladies and gentlemen, boys and girls," said the Half-Moon Man, "we come to our final entertainment of the evening. For this, I will need a member of the audience."

Moshe jumped up and raised his hand: "Me!" he shouted. "Take me!" Other spectators turned to look at him and sniggered. A Jew, they murmured. Do they have to let this filth in here?

Other hands shot up, but the Half-Moon Man had made his decision.

"You!" he said, pointing to Moshe. "Yes, you," the Half-Moon Man confirmed. "Come here, Jew boy."

Moshe ran down the aisle so quickly, he nearly lost his yarmulke, and he had to hold onto it with his left hand. The audience laughed. He reached the arena and, at a gesture from the Half-Moon Man, sat down on a stool. The magician turned and addressed the audience: "Ladies and gentlemen, the world is an enchanted place. A thin veil separates us from our dreams. What you are about to witness, ladies and gentlemen, will transform your life! Pay close attention!"

He turned to the wings and, with an impatient gesture of his hand, invited his assistant onstage. She was dressed in a flowing white dress. Her long black hair framed her pale skin and haunting green eyes. Princess Aryana of Persia lay down on a red recliner, placing her hand on her forehead, as if she were about to faint. Her dress shifted slightly, revealing a shapely leg. Moshe took a deep breath. The spectators whispered to one another.

The Half-Moon Man raised his cane and traveled the distance of her body with it, from her toes to her head. The cane never touched her. The orchestra was playing dark, mysterious music as the audience waited anxiously.

And then, to Moshe's amazement, the Princess began to levitate. She was lifted up and floated in midair. Her white dress and her luscious black hair flowed around her. It was the most beautiful thing Moshe had ever seen. He felt as if he was lifted up as well, by an unseen wave. He was in love. In love with the scent of the theater, the sawdust, the wood, and the stale sweat. With the glare of the footlights, the applause of the audience, but most important of all: he fell in love with Aryana, the Persian Princess.

He stood there, with his mouth hanging open, his mind not able to understand what his eyes were telling him.

The Half-Moon Man walked up to him, knelt down beside him, pointed at the Princess, and said, "What do you see?"

Moshe opened and closed his mouth. Finally, he said, "She is floating, sir."

"Do you believe it's a trick?"

Moshe shook his head. "No, sir," he said. "She's really floating."

Some in the audience laughed. The Half-Moon Man gave him a half smile.

His uncovered eye was fixated on Moshe; the other eye was

hidden in the gleam of the brass mask. Then, turning to the audience, he roared: "There you have it, ladies and gentlemen! The princess is floating!"

Applause thundered through the tent, and the bleachers were shaking with vibrations. Moshe felt his heart thumping in his chest.

The Half-Moon Man turned to the boy and said: "Before you go . . . would you like to kiss her cheek?"

Moshe looked at him uncomprehendingly.

The Half-Moon Man made an inviting gesture. Moshe hesitated, then stepped onto the stool, bent over the Princess, and nervously took her hand. He was afraid she might drop at any moment. He was trembling slightly. Her eyes were closed.

Her hand seemed to him the most precious thing in the world. It was pale and her fingers were long and elegant. It was a treasure, and he would have been happy to stand there for the rest of his life holding her hand and gazing upon her face.

"Well?" said the Half-Moon Man encouragingly. "What are you waiting for? Give her a kiss."

Moshe misunderstood that last remark. He bent over her and instead of kissing the side of her face, his lips very gently touched her mouth, for just a moment. A wave of bemused laughter ran through the crowd. The Half-Moon Man did not look pleased. But Moshe was certain that he could see the Princess smile, if only for a brief moment. He stepped off the stool and, in a sudden rush of inspiration, took a bow. The audience cheered and clapped. The Half-Moon Man, his smile now forced, took Moshe by the hand and led him to the edge of the arena. They bowed together, holding hands. Then the Half-Moon Man released his hand and bid him farewell.

Moshe, as soon as he stepped out of the arena, began to miss the footlights and the applause. It was as if he was awakening from a dream and finding himself in his cold, drafty room. The warmth of the adulation was over. The real world was beckoning. And he didn't like it.

When Moshe arrived home late that night, he found that his father was still up. Laibl was sitting at the kitchen table, looking worried.

"Where have you been?" Laibl said.

Moshe stared at the floor. He felt caught in the act. "I . . . I was out," he stuttered helplessly.

"Out?" Laibl asked. "Out where? I was worried sick about you!"

Gradually, the truth came out. That the Locksmith had taken him to see the circus. Moshe couldn't remember seeing his father this upset before. They got into an argument, and the evening ended with Laibl beating Moshe, harder and more severely than he ever had before.

That night, as he was lying on his bedstead by the stove, his behind aching mightily, Moshe began to devise a plan.

※

Over the course of the next couple of weeks, the animosity between him and his father escalated. Only now did Moshe realize that it had always been there, lying dormant under the seemingly placid surface.

One day, while Laibl was at temple, Moshe packed his few meager belongings—some provisions, his pocket knife, and his papers—and left his father's apartment. He went to the cemetery and stood by his mother's grave, asking her forgiveness for what he was about to do. He touched her headstone with his fingers, and then, with a heart both heavy and free, he turned around and walked toward the riverbank.

The tent was gone. The circus had already departed. All that was left behind was trampled grass, broken bottles, and trash. A sharp wind blew through the nearby alleys. Moshe walked around as if in a dream, and the small square seemed to him as barren and lifeless as a desert.

Then he noticed an advertising column nearby, covered with posters, circulars, and public notices. Approaching it, he saw an announcement for the Zauber-Zirkus, dirty and torn, flapping in the wind. The Half-Moon Man's smile was half-gone, and his face definitely had a diabolical quality to it.

Moshe tore off the announcement and rushed over to a newspaper kiosk at the far side of the square. A bulky old woman, her hair hidden underneath a cotton scarf, was sitting inside the dimly lit wooden booth, reading the paper. Max approached her and showed her the bill.

"Do you have any idea where the circus might have gone?" he asked.

The old lady looked up, glanced at the announcement, and slowly nodded.

THE MAGIC SHOP

S hortly before eight, Max arrived at the corner of Holly-wood Boulevard and Cherokee Avenue. It was already dark. A light rain had descended on Los Angeles. After the argument with his mother, he had climbed out the window and walked to the bus stop. His plan was as simple as it was daring.

He was now officially a runaway child. How exciting! The police were probably already after him, maybe even the FBI. His mom would be worried, but he couldn't think about that right now. He had to find Zabbatini, no matter what. If the man was even alive. And if not . . . dear God, Max hardly dared to think about it.

He had taken the 181 East bus, all the way to the final stop in front of that large, kitschy theater where they seemed to be showing *Cats* all the time. Two years before, Max had gotten the idea that he absolutely had to see that musical, and finally his parents had grudgingly taken him. But Max had been bitterly disappointed. Instead of cute little kittens frolicking about on a stage, he only saw big-breasted dancers in spandex outfits and glittery makeup. Who wanted to see *that*? Was it too much to expect cats from a show called *Cats*?

Max desperately hoped that his little adventure would turn out to be a success. When the doors of the orange-colored bus finally opened with a hiss at the last stop, he got off and began walking farther east. He knew exactly what he was looking for.

The Hollywood Magic Shop was a slightly run-down storefront on the south side of Hollywood Boulevard, with a broken neon sign above the door and a life-size Darth Vader costume in the window. An electronic doorbell sounded as he opened the glass door. It seemed oddly whiny, like a cat in heat.

Max timidly entered the store, feeling something bordering on awe. The shop was brightly lit with rows of neon tubes, and was lined on both sides with glass counters. Inside the glass cases behind the counters and stacked on long racks beneath the ceiling were magic boxes for kids, straitjackets, ventriloquist's puppets—monkeys in frock coats seemed to be all the rage—top hats with and without bunnies, flying broomsticks for witches, and endless books and DVDs. The walls were covered with faded posters advertising magic acts of yesteryear: Howard Thurston, Harry Blackstone Sr., Dai Vernon, Shadow Master. . . .

A young couple, dressed in Dolce & Gabbana, was looking at pairs of plastic glasses that distorted the eyes. Each time the man put on a new pair, the woman laughed and clapped.

Max walked through the room as if in a trance. He had never

seen anything like this. A bald pudgy man in his fifties who was dressed in black and had a pencil-thin moustache was standing behind the counter, performing card tricks for an elderly couple in brightly colored tracksuits. The husband took a sip of soda while his wife looked on with rapt fascination as the cards flashed this way and that. Max stood behind them and tried to peek.

"This," explained the bald man as he held up a card, "is the ace of diamonds." The couple nodded agreeably. Then he placed the card facedown on a square pad of green velvet and tapped it with his fingers. "But what if it weren't?" he asked with a theatrical flourish. The couple shook their heads and the man grinned from ear to ear. Then he lifted the card: the queen of diamonds. The couple oohed and aahed. After a few more tricks, they decided to buy a deck of cards, and then left the store.

The bald man turned his attention to Max. "Can I help you?" he said. His voice was pleasantly sonorous.

Max nodded nervously. "I'm looking for someone," he said.

"Who?"

Max opened his backpack and pulled out the record. He showed it to the man, who let out an appreciative whistle. He took the record from Max and examined it carefully, as if he were studying a religious artifact. "Zabbatini," he said. "I haven't seen one of these in ages."

"Do you know him?"

"Sure, we crossed paths. A long time ago." He held out his hand. "My name is Luis. You can call me Wacky."

"Wacky?"

"I used to be a clown," Luis said. "Wacky the Clown. Then I

became a magician. I spent most of my life trying to tell people, 'I am not Wacky.' But I could never shake it." He sighed. "I am Wacky," he said with an air of resignation.

"Are you the owner here?"

Wacky nodded. "Yes," he said. "I've had this shop for over forty years now." He gestured toward the other side of Hollywood Boulevard. "Zabbatini, he used to work at the Castle."

"The Castle?" Max asked.

Luis nodded. "Up there, in the Hollywood Hills. You can't see it from here. But it's there. The greatest magic club in town. Maybe even in all of California."

"This man, Zabbatini . . ." Max began cautiously.

"What about him?"

"Was he good?"

Luis seemed to ponder this for a moment, then he said, "No. Not especially."

"He wasn't?" Max was shocked.

"Not really. He had a brief moment of fame, back in the sixties or seventies. He was one of the first guys to be on TV. But no one could understand him. His accent, you see."

Max nodded. Yeah, that was certainly an issue.

"Where was he from?" Max asked.

Luis shrugged. "I don't know. Eastern Europe, maybe Germany. Somewhere like that. He came here after the war. It was hard for him, because he had a bad arm. There were a lot of tricks he couldn't do, like coin magic."

"Because of the bad arm?"

"Yeah, his left arm. He couldn't move it properly."

"And he wasn't a great magician?" Max asked in disbelief.

Luis shrugged. "He was okay, I guess."

"On the record, he said he was very powerful."

"They all say that."

"He said he could predict the future."

"Of course. He was a mentalist."

"What's that?"

Luis pointed to the displays near the entrance of the store. "What do you see there?"

Max looked. Then he turned back to Luis. "I don't know. Bunch of toys."

"Exactly," Luis said. "Toys." Then he pointed at the glass counter that he was standing behind. "And what do you see here?"

Max bent down and peeked into the glass case. He saw an assortment of coins and nondescript wooden boxes. He looked back up. "I'm not sure. Some stuff."

"Some stuff," Luis said with a sneer. As he continued talking, his voice took on the same enigmatic tone it had with the elderly couple. "This," he went on, "is far more than stuff. These are the tools of a mentalist."

Max blinked at him, astonished. Luis seemed a little blurry to him. Max realized that his glasses had fogged up in the rain. He took them off and wiped them on his shirt.

"When you enter the store, the first things you see are silly games," said Luis. "Toys for children." He made an airy gesture with his hand. "But the deeper you go inside, the more powerful the magical items are. Each step brings you closer to the threshold of mystery. Which is where we are now."

Max put his glasses back on. "All right . . ." he said uncertainly.

"It may not look like much, but mentalism—it's the highest order of magic there is."

"And what does a mentalist do, exactly?" asked Max.

Luis looked at him closely. "I want you to think of a vegetable."

"I'm sorry, what?"

"A vegetable, it doesn't matter which one. Just don't tell me."

Max concentrated. The first thing that popped into his mind was a carrot. He nodded at Luis.

Luis seemed to stare right into Max's head.

Then he took out a yellow Post-it and wrote a word on it. "Is that what you were thinking of?"

He showed him the Post-it. It said, *Carrots*.

Max gasped. "How did you know that?" he asked, genuinely astonished.

"This," said Luis and tapped against his temple with two fingers, "is what a mentalist does. He's a magician of the mind. Someone who unlocks the mysteries of the soul. Mentalists are fortune-tellers, mind readers, hypnotists. The greatest among them are rightly feared, for they can manipulate your thoughts and look into your heart."

That's exactly what I need, Max thought. "And Zabbatini, he's a mentalist?"

"Yes," said Luis. "He is a mentalist. He's the . . ." He paused. "Well, not the greatest," he murmured pensively. Then he collected himself and loudly exclaimed, "The Great Zabbatini is the most mediocre magician who ever lived!"

That sounded impressive enough, Max thought. "Do you know where I can find him?"

Luis shook his head. "I have no idea. Is he even alive?" He sighed, then looked at his watch. "Sorry, I have to close up now."

Max watched, with an air of sadness, as Luis put on an ill-fitting trench coat and proceeded to lock the glass cases.

When he was finished, they went outside and Luis pulled down the metal grating over the shopwindows. It was raining more heavily now. Max had no idea where to go. He said good-bye to Luis and started walking away, his head hanging low. His quest was over before it had even begun. Moments later, he heard heavy footsteps behind him.

"Wait!" called Luis. "Just a minute!"

Max turned around. "Yes?"

"If I were you," he said, "I'd look in an old-age home."

"Yeah, but where?" Max asked. "There's got to be hundreds."

"True," said Luis, sounding perplexed. "It would have to be cheap. He never had any money."

Suddenly, his face lit up.

"Hey! Try the King David!"

"The what?"

"On Fairfax," Luis said. "The King David Home for the Elderly. A lot of old actors live there." He dug into his pocket and pulled out the Post-it with the word *carrots* written on it. Turning it over, he scribbled on the other side: *Zabbatini, King David, Fairfax Avenue.*

"Good luck," he said, handing it to Max.

"Thanks," said Max, and went on his way.

He was soon swallowed by the hazy October night. And all the lights and broken promises of Hollywood Boulevard were gleaming in the distance.

THE PERSIAN PRINCESS

On a field outside of the city of Dresden, Moshe finally caught up with the circus. He had been traveling for what seemed like an eternity to him. He was weary and exhausted, his feet hurt, and his body felt worn out. He had never been so far from home.

Moshe had learned one thing: he didn't like the countryside. He was a city boy, he realized, and felt most at home on cobblestone streets, among throngs of people. The countryside had little to offer him, except drastic temperature changes, too much rain—which turned the forest floor into a soggy mess—and a noticeable lack of toilets. He had diligently followed the Vltava River north for a few days, always stopping at inns and farms to ask if the circus had come through. Some of the people he encountered were very helpful, even offering him food and shelter. Others would spit over their right shoulder and drive him away.

A baker's wife in the town of Mělník had told him that, indeed, the Zauber-Zirkus had come through on its way to Dresden.

On his journey through Bohemia, he followed the Elbe River and soon came across a group of traveling Roma gypsies. Their friendliness and openness touched him deeply. They shared what little food they had with him, and allowed him to sleep in their camp that night, alongside the animals. In the evening, they made a fire, and ate goulash and drank grog. An old man with rotting, stinking teeth was playing violin, making awful screeching noises, which nonetheless seemed to delight the gypsies and bring tears to their eyes. Moshe felt desperately lonely. He missed his mother, who had abandoned him, and he missed his father, whom he had abandoned. He wanted nothing more than to be back in Prague.

∗

A few days later, at Hřensko, he reached the border of the German state of Saxony. The Elbe Valley was breathtaking, with the trees already a vibrant green and the sunlight glistening serenely on the still river.

The border crossing itself was no more than a shack with a wooden barrier at the end of a dirt path. On the left side of the path, Moshe saw an inn; to the right, train tracks and a small station. The German border guards, who were lolling about in front of their shack, refused him entry. He had, they claimed, no valid travel visa. His identity papers from Prague labeled him an "Israelite," meaning he could not enter the Reich without special permission. Had he been a "Sudeten German," they said, it would have been a different matter. The guards seemed to find the whole thing embarrassing. Moshe thanked them politely and turned back, heading for the inn.

After entering the noisy smoke-filled hall, he found a seat on a bench, near the fireplace. He shared the table with two drunken bricklayers from Bratislava, who told him that they regularly went to Prague, Warsaw, and Dresden seeking work. They were wearing coarse overalls and had brick dust under their fingernails and in the creases of their ruddy faces. One of them, a heavyset, toad-like man with wild gray hair, threw an arm around Moshe and began singing "Nad Tatrou sa blýska." Moshe had heard the melody before, at U Fleků and other beer halls of the goyim, but he didn't speak much Slovakian, so as the bricklayers sang their national anthem he hummed the Hebrew "Hava Nagila" instead. When the inn-keeper, carrying a tray with full beer glasses, came to ask him what he wanted to drink, Moshe smiled politely and shrugged. He had no money. The other bricklayer, a tall, gaunt fellow, would hear none of it. "He is my guest," he informed the innkeeper in shaky German.

"And what," said the innkeeper, "will your guest have?"

Moshe decided on a Radeberger Pilsner, brewed locally, the innkeeper informed him, just outside of Dresden.

"Nothing to eat?" the innkeeper asked, sounding as if it were an offense to decline his food. Moshe shook his head. He knew the Bohemians, and he assumed the German goyim were no different: they would eat absolutely anything, even pigs. One of their sausages was called "blood pudding." Disgusting. But he was hungry, and the tall bricklayer managed to convince him to eat at least some black bread with cheese and mustard.

The drunken Slovaks continued singing and swaying. At one point, they were swaying so hard that Moshe's yarmulke fell off his head.

The rotund bricklayer picked it up and gazed at it with astonishment.

"What is this?" he asked.

Moshe felt himself blush. "My hat," he whispered, and averted his eyes.

"Only Jews have such hats," said the second bricklayer. "You are not a Jew, are you?"

Moshe nodded. "Well," he stammered, "I'm afraid I am. I'm sorry."

The bricklayers were silent for a moment. This information seemed completely puzzling to them, even though the fact that Moshe was a Jew was readily apparent to anyone sober. Not only was he wearing a yarmulke, but he had *payos* dangling from his temples and was dressed in the black overcoat of the Orthodox. But, apparently, for the drunk, such mysteries were revealed only in good time.

After an awkward silence, the first bricklayer threw Moshe's yarmulke into the fire. "Bah!" he exclaimed.

"Bah!" said the second one in agreement.

Moshe watched his yarmulke burn, feeling as if something in him was being devoured.

"You are not a Jew anymore," proclaimed the first bricklayer.

"Because Jews are shit. Now you are one of us." He raised his tankard. "Cheers!"

"Cheers!" proclaimed the second.

Timidly, Moshe raised his tankard as well. Perhaps it was better that he was not a Jew. After all, who wants to be shit?

"Cheers!" he shouted. He would become someone else today. Someone new. He was no longer a member of the Mosaic tribe, an Israelite, standing in line for special forms and the small mercies your government was willing to extend to you. He didn't want to be a beggar anymore—he wanted to drink pigs' blood! Today, he was a goy!

After a few hours of vigorous drinking, Moshe the Goy shambled into the woods behind the inn to relieve himself. Afterward, he sat down against a moss-covered tree trunk and gazed up at the stars. The world seemed infinitely vast and filled with possibilities. He closed his eyes and fell asleep.

$$\ast/\ast$$

The next morning, he awoke with a terrible hangover. The sun was shining awfully bright, piercing his eyes. He got up and stumbled in the direction of the inn. Its doors were locked and its windows shuttered. Everything was quiet.

Moshe went to the outhouse. When that was done, he stumbled to a trough full of water, because his throat was parched. He saw his reflection in the water and then the events of last night came back to him. The drunken bricklayers who had burned his yarmulke. Then he thought he could see his father's face on the surface of the water, and he felt a pang in his heart. Moshe missed him so much, tears came to his eyes and the reflection became blurry. Then he remembered: he had vowed not to be a Jew anymore. He took his pocketknife out of his backpack and cut off his *payos*. Then he took off his black overcoat and looked at himself again. Now he was only wearing trousers and a white shirt. He still looked Jewish, he thought. Apparently, it wasn't something one could get rid of in a day.

He started walking toward Saxony. Since he knew that he couldn't cross at the border checkpoint, he decided to stay in the woods.

By afternoon, he had left Czechoslovakia and was deep within the Saxon forest. Then he heard a man's voice.

"God bless you, traveler!"

"Who? What?" Moshe blurted out. He turned around but didn't see anyone.

"Up here," said the voice. Moshe peeked up through the branches of the birch trees and saw a man wearing an outfit of green wool, as well as a hat with something like a shaving brush sticking out from the rim. The forester climbed down from his lookout post, shouldered his rifle, and held out his hand. Moshe timidly accepted it. This was new to him. Normally, the goyim didn't like touching you.

"Where are you headed?" asked the forester.

"To Dresden," said Moshe.

The man was kind enough to point Moshe in the right direction. Then he gave him some water and bade him farewell.

Moshe continued his journey. At nightfall, he finally caught up with the Zauber-Zirkus. The tent was pitched on an open field, and he recognized immediately the ragged cloth, the poorly sewn stars and symbols. He heard applause from inside. A warm glow was emanating from the tent and Moshe could hear the applause, but he knew that this time he would not be allowed inside, for he had no ticket. Cautiously he explored the surrounding area and saw a few circus wagons, some mules and horses, and a cart filled with hay. He snuck up to the back of the tent and heard shouts and applause. Taking a deep breath, he knelt down and lifted one of the tent flaps ever so slightly.

He was behind the circus arena, near the artists' entrance, underneath the orchestra. He could see the Half-Moon Man from behind, a dark shape against the colorful and seductive flare of the footlights.

And then he saw the Persian Princess, afloat in midair. A boy from the audience was standing near her, in awe, trying to understand the impossible. How could this woman just hang in the air like that? The boy had the same look on his face as he himself must have had, just recently. Moshe felt the sting of jealousy in his chest as he watched the boy kiss the Princess and walk back into the audience, which erupted into thunderous applause.

The show was soon over. The curtain was lowered and the lights went out. For a moment, Moshe couldn't see anything. Then he saw the Persian Princess walking toward him at a brisk pace. He gasped and let the tent flap drop. But it was too late to hide. A moment later, a hand tapped his shoulder from behind and Moshe found himself face-to-face with the Princess.

As she glared at him, he was dumbstruck by her magnificence.

She had a passionate gleam in her eyes, and her black, flowing hair was moving slightly in the wind.

"Who the hell are you?" she snapped at him in German, bringing him suddenly back to reality.

"I'm . . . I am . . ." stuttered Moshe.

The Princess reached into her hair and, before Moshe could say or do anything, pulled it off her head. Moshe was shocked. It was a wig. Underneath, she had short, blond hair, which was covered in sweat and powder and sticking up at all angles.

"I've seen you before," she said.

Moshe nodded. Her voice. There was something in her voice that moved him. He had never heard anybody speak German like that before. The Persian Princess came from the streets of Berlin, and she spoke the language of the local alleys and factories, perfectly suited to both tenderness and bitterness.

"You're the little Jew boy," she said suddenly. "From Prague. The one who kissed me. What are you doing here?"

Moshe shook his head. "I'm not a Jew boy."

"You look like one."

"I'm not anymore," Moshe said. "Now I'm normal."

"That so?" said the Princess. "Why don't you lower your pants and show me how normal you are?"

Moshe blushed and took a step away. The Princess started laughing, the sound coarse and ringing, then turned around and tramped over to her wagon. Moshe watched in amazement as she climbed wooden steps to her door. All the grace and agility she had as a princess had left her body. It was as if, in taking off the wig, she had become an entirely different person.

Moshe was utterly confused, but intrigued. The woman turned around and looked at him.

Reaching inside her dress, she took out a pack of cigarettes and removed one. Striking a match against the doorframe, she lit the cigarette, inhaling deeply as she gave Moshe the once-over. Evidently amused, she exhaled smoke through her nostrils.

"Are you coming or not?" she asked.

"Can I keep my pants on?" Moshe asked.

"I'll beat you if you don't," she said.

THE MENTALIST

The King David Home for the Elderly on Fairfax Avenue had been built in the sixties, and looked it. When Max opened the glass entrance door, he found himself in a lobby decorated with brass and chintz. A palace of kitsch, he thought, observing the giant bronze chandelier above him. The walls were adorned with faded, autographed black-and-white pictures of long-dead crooners and Western actors, their faces blanched. Probably former inmates here, Max thought. A purple velour sofa stood in the entrance hall, next to some folded-up wheelchairs with a handwritten sign that said, NEEDS REPAIR. The room smelled of cloyingly sweet air freshener. The King David was the end of the line, a depository for the old and the unwanted. Before coming in, Max had seen two withered old ladies through the window, shuffling about like zombies in flower-covered aprons. The doors still had last year's Chanukah decorations attached. Depressing.

Who likes old people? Max wondered. In his experience, they were maudlin and they smelled funny, like his grandpa Herman before he died. Max remembered having to kiss his stubbly cheek. Gross.

The front desk was at the end of the lobby. A bored-looking nurse in her late twenties sat in an office chair, painting her nails. Probably the night nurse. Max clutched the straps of his backpack as he timidly approached her. In his right hand, he had the Post-it that Luis had given him.

The nurse blew at her nails and said, "Yes?"

"I'm sorry," Max said. "Maybe you can help me. I'm looking for someone."

The nurse shook her hand to better dry the nail polish. "Who?" she asked.

"A man named Zabbatini."

"There's no one here by that name," she said.

Max looked at her, aghast. "Are you sure?" he asked. "Maybe it's not his real name. He's a magician."

"Aha," said the nurse with a tone of boredom in her voice. She pressed a button on the intercom, summoning her boss.

Then she went back to doing her nails, ignoring Max. He felt uncomfortable.

He saw a clipboard with a sheet of paper lying on the counter. The visitors' log. Max realized he was supposed to write down his name and address. Folks here probably needed to know who came and went. Max obediently wrote down his information, then put the pen aside and began gently bouncing on the balls of his feet.

After a while, a portly man with a bushy moustache, a striped shirt, and a stained white coat walked around the corner. He had a sandwich in one hand.

"This better be important," he said, chewing.

The nurse nodded toward Max. "Kid's looking for someone."

The manager glared at Max with barely concealed hostility.

"A magician," said Max.

"What?" said the man.

Max held out the Post-it. "Look," he said. "It says it right here."

The man picked up the paper and glanced at it. "It says, 'Carrots'."

"The other side."

He turned it over, then shrugged. "There's no Zabbatini here."

"Like I said, maybe it's not his real name. He's a mentalist. He can read people's minds. His left arm is busted, somehow. And I thought . . ."

What? What did he think? Max was looking for a needle in a haystack. Why should Zabbatini be here, of all places? Maybe he had left LA. Maybe he had moved somewhere else. Maybe he was dead.

But, to Max's surprise, the manager raised his eyebrows. "Left arm?" he said. Then he went to a door and held it open for Max. "Try Bungalow 112," he said, pointing toward the courtyard beyond. "But that guy doesn't read minds. He only reads girlie mags."

Max thanked the manager and proceeded through a short walkway. The courtyard on the other end, overgrown with palms, had a fountain burbling in one of its far corners and a swimming pool at its center. The rooms and bungalows had been constructed around it.

Max approached a small bungalow marked 112. He knocked and waited. Then knocked again. No response. He looked around and realized he was alone in that tropical courtyard. The only sound came from the small fountain. Max snuck up to one of the windows of the bungalow and peeked inside. He saw an old man's leg lying on the floor. That's all he could see, just the leg. The skin was pale and wrinkled and covered with blue varicose veins. The leg protruded from a pair of white cotton shorts, and its limp foot was wearing a cheap, bright blue plastic sandal. The rest of the body was hidden behind a wall. Max was worried. He wondered if he should inform the nurse or her boss. Maybe that would take too long. What if there was a serious problem? Should he break down the door? On the other hand, if he did break down the door, the fat man and the nurse might get upset.

Maybe the guy was only sleeping. Maybe he was enjoying a well-deserved rest after a long day.

On the floor?

Then he smelled gas.

Max pounded against the door as hard as he could. "Hello!" he called. "Hello!"

The man on the floor did not respond. Max turned around, clutching his backpack, and ran back to the lobby. The nurse was gone. Max timidly touched the bell standing on the counter, but the sound trailed off unheard.

Nothing.

He ran back to Bungalow 112. Now what? he wondered. Maybe he should break the door down after all. This was the sort of thing he had only seen in action movies, but never in real life. He rammed against the door with his left shoulder, and immediately felt a sharp shock of pain. He was too weak. Near the pool was a plastic lawn chair. Max grabbed it and smashed it against the door. This, too, produced no discernible result. He put the chair down and started kicking against the door.

"What," said a voice, "are you doing?"

Max shot around. The manager was standing behind him, glowering at him.

"Do you smell that?" Max asked.

"Where are your parents?"

"It smells like gas," said Max. He leaned against the door, which suddenly gave in. For a brief moment, Max felt suspended in midair, like an astronaut. Then he crashed down to the ground.

"You're going to pay for that," the manager informed him.

"Look!" Max pointed at the motionless leg.

"Moshe!" the man yelled at the leg and came charging into the room like a mad cow. "Wake up! Moshe!"

※

At some point in his life, Moshe Goldenhirsch of Prague, son of Laibl and Rifka and possibly the Locksmith from upstairs, had realized that it was better to be a "Zabbatini" than a "Goldenhirsch." It had taken considerable effort to become the former and run away from the latter. Not that it did him much good at the moment. Right now, the Great Zabbatini was lying on a wall-to-wall carpet, as good as dead. And it felt great. As if he was floating above it all, above Fairfax Avenue with its retirement homes, its thrift stores and kosher delis. He was looking down into the courtyard, feeling oddly at peace, watching Ronnie, the manager of the King David, dragging his lifeless self out into the courtyard. A boy was helping him. Little brat, Zabbatini thought. But so what? None of this concerned him any longer. He was free.

And he turned around and started to float away into the evening sky. He didn't get very far. He suddenly felt pulled down by the ankles, which strongly impeded his ability to float. He flapped his arms like he'd seen penguins do in nature documentaries, but that didn't help. It didn't help the penguins either. They were flightless birds. And he was a flightless man.

Everything around him went black.

⁂

The manager grabbed the old man by the legs and dragged him outside, with Max's help. The bungalow consisted of two rooms, a kitchen and a bedroom. The old man must have been standing between the two rooms when it happened. Ronnie went back inside and closed the gas line with a wrench.

The man moaned. He must have been well over eighty, and probably had been a good-looking guy in his youth. Now his face was sagging and sad, distorted by old age and years of disappointment. He had a nearly bald head, bushy eyebrows, a bulbous red nose, and thick black glasses that hung from his ears. He was wearing a faded Hawaiian shirt and a gold chain with a small Star of David around his neck. His left arm was distorted and withered like a gnarly tree branch, sticking out from his body at an odd angle.

His arm! Max thought, and his heart skipped a beat. This must be the guy!

The manager and Max managed to lift him up and put him in one of the lawn chairs that were standing around the sad, green swimming pool.

"Moshe!" the manager called. "Wake up!"

The old man moaned, but showed no sign of coming to.

"We have to wake him," said Max. "Maybe you should slap him."

"He's your friend," the manager said. "You slap him."

Ronnie didn't particularly like the *alte kaker*. Moshe still owed back rent.

"Me?" Max said. "I don't even know him."

"What, you never hit a guy before?"

Max had indeed once hit a guy, little Willie Bloomfield in the class below him. Willie had run to Mrs. Wolf and ratted on him, but he couldn't really count that incident as proper violence. Willie was, after all, an idiot.

Max shook his head.

"It's easy. Look." The manager proceeded to demonstrate. A powerful blow caused the old man's body to jerk like a helpless puppet.

"Like that," he said.

"Okay," Max said. He touched the old man lightly on the cheek with his fingertips.

"Not like that," the manager said. "Harder."

"My shoulder hurts," Max said by way of apology.

"Put some juice into it," said the manager. "I'll get some water. Be right back."

Max watched as the man headed toward the lobby. There was something waddly about the way he walked. He seemed to be very content and at peace with himself. Max stood back and took a deep breath. He remembered watching old episodes of *Kung Fu* on TV. He remembered David Carradine who, when forced to use violence, would first gather his thoughts and then strike with great precision and accuracy. Max closed his eyes and inhaled. Then he let the air out, opened his mouth, and hit the old man as hard as he could. His glasses were flung off his face and fell into the pool, sinking down with a sad gurgle.

"Ahhh!" the old man screamed indignantly.

He opened his eyes and looked up at Max, his gaze deeply confused and filled with despair.

Max stood in front of him, his hand still raised.

This, he thought, is very awkward.

Max cleared his throat, lowered his hand, and tugged help-lessly at his T-shirt. His hand had left a red mark on the old man's saggy cheek. The old man glanced around disoriented. Then he muttered, "I love you."

He put his face in his hand and began to sob.

Max kneeled next to him and gently put his arm on the gnarled shoulder. "I . . ." he began. "I love you too."

The old man raised his head and looked at Max with great disbelief and contempt. "Not you!" he said.

"I saved you . . ." Max added timidly.

The old man gave a dismissive wave. "That's a mitzvah? I want to be saved? Look at me. This is a life?"

"But the gas . . ."

"I wanted it should kill me," the old man lamented. "That was the idea! Life is shit."

"I'm sorry."

"You should have left me to die!"

"It won't happen again," said Max. The man had the exact same accent as on the record.

The old man leaned back in his lawn chair and stared at the cracked cement floor, brooding.

Max got up silently. "Are you the Great Zabbatini?" he asked.

"Shut up your mouth. Always with the talking," said the old man.

Max did as he was told. Both of them seemed lost in thought. And neither of them noticed the manager approaching with a bucket of water.

Max heard a splashing noise, and when he looked up, the old man was completely drenched. He sat in his deck chair with a resigned look on his face. He looked down at his Hawaiian shirt. He wiped the few wet hairs from his forehead.

The manager dropped the bucket with a loud clatter. "I'm so sorry," he said.

The old man stared at him and Max reproachfully. "You beat me," he said.

The manager pointed at Max. "That was him!"

"And now you try to drown me." The old man's voice got shrill.

"You were unconscious," the manager responded.

The old man made a dismissive gesture. "It is no matter," he said. He lifted himself laboriously from his deck chair and shuffled toward his room.

"And why is broken my door?" he asked.

"Well . . ." Max began. But the old man gave an exhausted wave. Water dripped from his arm. Max closed his mouth.

"Nothing matters," the old man said. "Nothing matters at all."

"There's gas in your room," Max said.

"So what?" said the old man. He shuffled into his room. "Wake me when there's pancakes," he told the manager. Then he put his hand in his pocket and took out a pill for his heart. After all, who wants to have a heart attack?

AN ARTIST

Moshe found out that Princess Aryana's real name was Julia Klein. She was not from Persia at all, but rather from a working-class neighborhood in Berlin-Spandau. She had met the Half-Moon Man at the Wintergarten-Varieté on Friedrichstraße, a well-known vaudeville cabaret.

The Wintergarten was located on the ground floor of the Central-Hotel, and for many nights, after her shift at the store was over, Julia would stand in front of its stone columns, where a uniformed doorman held open the doors of carriages and automobiles, so that the elegant ladies and gentlemen of Berlin society could make their proper entrances. The ladies wore mink coats and ornate hats with peacock feathers; the gentlemen were dressed in frock coats. Arm in arm, the couples would enter through the imposing and ornate double doors and vanish in the dark. Julia would stand and watch. She could feel the warmth and hear the laughter and music from inside, and she even smelled the faint cigarette smoke. She longed to go inside, to enter this sophisticated world, seeking a refuge not only from the cold and rain, but from her life. She would study the playbills posted in front, riveted by what she read. Transvestite shows! Jazz! Magic! One night, after borrowing an ill-fitting dress from her friend Dagmar, she ventured inside.

The Wintergarten was smoke-filled and poorly lit. Hurried waiters in tuxedos rushed about. People jostled, and rudeness was de rigueur—this was Berlin, after all. Julia, who wasn't used to wearing heels, stubbed her toe looking for a seat, and a pudgy waiter with a large tray and a white cloth grudgingly assigned her a place in the back, rolling his eyes. She could barely see the stage, since a round lamp illuminating her table almost completely blocked her view. In the orchestra pit, the musicians were playing a jazz hit of the day: "Yes! We Have No Bananas." Julia was astonished to see that the musicians had dark skin. She was puzzled. Were they Africans? She'd seen Africans before at the Berlin Zoo. Or perhaps they came from America. Everything inexplicable came from America: the latest music, the latest automobiles, Lucky Strike cigarettes, Coca-Cola.

After a few more songs, the red curtain opened and an announcer entered the stage and took the microphone. He was a small man with blond slicked-back hair and he wore a frock coat.

"Ladies and gentlemen," he purred into the microphone, "welcome to the Wintergarten. Allow me to introduce a man of magic and mystery. . . ."

He continued in this vein for a while, and then introduced

"Kröger the Great," adding, "We guarantee that this gentleman will change your life."

This was no lie: he did indeed change Julia's life. But what she saw that night wasn't very promising. Kröger appeared in front of a rather small audience, and they seemed to be mocking him. Still, he kept his cool, smiling and bowing. She was oddly intrigued by his hapless performance, which must have triggered some maternal instinct in her, for she decided, right then and there, that this man needed her help, whether he wanted it or not.

She came back, night after night, watching the Great Kröger and spending the money she earned as a shopgirl.

One day, after another disastrous performance, she gathered her courage and went to his dressing room. In the narrow hallway backstage, she ran into some of the musicians, who were washing their faces. Only then did Julia realize that they had been wearing makeup, as the black dissolved to reveal white skin underneath. When she asked for Herr Kröger's dressing room, one of the musicians pointed down the hallway with his thumb.

"That way," he said in a thick Berlin accent.

Julia knocked on his door. And so it began.

"Come in," said Kröger the Great.

Julia timidly entered and curtsied, just like she had learned in school.

"What do you want?" asked Kröger. His first name, she would learn, was Rudi.

He wasn't looking at her; he was only looking at himself in the mirror, as he was removing his stage makeup. She didn't know how to begin. What could she possibly say? That she hated her home and that she wanted to run away? That would sound foolish. But she knew that men usually found her attractive, and that all she needed to do was keep her mouth shut. The less she said, the easier it was for her to get her way.

It worked. That night, he took her out for dinner. They had champagne and lobster—on credit, of course. Julia Klein was enchanted, and did her best to enchant Kröger, whom she saw as her way out.

She was getting tipsy and she began telling him about her family. Her father had fought at Verdun; now he worked in a factory. He often came home drunk and berated the family, making Julia blush with shame. With an iron will, he enforced his ideas of discipline, even raising his hand against his own daughter on occasion. One time, she confided to Kröger, he had even smeared his feces all over the bedroom wall, throwing it everywhere. Everyone thought he was insane. He wasn't. No one in her family realized that flinging around excrement was a perfectly reasonable response to the events of the twentieth century.

Julia, like most people, was not very interested in politics—or feces, for that matter. She was, however, very interested in leaving behind her bleak world. She told Kröger that she wanted to run away from home, and that it had not escaped her attention that he, a magician, might be in need of an assistant. That night, they kissed under the stars that hung above the Brandenburg Gate.

A mere five days later, Rudi Kröger and Julia Klein left their lives and names behind. They reinvented themselves—as Baron von Kröger, the legendary Half-Moon Man—and the Persian

Princess Aryana. The name Half-Moon Man had been Julia's idea. She knew that Rudi was a war veteran and that many veterans had disfigured faces. Why not play with that? In a shop selling carnival supplies, she found a Venetian brass mask in the shape of a half-moon. From now on, Kröger would pretend to be a nobleman with a tragic past whose face had been forever destroyed by the enemy's weapons.

Kröger envisioned himself in the tradition of the great European masters of magic, such as Bartholomeo Bosco, the Maskelynes, and Jean Eugène Robert-Houdin. Julia was fascinated as Kröger led her through the history of magic and, later, to his bed. It was her first time, and happened a few weeks after their first meeting at the Wintergarten. In her dreams, this had been a moment of enormous importance, but it turned out be to oddly uneventful in real life, and slightly uncomfortable.

Is this it? she thought. Are we really making love?

Before she knew it, it was over. She got up and went to the bidet in the small bathroom of the hotel they were staying at and carefully rinsed herself.

Kröger was hardly a magician between the sheets, but anything was better than living under the same roof with her increasingly demented father and tormented mother. Still, Kröger's occasional outbursts of anger kept her on edge. One moment, he would be sweet as a lamb; the next, some trivial incident would send him into fits of fury. A real artist!

Together, they worked out a nearly seamless magic act, tried and tested over hundreds of performances. Gradually, a structure emerged that seemed to be pleasing to the audience. In addition to playing the Wintergarten, they appeared in various other clubs and cabarets around Berlin, saving up enough money so that they could buy an old army tent, which Kröger and Julia painstakingly repaired and turned into something resembling a circus tent. And thus the Zauber-Zirkus was born. Cobbling together a small group of musicians, acrobats, and animal trainers to flesh out Kröger's show, they proceeded to go on tour. It was the best time of Julia's life so far. They traveled through Galicia, Belorussia, Hungary, and finally Czechoslovakia.

And that was where Moshe Goldenhirsch appeared, and kissed the sleeping princess awake.

Now, young Moshe, at the tender age of fifteen, was sitting in Julia's wagon, drinking a hot tea spiked with brandy. He felt incredibly lucky to be in her presence. Moshe didn't realize it, but luck had nothing to do with it. Julia had noticed at once that Moshe had a crush on her. She was only eighteen herself, and desperate for the attention of boys, so that she could scorn them.

But she did not scorn Moshe. No, Moshe was a gift from heaven. There was one thing in the Zauber-Zirkus that she hated, and that was shoveling horse manure. It seemed there was no end to it. Men and horses were incredibly prolific producers of shit. And since everyone else in the troupe was a "highly trained specialist," whose skills and experience were far too valuable to be wasted on shoveling, the task had always fallen to her, the youngest and least experienced member. This was where Moshe came in. And so, she did everything in her power to make him feel warm and welcome in her wagon, which she had to share with Mrs. Arndt, the ticket-taker and cook of the troupe. Julia didn't have to do much to persuade Moshe. The little Jew was clearly beguiled by her.

"What a glamorous life you must lead," Moshe said, awestruck.

"Every day is an adventure," Julia said, but wisely didn't mention what kind of adventure.

Her face had an almost classic beauty to it, with deep-set green eyes. Moshe feared that he would drown in those eyes. The boy lowered his cup and stared at the wooden planks beneath his feet. Julia knew what was coming.

A warm, pleasant fire in a steel oven was warming up the tiny wagon, which was stuffed with pots and pans and the clutter of everyday life. Moshe glanced at the makeup table, the costume racks, the sacks of hay on which Julia and Mrs. Arndt had to sleep, the colorful playbills and programs pinned to the mirror, the masks and costumes. He was enthralled.

"Do you think I could join your circus?" he asked timidly.

Julia averted her eyes. It was important not too seem too eager.

"I don't know," she said in a whisper. "I'll have to ask the boss."

❋

The boss was standing with some members of his troupe in the middle of the empty circus arena. He was not pleased. One of the tricks had not worked properly: the Princess's appearance from the overseas trunk had drawn sniggering from the audience. That meant either that Conradi-Horster had screwed up, which was unlikely, or that the trunk had been placed at the wrong angle, and that some audience members had been able to see into the safe zone. Kröger was in the midst of yelling at his colleagues when Julia and Moshe approached him.

"*Liebling*," said Julia in her smoky voice, the voice that drove Kröger mad. And also Moshe. Julia had the slender, graceful body and delicate features of a dancer, despite her odd tendency to tramp about gracelessly. Her short blond hair was unruly, giving her a slightly impish appearance. She wore a white undergarment specifically chosen to accentuate her breasts, as well as tall rubber boots, because life in the circus was no picnic, and one was likely to step into all kinds of things. She had wiped the sweat, makeup, and powder off her face and was sucking lasciviously on a cigarette.

"*Liebling*," she said again.

Kröger turned around and looked at her. "The audience saw you. In the trunk."

She shrugged, disinterested. "I did everything like I always do."

"I know, my treasure," the Baron cooed. "It's not your fault."

Up close, his brass mask gave off an eerie gleam. His makeup had blended with his sweat, becoming runny, and turned his face into something demonic. At last, Kröger noticed the boy.

"Who is that?" he asked.

Julia took Moshe's shoulders and pushed him toward Kröger. "I found him behind the circus. He wants to join."

The Baron stared at the boy. He smelled of old stale sweat and schnapps.

Moshe, terrified of the man, was breathing heavily.

"Who are you?"

"Sir!" Moshe called out. "I left my father to join the Zauber-Zirkus."

"Are you a Jew?"

"I used to be . . ." Moshe said in a quavering voice.

But Kröger gave a dismissive wave of his hand. "Spare me. We're circus folk. We're all equals."

Moshe had never heard that before. "Really?"

"Really. Can you shovel shit?"

"Me?"

"Yes, you. Do you see anyone else here?"

"Are you really a baron?" Moshe asked tentatively.

"In the theater," Kröger said, "everyone is a nobleman. We are artists, and there is nothing nobler than art."

That made sense to Moshe.

"Horst!" Kröger called out. An old man with a broom who was sweeping the bleachers looked up. "The boy here wants to know what you are!"

"An artist," Horst called back in a squeaky voice, then continued sweeping.

"You see?" the Baron said. "The man who sweeps the floor is an artist. Everyone here is an artist."

Moshe could scarcely contain his excitement: "I want to be an artist, too!" he said.

Kröger smiled and handed him a shovel.

"Welcome, Maestro," he said.

A THOUSAND LIGHTS

Max Cohn and the old man were sitting over roast beef sandwiches, french fries, and pancakes in a booth at Canter's Deli on Fairfax Avenue. It was shortly after ten, but the place was still bustling. The room was lit in subdued shades of yellow and orange, which gave the old man's skin a deathly pallor, and the seats were covered with brown fake leather. Small bottles of mustard and ketchup stood on the table in the midst of their half-eaten food. In the distance, Max could hear the clatter and hushed murmurs of other customers.

Max was drinking Coke. The old man pulled the onions from his sandwich and put them on the table next to his plate, shaking his head disapprovingly.

"Onions make me fart," he declared.

Max nodded.

"They're everywhere," said the old man with an air of melancholy. "On everything."

Max took another sip of his soda. "Are you a magician?"

The man ignored the question. He carefully lifted a slice of rye bread off his sandwich and peeked under it. An elderly waitress approached the table, sighing dramatically. A yellow apron covered her large, sagging bosom; her hair had been dyed bright red; and her lipstick was a dazzling shade of fuchsia. She leaned on the table with her left hand as she fumbled for her notebook.

"My hip," she said. "It's just not getting any better."

"What's with all the onions?" the old man said. "This is shit."

"Watch your language," said the waitress. "There's a kid sitting there." And then she added, "Is there anything else I can get you gentlemen?"

"Why always put you onions on everything?" the old man demanded, apparently unwilling to drop his line of inquiry.

"People like onions. Normal people. You want coffee or something?"

"Coffee?" the old man asked indignantly. "So I should stay up the whole night?"

"I'm just asking," said the waitress.

Max found it odd that she didn't lose her calm. He personally felt embarrassed by the old man's behavior. But apparently, at Canter's it was quite normal.

"Bah! Coffee," the old man said contemptuously. "Go away."

The waitress put the check on the table and left.

Max repeated his question. "Are you a magician?"

The old man shook his head. "No."

Max was confused. Did he have the wrong guy? But Luis, aka Wacky the Clown, had said that he had a bad left arm. That seemed to fit the bill.

"Do you know the Hollywood Magic Shop? A guy named Luis?" Max asked.

There was no reaction.

He added, "Luis is amazing. He asked me to write down a vegetable—"

"What, again with that stuff?" the old man said loudly. "Leave me already in peace."

"So you're really not a magician?"

"Look at me! Do I look like a magician? I'm an old man. I want to die! But no, you stopped me, you stupid boy!"

Max opened his backpack and pulled out his record. "That looks like you."

The old man barely peeked at the record. He took a bite of the pancakes. His mouth full, he grudgingly said:

"Yes, it is I."

"So you *are* a magician."

He shook his head. "No. I *was* a magician. I'm retired. Enough already."

"See," Max started to explain, "I have a problem. And I was hoping you could help me."

"I don't help people."

"It's about my parents," Max went on undeterred. "They're about to get a divorce."

"Good," said the old man. "You know why a divorce so expensive is?"

Max shook his head.

"Because it's worth every penny," Zabbatini said with a grin.

Max could see the chewed-up pancake in the man's mouth. Somehow, this conversation wasn't going as he had hoped.

"I don't want them to get a divorce."

"And I want that my shit should smell like gold."

Max decided to make one last attempt. "On your record, there's a spell. Eternal love. I was going to listen to it and then . . . well, use it, somehow. But the record is scratched. I thought, I was hoping . . ." His voice trailed off. Gathering his courage, he said, "I was hoping you could perform that spell, so that they'll be in love again. So that Dad won't leave me."

Zabbatini glared at Max. He pointed his fork at him and said, "That's the dumbest thing I've ever heard."

Max turned red and fought back tears. There was a silence.

Then, Zabbatini said, "Carrots."

"What?"

"The vegetable that you wrote down. It was carrots, no?"

Max nodded, wiping away a tear. "How did you know?"

"It's always carrots. That's what always everybody writes. Why, I don't know. Stupid carrots."

Max smiled appreciatively, and Zabbatini indicated a bow. A brief smile flickered over his face, wiping away the years. He didn't seem quite as unfriendly when he smiled.

"Tell me about yourself," Max said, hoping to seize the moment. "How did you come here?"

Zabbatini looked at him, puzzled. "I walked. With you. I was hungry."

"No, not to Canter's," Max said. "America."

"Ah," said Zabbatini. "I came with the U.S. Army."

"You were a soldier?"

"No." He shook his head. "I was a prisoner."

Max was shocked. "Did you do something bad? Were you a gangster?"

"Nonsense," Zabbatini replied gruffly. "I was a Jew."

"Me too!" Max said, happy that they had something in common.

"Back then," Zabbatini continued, "it was not good to be a Jew."

Max nodded. His grandma had said something along those lines.

Zabbatini told Max about the day of liberation. January 27, 1945. A day he would never forget. Zabbatini had been in a concentration camp, along with thousands of others. He was young and able to work, which helped him to survive. That, and a lot of luck.

"Then came the Red Army," Zabbatini said, and took another bite of his pancakes.

"What?" Max asked.

"What?" Zabbatini repeated dismissively. "The Russians!"

In the last days of the war, Zabbatini had gotten dysentery. He had been lying in the barracks, in a weakened state. He had terrible diarrhea and was afraid of dying. If the disease didn't kill him, the Germans would, the next day, during morning roll call at the latest. They would shoot him like a dog. But there was no more roll call. Zabbatini was lying there, feverish and whimpering, and when he lifted his eyes, he saw a man looking at him. A man in an odd uniform.

"He looked Chinese," Zabbatini said.

"Chinese?" Max said. "I thought he was Russian."

"He was," Zabbatini said. "A Soviet citizen, from Mongolia or God knows where. One of the New People. Russia is huge." Max nodded.

Zabbatini could see it all now, as clear as day. The smelly barracks, the wooden bunk, the big man in the uniform who winked at him. He had said only one word: *"Tovarish."*

"What does it mean?" Max asked.

"It's Russian," Zabbatini explained. "It means 'friend.'"

At that moment, he had known that he was saved. A feeling of joy, unlike anything else he'd ever felt, had rushed through his body. The Russians brought him to a field hospital and gave him medicine, even some soup. After a few days, he began regaining his strength. He spent a few more weeks in a camp for displaced persons, then made his way west. A long and arduous journey. Germany was in ruins.

Near Hannover, he saw a dead body strung up in a tree. The sight disgusted him, but he couldn't resist a second look. The man had been hanging there for a few days, and Zabbatini gasped in shock when he saw who it was. The crows had already picked out the man's eyes, but Zabbatini still recognized him.

Then he heard a voice coming from behind.

"You know him?"

Zabbatini turned around. The man had spoken English, not German. He was wearing an American uniform. A major, apparently. He was just buttoning his pants. A few feet away stood a jeep. The man must have been peeing, Zabbatini thought. Two other soldiers were sitting in the jeep, having a cigarette.

Zabbatini nodded. He had to fight against the urge to vomit. The wind carried the sweet scent of decay.

"Who is he?" the major asked.

"Inspector," said Zabbatini, who had learned only a few words of English in his time in Berlin. It had been a very fashionable language for a while, but the Nazis put an end to that. They put an end to everything.

"A policeman?" asked the major.

Zabbatini nodded.

"A Nazi?"

Again, Zabbatini nodded, though with some uncertainty. Yes, strictly speaking, the man had been a Nazi. Strictly speaking. Zabbatini turned away. The sight of the dead man made him infinitely sad. He had liked that man.

"What was his name?" the Major asked.

"Erich Leitner," said Zabbatini, and added in German: "I helped him catch a murderer."

The major seemed to understand. "You're a policeman, too?"

Zabbatini shook his head. "No," he said. "Mentalist."

"What?"

In an awkward mélange of English and German, Zabbatini explained to him that he had the ability to read other people's minds. The major seemed unconvinced.

"You have a paper?" Zabbatini asked. "And a pen?"

"Sure," said the major.

"I want you think of a vegetable. No matter. Any vegetable. Write it down, please. . . ."

☼

Zabbatini seemed to relax somewhat. The conversation picked up as he told a few more anecdotes from his life. Old people loved talking about the past, that much Max knew. They lived in the past, because their limited future featured mostly bedpans, walkers, and various ailments.

Zabbatini told Max how he'd come to this country, after the war.

"Major Forman helped me." He ate another piece of his pancake, a distant look on his face. "After the war, I was a colonel in the American army. I had even a uniform. It was nice. Very green."

Max was impressed. "Cool. What did you do?"

"I found Communists."

"What?"

"Communists. I found them."

"What's a Communist?"

"A Communist is a someone who dreams of a better future." Max scratched his head. "I don't get it," he said.

"Neither do I. But it is forbidden."

"What, the better future?"

"No, the Communism."

Zabbatini went on to explain that after meeting Major Forman, he had worked for the U.S. Army as a mind reader. His job was to weed out Communist infiltrators. For that, he was given a uniform, a rank, a paycheck, and, last but not least, American citizenship.

In 1948, he went to New York.

"I cannot describe to you," he said to Max, "the seeing of the Statue of the Liberty for first time. I was on a boat from Hamburg. It was night when we arrived in the New York Harbor. It was very cold, and windy. And it was raining. But everyone, no matter, old, young, sick, no matter, everyone came on deck to see it."

He took off his glasses and wiped them with a paper napkin.

"It was beautiful. Manhattan was shining like a diamond in the dark. We could see a thousand lights glowing in the mist. And the statue, she looked down on us, and it was as if she made us a promise."

"What promise?"

Zabbatini shrugged. "A better future?"

"So the Statue of Liberty is also a Communist?"

Zabbatini shook his head. "No, not like that. When I saw it, I thought, Maybe now, there is a little bit more freedom, a little bit less Nazis."

He paused, and stared off into his distant, dreamlike past. Then he told Max how he joined Project MKULTRA.

"Project what?" Max asked.

Zabbatini tapped against the side of his head. "Mind control. The CIA. It was a secret project for the control of the minds of the stupid."

"Control of the minds?" Max was in awe.

"Yes," Zabbatini said.

"And?" Max asked. "Does it work?"

"Of course not, you schmuck! That's why I left the CIA and joined the CBS." He slurped his iced tea and said, "It is all a big bullshit. Dumb tricks. There is no magic. Your dad will leave you, and you can do nothing. Now pay the money so I can get out of here. I must now go to toilet."

Choking, Max said, "There's nothing you can do?"

Zabbatini shook his head. "Nothing." He tapped the bill. "Money."

Max looked at the bill, somewhat startled. Was he really supposed to pay? Normally, the adults in his life paid for everything. He timidly lifted up the bill and looked at it. Then he said, "I can't afford this."

"What?" Zabbatini practically screamed. "You bring me to the eating and you cannot pay it?"

"I didn't bring you," Max said.

"It was your idea!"

"You wanted pancakes."

"Of course. I always want pancakes. Who doesn't want pancakes? Pancakes and pussy."

"But I can't afford this."

Zabbatini looked at him and said, "Not my problem."

With that, he got up and casually walked out of the deli. Max was left sitting there, wondering how to proceed. He really didn't have enough money, only five dollars. After a few seconds of agonized pondering, he came up with the only plan that made any sort of sense.

He could feel his heart beating in his chest. He looked at the waitress. When she turned around, he suddenly leapt from the imitation leather set and ran as fast as he could toward the glass door.

He didn't get very far. The waitress's hands were on him before he could run to safety.

"Where do you think you're going?" she said. She had his shoulder in a tight grip.

Max blushed. "I . . ." he began. "I was just going for some air."

"First you pay your bill," she said. "Where's the old guy?"

Max stared at the tiled floor. "He left."

"He left? So are you going to pay or what?"

Max began to stutter and gasp for air. "I don't have any money," he finally said.

"Oh," the waitress replied. Max thought he could hear a sarcastic tone in her voice. "Eating roast beef sandwiches and pancakes, but no money. Where are your parents?"

Max tried to explain that he'd run away from home to look for a retired magician to perform a love spell on his separated parents, but somehow his story didn't really hold the waitress's attention. She called the manager over, a middle-aged, bony man with bushy eyebrows, who wore a yellow Canter's T-shirt. On the spot, the manager started interrogating Max, who immediately broke down and revealed his mom's phone number. Max was taken into the manager's office. It was filled with old photographs and piles of papers. Buried underneath a stack of files was an old-fashioned black phone. Apparently, Canter's was the deli that time forgot. The manager dialed the number and handed the phone to Max. His mom picked up on the first ring.

"Hello?" Her voice sounded frantic.

"Mom, it's Max."

He could hear her exhale sharply. Was she angry? Or relieved?

"Where are you?" she asked in a shrill voice. "I'm worried sick about you!"

"I'm at Canter's," said Max.

"Canter's?" she said in disbelief. "What in God's name are you doing at Canter's?"

"I ate a roast beef sandwich," Max explained. "And pancakes."

It took a few minutes for her to calm down. She was seething with rage. She told Max he'd be grounded for at least two weeks, including "no TV, no internet." Then Max put the manager on the line to negotiate the details of the ransom payment. Mom said she was on her way, and the manager gave the phone back to Max, but Mom had already hung up. Max slowly put the receiver down, cursing the old fool of a magician.

THE BEAUTIFUL LIE

Moshe Goldenhirsch soon came to realize that life in the circus was much harder than he had anticipated. But he enjoyed it. He liked the traveling life, and he liked the people. Still, there were times, in the quiet hours of the night or shortly before dawn, when he saw his father's face in his mind's eye. He imagined the poor, lonely man stumbling through Prague, looking for his lost son. Moshe decided to write him a letter. He begged forgiveness for abandoning him, but he also explained that he had been looking for his own life, and now he had found it. He had left behind not only his father, but also his Judaism, once and for all. And now he was walking his own path, toward his own destiny.

Moshe didn't realize what his words would do to his father. He had cast aside all that the rabbi believed to be true and right. Moshe had walked away from the core of decency, he had shut the light of God out of his heart. The rabbi had turned old and gray in recent days, and when he read the letter, his fingers trembled and tears ran down his cheeks. Then a scream came forth from his body, his deepest soul. He collapsed. A dark abyss opened in both his eyes and his heart. Nothing could have hurt him more, after these weeks of agony, than this apostasy. He tore apart the letter, his hands moving meticulously, and burned the shreds in his oven. From now on, Laibl knew, he had no son.

Moshe, meanwhile, was enjoying his new worldly life. The circus troupe consisted of the Baron and his assistant Julia, four orchestra musicians, and Mrs. Arndt, who did the cooking and washing and also tore the tickets. Then there was a morose, chain-smoking clown named Siggy; an alcoholic acrobat named Hilde; a lion tamer, who, ironically, was called Löwitsch; and Horst, the artist, who took care of most of the menial tasks that other members of the troop would refuse.

And now there was Moshe the little Jew boy, who grew less Jewish with each passing day. Julia, intent on reshaping him in her image, gave him baggy pants, an old frock coat, and a haircut. His tender fingers, which thus far had only been turning the pages of the Torah, grew blisters and a tough layer of hardened new skin, which Moshe was very proud of. His muscles developed with each shovel of horse manure. A few months into his new life, the little *Bocher* from Prague was unrecognizable. Taller, stronger, more confident. He was no longer a boy, but a man.

However, there was one thing about him that irked the Baron: his name.

"Moshe just sounds so . . . so different."

Moshe shrugged. "But that is my name."

"Names are sound and smoke. They are nothing. But they need to sound like everything. Moshe Goldenhirsch," von Kröger grumbled. "What kind of name is that?"

"Mine," said Moshe hesitantly.

They were sitting in the Baron's circus wagon, a large mahogany cart with a tiled oven and even a private toilet, which had to be emptied once a day. The Baron was reclining in a red, plush armchair, smoking a pipe, while Julia tended the fire. The flames reflected eerily off the Baron's brass mask as he stirred his tea. He placed a piece of candied sugar in his mouth and crunched down on it, then sipped his tea. Moshe had never met anyone who loved sugar as much as the Half-Moon Man.

"Your name is your true self," explained Kröger. "It is the first thing people learn about you. Your name must convey who you want to be. Who you are."

"I am Moshe Goldenhirsch."

"No. You are not. You joined my circus so that you would not have to be Moshe Goldenhirsch any longer. You can be whatever you choose to be. The question is, What?"

Moshe hadn't really thought about it. He looked at Julia, her graceful features illuminated by the soft glow of the fire. What do I want to be? Her lover, that much he was sure of. But he'd made no progress in that respect. And he had no idea how to proceed. So he only said, "I don't know."

"Well, think!" snapped Kröger. "You don't want to be shoveling horseshit forever, do you?"

Moshe shook his head. "I want to be a magician."

Julia smiled.

"A magician?" The Baron frowned. "You couldn't be a clown?"

Moshe shook his head. "I want to be like you."

The Half-Moon Man nodded, somewhat pleased. "I see," he said. "You wish to be my apprentice."

"Yes."

The Baron tossed a coin toward Moshe. Moshe caught it.

Kröger nodded. "Again."

He tossed the coin several more times, and each time Moshe was able to catch it.

"Not bad," said the Baron. "Let me see your hands."

Moshe held out his hands. The Baron took them, pulling Moshe closer, roughly examining his palms and fingers. "All right," he finally grumbled and pushed Moshe away. "That will do. I will consider your proposal. But!" He held out his middle finger. "It means I will get to choose your name."

Moshe was puzzled, and the Baron explained, "It has always been the custom that the noble lord chooses a new name for his loyal serf."

Moshe hadn't heard that before. "Really?"

"Do I detect the faint scent of rebellion permeating my chamber?"

"I don't smell anything," said Moshe.

"You're not a Bolshevist, are you?"

Moshe shook his head.

The Baron nodded. "Massage my feet," he said to Julia, who sat down next to his chair and started pulling on his left riding boot. She had to use considerable effort, but at last, the boot came off with a satisfying thud. A scent permeated the chamber, but it was not of rebellion.

"Something Persian," said the Half-Moon Man pensively.

"Persian?" Moshe asked. "Why Persian?"

"I already have a Persian Princess," explained the Half-Moon Man. "Maybe you could be her dim-witted half-brother, yes?"

Moshe said nothing. He wasn't sure whether he wanted to be a dim-witted half-brother.

"These are strange days, my friend. The Nazis won the election last year."

Moshe had heard all about it. He knew that these were not ideal times to be Jewish. Everywhere he looked, there was propaganda and hate. But here, in the circus, he felt safe, as if the outside world could do him no harm.

"They believe themselves to be the descendants of Aryan tribes. From Persia."

"Are they really?" asked Moshe.

"Of course not. They're illiterate pig farmers, that's all. But they're also our audience, and if they want to hear that they are princes, then by God, they are!"

Moshe nodded. Give the audience what they want.

"But," continued the Half-Moon Man, "the true princes of Persepolis are sitting right here, in this room."

"Who?"

The Half-Moon Man made a grandiose gesture that included everyone here. "Us," he said. "We are the Aryans."

Moshe looked at him, puzzled.

"We are magicians, are we not?" said the Baron. "And the first magicians were the Magi, the high priests of Persepolis."

Moshe was delighted. Within minutes, he had graduated from dim-witted half-brother to high priest.

"We are their children, at least in spirit. We are the speakers of the gods and the guardians of a timeless truth."

"Yes?" Moshe asked excitedly. "What truth?"

"The truth of lies."

"How can lies be true?"

"How can they not? People are desperate to be deceived. They want to believe in something greater. We give them something lesser, and that is why they come back. Magic is a beautiful lie."

※

One morning a few days later, the Zauber-Zirkus stopped at Würzburg and Moshe began cleaning out the lion cage. Ludwig the Lion was an old, nearly toothless animal whose only interests after his many years of incarceration were his next meal and subsequent nap. Suddenly, Moshe noticed the Half-Moon Man walking up to the cage and looking at him through the bars.

"Boy," said the Half-Moon Man. His shirt was open, revealing his ample, rosy belly. His mask shone in the pale morning light. He was smoking a pipe and staggering slightly.

"Yes?" said Moshe.

"Come here," said the Half-Moon Man. Moshe got up and scurried outside. He clutched the shovel in his left hand. It was still early. The day was gray and overcast. He could hear the cries of the ravens in the nearby forest, and he could feel the cold wind tugging at his shirt.

"What day is this?" asked the Half-Moon Man.

"Saturday," Moshe replied.

"Is it not against your religion to work on a Saturday? On the Sabbath?"

Moshe shrugged. "I have no religion."

The Baron smiled. Obviously, it was the answer he'd wanted to hear. "Kneel," he said.

Moshe looked at him and blinked.

"Kneel!" the Half-Moon Man suddenly roared. "I am your liege!"

Intimidated, Moshe knelt down in the hard, cold mud.

"Give me the shovel," said von Kröger.

Moshe did as he was asked. The Baron took the shovel and held it near Moshe's head. Moshe was getting nervous. What was all this? Did the Baron want to bang him on the head? If so, why?

"Repeat after me," said the Half-Moon Man solemnly. "As a magician . . ."

"As a magician . . ." Moshe repeated.

"I swear never to reveal the secret of any illusion to a mortal . . ."

"Mortal?"

"Shut up and repeat," said the Baron.

Moshe dutifully did as he was told.

When the long oath was finished, the Half-Moon Man solemnly lifted the shovel and tapped him lightly on each shoulder, then on the head. Moshe beamed. He had been knighted, right here, in the mud! He was a magician!

"Henceforth . . ." began the Baron. He paused to take a sip from his flask, then burped and went on. "Thou shalt be known as Zabbatini."

"As what?" asked Moshe, incredulous.

"Zabbatini," the Half-Moon Man repeated. "Like the Sabbath, only with an *ini* at the end. And maybe a *Z* at the beginning. It's nice, no?"

"I don't know . . ." Moshe murmured, scratching his head.

"Enough!" roared the Half-Moon Man. "It's brilliant. Mellifluous. And it sounds Persian."

"If you say so."

"I damn well say so," insisted the Half-Moon Man.

He threw the shovel away and stalked off, while Moshe Goldenhirsch, henceforth known to the world as Zabbatini, remained kneeling in the mud.

THE BELIEVER

After dinner, Zabbatini walked back to the King David in a gloomy mood, despite the free pancakes, courtesy of that idiot kid. He was eighty-eight years old and his mind was as active as ever. His body, however, was giving out. It was the greatest failure of his life, this betrayal of his own flesh. It felt as if there were weights attached to his bones, and his joints were like creaky hinges. He was tired of life. He didn't want to go on this way, not really. After all, he hadn't opened the gas valve by accident. He spent most of his days drunk, with little to look forward to. Only quiz shows and whiskey, cancer and incontinence.

An unpleasant surprise awaited him when he entered the lobby of the King David. Ronnie, the manager, was already expecting him. He held up a piece of paper.

"What's this with the gas leak?" Ronnie asked accusingly.

"Leave me alone," said Zabbatini, his usual opening gambit to almost any question.

"And you're going to pay for the door," Ronnie said.

"It's a miracle I'm alive," said the old man loudly. He threatened to sue the King David on account of the "gas leak," but Ronnie seemed unimpressed, realizing that someone had tampered with the valve. And he had a strong suspicion of who that someone might be.

"I only twisted the knob," said the old man by way of defending himself.

"You removed the knob!"

"The plastic thing came off, that's my fault now?"

Ronnie slammed the paper he had been holding down on the desk. It was an eviction notice. Zabbatini had twenty-four hours to find a new home.

Zabbatini waved dismissively. Leave me alone, he thought as he shuffled to his room. He wanted to slam the door shut, but there was no more door to slam. Only pieces of wood on the floor. He grabbed the bottle of whiskey, turned the television on, and sank into his chair.

I want to die, Zabbatini thought, bringing the bottle to his lips.

❧

Despite her misgivings during the early stages of her pregnancy, the day that her son Max was born was the happiest day of Deborah's life. That was partly due to the amazing drugs they had given her at Cedars-Sinai. But only partly. The birth hadn't been as bad as she had feared, and when it was all over, a nurse had come in and handed her a baby. Not just any baby, *her* baby. Max Cohn. Deborah was initially puzzled, but her bewilderment soon gave way to a deep, warm pride, unlike anything she had ever felt before. She was, in many ways, emotionally unprepared for Max's arrival. He had suddenly arrived, turning her life upside down. But he *was* there, and Deborah and Harry loved him. In the beginning, it was all relatively easy. Of course it was exhausting to be awoken in the middle of the night by a screaming newborn, but at least Deborah knew what was expected of her. There were diapers to change, and the baby had to be fed. Later came the arduous task of spooning baby food from bottles with misleading pictures of rosy-cheeked children into little Max's tightly shut mouth.

She and Harry got married a few weeks before his birth. It was a simple and surprisingly moving ceremony at an ashram in Malibu, with a view over the beach. They stood in the grass, in the soft breeze, under the traditional wedding chuppah, with the sun on their faces, and she wore the most glamorous retro-seventies dress ever over her round belly. She and Harry both said, "I do," and then the guru pronounced them man and wife and proclaimed, *"Om mani padme hum."*

Even though Deborah called herself a Buddhist, there was no denying what she truly was: a Jewess of Beverly Hills. Her father was a prominent dentist, and young Deborah had been raised on the not very mean streets of 90210, subject to constant displays of ostentatious wealth and a great deal of peer pressure. Her family was conservative, and it was probably a response to her strict upbringing—in a walled house with separate refrigerators for meat and dairy products—that Deborah had developed a fascination with Dharmic religions.

Buddha or no Buddha, when Max was born, there was never any question that he would be raised in the Jewish faith, with a bit of Eastern mysticism thrown in for good measure. She and Harry moved to the east side, beyond the socially dividing line of La Cienega Boulevard, and the first thing they did was find a Jewish day care center for Max. Both felt they should provide a stable, somewhat traditional, and spiritual home for their child. Deborah's mother was initially unsure of her choice of husband, but Harry was a child of Holocaust survivors. Survivors were seen as something akin to nobility in the Jewish community of West Los Angeles. Marrying the child of a Holocaust survivor was like marrying a Kennedy.

At first, things had worked out remarkably well. Harry was a loving husband and father, and most of all, he was fun to be around. He'd once had aspirations of becoming a musician, but his dreams soon faded and he was simply forced to support his family. He was a grown-up now. He studied law and found work as a music licensing attorney, at a firm that sold jingles to commercial houses and movie studios. With the generous support of Deborah's parents, the young couple bought a house in Atwater Village. Deborah opened her shop, Om Sweet Om. It did all right. As did Harry's career.

They'd had a few good years, she now realized, not without regret. Where did we go wrong? she wondered.

Whatever the secret to a happy marriage might have been, they were unable to hold onto it. She remembered her wedding, standing there, looking out at the ocean, thousands of sparks of sunlight glittering on the Pacific, watching the beautiful high waves coming in. And then seeing where they broke and rolled back and dissolved, just like their happiness, just like their life together.

All that was left now was arranging drop-offs and pickups with Harry, shuffling through the vast concrete wasteland of Los Angeles to Gutierrez & Partners in her old Jeep Cherokee, the very same car in which Max had been conceived. Mr. Gutierrez was a patient man: in his office, she was allowed to cry to her heart's content. It was like therapy. And he always had a box of Kleenex ready for her. One of the tools of his trade.

✲

When Deborah had knocked on Max's door after their fight to apologize for her nasty remarks, she'd gotten no response. He's probably sulking, she thought. She lit some scented candles and meditated for twenty minutes. Then she called him, and when he didn't respond to further knocking, she got fed up. She opened the door and went around outside to his window.

"Who do you think—" she said and then stopped. Max was gone. The window was open and his curtain was flapping in the evening wind. She became immediately alarmed. She searched the house and garage for him, then the neighborhood, calling his name with increasing desperation.

As a young girl, she had witnessed a neighbor get two of his fingers cut off by a lawn mower. He had stuck his hand in, because the machine hadn't been working properly, and he didn't realize that it was still turned on. Deborah had watched with morbid fascination as the neighbor's fingers flew through the air like little pink hot dogs and landed in the grass. The wife had gathered them up. Paramedics had taken the bleeding man to the hospital, and the fingers were sewn back on. Ever since then, he had scars on his fingers and could hardly move them. She would never forget the feeling of nausea she had back then, deep in her stomach.

Now she felt the same way. Worse. Now she was the one who had stuck her hand in the lawn mower. Her son was gone, and it was as if someone had torn a limb from her.

She called his father, who was puzzled and useless, as always. She heard people in the background. Where was he? A bar? A restaurant?

"Where are you?" she snapped at him.

"None of your business."

"I can't find Max. Is he with you?"

"Why would he be with me? It's your day today."

"He's gone. He's not at home. Where the hell is he?"

"I don't know," said Harry, worried now. "Why didn't you pay attention?"

Before the argument could escalate, Deborah said she had to hang up now. She had to call the police. Harry promised to come by as soon as he could.

The cop on the phone told her not to panic. She had to wait twenty-four hours before filing a missing persons report. It was far too soon to assume the worst. For Deborah, however, it was never too soon to assume the worst. She decided to comb the neighborhood one more time. Maybe she had overlooked something. This time, she knocked on the neighbors' doors, but no one had any idea where Max could be.

Then Harry showed up.

"What took you so long?" she said accusingly.

"Well, excuse me!" he said indignantly.

"Your son is gone," she snapped. "Where were you?"

Harry Cohn had been out for dinner with his mistress, the infamous yoga instructor. Of course, he didn't tell Deborah that. The evening with Eleanor—that was her name—had not gone particularly well. He had asked her how she would feel if he moved in with her. And she had said nothing. Not a good sign. When he reached for her hand to tell her that they could start a new life together now, she had pulled back. Icy silence. Seconds later, when Deborah called, Harry was relieved to end the awful dinner with Eleanor. He paid the bill and rushed over to his former house.

He and Deborah went in her car to check out all the places where Max liked to spend time: playgrounds, cinemas, comic book stores. Nothing.

In despair, they had driven back to the house. And then the phone rang.

It was Max! He was at Canter's, unable to pay his bill. After

Deborah berated her son for a few minutes, the manager of Canter's came on the line and demanded money, asking what kind of brat was she raising there?

Feeling more relieved than ever before in her life, Deborah swore she'd kill the brat!

※

Deborah and Harry didn't utter a single word during the whole drive home. Max's parents sat in stony silence, like the Frost Giants from the *Thor* comics. Max wished he could teleport himself somewhere else—Grandma's, for example. Teleportation was a wish he harbored often. It seemed like an awesome superpower to have, and Max couldn't understand why science was taking so long to catch up to the promise of comic books. Also, he thought, fireballs would be good. You could throw them at teachers. And parents.

Deborah made a left on Edenhurst Avenue and pulled up in their driveway. When the car came to a halt, she suddenly yelled at him:

"What the hell were you thinking?"

"Answer your mother," said Harry in a rare moment of parental harmony.

Max lowered his head and mumbled an apology. Now was the perfect time for a fireball.

"I thought you were dead," Deborah said.

I wish I was, Max thought.

His parents wanted to know why he had run away. Max stuttered, unable to come up with a convincing defense. They

besieged him with questions. What was he doing at Canter's? Did
he intend to eat the place clean?

Finally, Max came out with the truth. "I was looking for a
magician," he said.

His parents exchanged a puzzled look.

"A magician?" Mom said. "What on earth for? Who needs
magicians?"

She unlocked the door and they went inside. Just like the old
days, Max thought bitterly.

He told them about Dad's record and that he had wanted
to meet the Great Zabbatini. He didn't mention the love spell.
Mom looked at him as if he'd lost his mind. Dad sat miserably
on the sofa. Mom went into the kitchen, opened the fridge, and
took out a plate.

"Eat your dinner," she said with an air of resignation.

Max poked sullenly at his cold mashed potatoes.

Deborah sent him to bed and sat down next to her soon-
to-be ex-husband. They couldn't explain their son's behavior. But
they both felt guilty. They knew that Max's escape attempt had to
do with their divorce. But why a magician, of all things?

They didn't realize that Max was listening to their conversation through his bedroom door. After Dad left, he went to bed
and fell into a restless sleep.

∗

The next day in school, Max sat brooding on a schoolyard bench.
His plan had failed. The Great Zabbatini had turned out to be

anything but great. Max had to face the fact that there would never be a love spell.

He was at that age when dreams slowly give way to the harsh realities of the world. Only last year, Max had discovered a major scandal that had rocked his world: there was no Santa Claus. It was all a lie—the man he had mistaken for Santa Claus had turned out to be his dad in a ridiculous costume. Max had suspected as much for a while now; he had been baffled that Santa Claus bore such a strong resemblance to his father. His voice, his movements, his scent. And why was his dad never around when Santa showed up? Last year, during the holiday season—the terror of Christmas was so all-pervasive, even a Jewish family such as the Cohns found themselves succumbing to Santa—Max had opened the door to his parent's walk-in closet. He had been looking for Bruno the Bunny, who had hopped off as Max was cleaning his cage. Inside the closet, Max found his dad, fumbling with the familiar red costume and white beard.

Despite this spiritual setback, Max retained a deep desire to believe in something better than the known world. He just couldn't keep his fingers out of the cookie jar of irrational beliefs. And the more his parents' relationship deteriorated, the more irrational Max became. The real world around him was collapsing like a house of cards, and he was looking for salvation in other places. There was a schism of faith within him. Max the Believer vs. Max the Pragmatist. It was the Believer who had pinned his hopes for happiness on a scratched record, who had run away from home and endured the company of a smelly and cantankerous old man. He wasn't the first person to succumb to the lure of silly beliefs: some people never outgrew this awkward phase. Max was afraid of waking up, of facing the end of childhood. He wanted to keep on dreaming for a while longer, covered by a comfortable blanket of lies. He didn't want to get out of bed and feel the cold floor under his naked feet. Not now. Not yet.

Somehow, and in the face of overwhelming evidence to the contrary, Max had managed to cling to his belief in the impossible.

Myriam Hyung walked up to Max and sat down next to him. She fed crumbs of toast to the squirrels.

"How are you doing?" she asked.

Max shrugged. He didn't want to talk to her. Something about her made him nervous. She could be irritable. Like that time when Joey had asked if they had refrigerators in North Korea and she had yelled at him and called him a moron. Her family, she said, was from Seoul, one of the coolest cities in the world. And amply equipped with refrigeration.

But now, she was as peaceable as a lamb. "How are your parents?" she asked.

What could he say? "I dunno," he said evasively.

They both stared silently at a squirrel as it happily chewed on a piece of bread, its tail bobbing. Grandma hated squirrels, calling them "rats with bushy tails." Weird, Max thought. They're so cute.

"My mom said I should try and cheer you up," said Myriam Hyung.

Max replied with a noncommittal grunting noise. Suddenly, Max said, "I miss him." His voice was weak and thin. It was difficult for him to admit it. And he was surprised that he would admit it to Myriam Hyung, of all people.

Myriam took his hand. He put up no resistance. That surprised him, too.

Then she said, "Do you have any more bread for the squirrel?"

SOMETHING FROM NOTHING

The Zauber-Zirkus continued its tour through Europe, traveling through Bavaria, Austria, Hungary, and finally, after a detour over to Zagreb, back to Germany. These were hard years for Moshe Goldenhirsch, for the Half-Moon Man was a stern teacher. But, to his own surprise, Moshe turned out to be an able student. It was the first time in his life that he was good at something.

In the beginning of his apprenticeship, the Half-Moon Man had led Moshe into the empty circus tent. Standing in the middle of the arena, the Baron took out a red handkerchief and pulled it through his fist, twice. On the third pass, it suddenly became blue. This was called "transformation." Moshe nodded, and the Half-Moon Man gave a slight bow, his mask catching the afternoon sunlight. Then, there was "teleportation," where an item would suddenly vanish, only to mysteriously reappear somewhere else.

And, of course, "levitation," which involved objects floating in midair. To Moshe, this was one of the most beautiful and mystifying tricks. He would always remember his first sight of the Floating Princess as the moment he fell in love.

Then there was "production." The Half-Moon Man illustrated this by simply producing a bouquet of paper flowers from seemingly thin air. "In magic," explained the Half-Moon Man, "we create something from nothing." The opposite of this was a "vanish," when an object is made to disappear or to become invisible. Von Kröger opened the large overseas trunk, out of which Julia emerged every night. Moshe peeked inside.

He saw only the lining. "There's nothing here."

"Exactly," said the Baron. He placed the paper flowers inside the trunk. Then he closed it and opened it again.

The flowers were gone.

Moshe blinked. "How is it done?" he asked.

The Half-Moon Man reached inside the trunk. Suddenly, Moshe saw the reflection of his fingers.

"It's a mirror!" said Moshe.

The Baron nodded. He pushed the mirror in. "A hidden flap inside the lid. One side has a mirror attached. When the trunk is closed, it moves down automatically. The mirror reflects the lining. It looks as if the trunk is empty."

"I see," said Moshe, nodding. This seemed very mundane. Once he understood how a trick worked, it lost all its magic.

"But this is no true magic," said von Kröger dismissively. "It is a device. Anyone can buy a device. True magic," he continued, "is spectacle, illusion, entertainment."

"What about the sword?" Moshe asked.

Every evening, the Half-Moon Man would plunge his sword into the trunk, leaving neither wounds nor blood. Von Kröger showed Moshe two identical sword canes. One of them, his real one, had an actual saber inside it. The other one contained a dull blade. The Baron touched its tip with the palm of his hand and effortlessly slipped it into the cane. "The blade is retractable," he said. "I cut the ribbon to prove that it's the real thing. Then I switch canes right before the trick. I do it while I adjust my cape. I hide the real sword cane behind the trunk."

In addition to various tricks and methods, Moshe learned what his mentor called "the history of the art." He discovered that the traditions of stage magic originated in Babylon. Many of the high priests came from a tribe of the Medes called the Magi, and this is where the word *magician* was derived from. It was the beginning of an unfortunate tradition—mixing stage magic with religion.

The Half-Moon Man told Moshe about an ancient Egyptian soothsayer who claimed to have the power to raise the dead. "An old canard. Priests and prophets have always claimed to have the secret to eternal life. It's part of our repertoire. Everyone is afraid of dying. Our audience will happily surrender their hard-earned coins for the promise of a second life, preferably one that's less inconvenient than the present one. Otherwise, we'd all be unemployed."

The Egyptian soothsayer, however, nearly lost his head. He was summoned to the court of the Pharaoh, who wanted to see these feats of magic with his own eyes and offered a few slaves to be executed, in hopes of a quick resurrection. The soothsayer managed to convince the Pharaoh otherwise. Instead of slaves, he used ducks to perform his trick. And a cow, according to legend.

"He probably just switched the birds at the right moment."

"But a whole cow?" Moshe wondered.

"Size is irrelevant. Houdini even managed to vanish an elephant."

"A whole elephant?"

"On a stage in New York," said the Baron. "Her name was Betsy."

The Half-Moon Man then talked about "the golden age of magic." During the nineteenth century, as a new era of reason dawned in Europe, the face of magic changed. Thanks to men like the Italian magician Bartholomeo Bosco, magic moved away from cheap superstition. Bosco believed in "honest magic." This new breed of magicians never pretended to be anything more than entertainers. The Baron explained that many of the famous magicians came from mechanical trades. The best-known magician of the golden age, Jean Eugène Robert-Houdin, was the son of a watchmaker. His exploits, and his name, were a source of inspiration for Ehrich Weiss, the Unseen Art's shining star, the great Houdini. "Here is a man," the Baron remarked, "who needs no explanation. He could crack any lock."

Moshe suddenly thought of the Locksmith, back in Prague.

He wondered what had become of him. And of his father? The faces of all those he had left behind kept appearing in his dreams.

Moshe Goldenhirsch remained with the Half-Moon Man for two years. He learned that magic was nothing more than a form of storytelling. Each trick was a drama. In the first act, the magician set up an expectation, which he simultaneously fulfilled and subverted in act three. Moshe realized that the real trick happened inside the audience's mind. The art did not, in fact, consist of a simple transformation through mundane mechanics or props. No, the art itself was the transformation of feelings. It meant saying the right things. Or, more to the point, not saying much of anything.

"Magicians," the Half-Moon Man told him one night after a performance, "are scared of only one thing."

Moshe regarded his mentor, who was reclining in his red armchair.

"Magic," he said. "Magicians are afraid of magic. Instead, they fill their acts with vaudeville and mindless blather."

The Half-Moon Man taught Moshe that the best way to lie was not to lie. "Stick to the truth, but don't say more than you have to. Just show them the object, wave it around, and keep your damn mouth shut. Works every time."

Moshe nodded.

Moshe felt at home. He felt like he had arrived. While he was still responsible for the animal manure, he was, toward the end of his apprenticeship, given his own slot in which to perform, before a live audience. Only one thing was forbidden to him: he could not perform "true stage magic." That was the Baron's prerogative, and his alone. So Moshe had to work the tent as a "magical clown." He wore a ridiculous costume, identifying him as a buffoon. A top hat, floppy shoes, and white bathing trunks with red polka dots. He would scurry around the audience and do card tricks and pratfalls. People would laugh at him and, on occasion, even throw things at him. But he didn't mind. Their scorn hardened his soul.

One night, however, turned out to be different from all the other nights. They were performing in Hesse, in a small town named Gießen, north of Frankfurt. Earlier that afternoon, they had pitched their tent on the fairgrounds near the River Wieseck. The townsfolk, a notoriously rude bunch even by the low standards of Hesse, prided themselves on their inquisitiveness and were highly suspicious of anything that smelled of deceit. They were mostly farmers, proud, stubborn, and set in their ways, but those who were not farmers were something far worse: intellectuals.

That night, the local chapter of the Nazi Brownshirts had come to enjoy an evening of magic and diversion. Over the last few years, the mood in the country had changed. The NSDAP, the Nazi Party, kept growing in numbers. Its message, for one, was very popular: Blame the Jews. In addition, the party was not particularly choosy. Thugs, thieves, and sadists were not only tolerated, but welcomed with open arms. The party offered them a home, a place among like-minded people. But others joined, too, respectable folks, average Germans. The party promised a better future, a well-earned place in the sun. As a party member, you weren't a failure, you were a member of the master race. Ugly ducklings turned into ugly swans. Nationalists, students, scholars, farmers, factory workers, lawyers, businessmen—the party offered something for everyone. The party was the answer they had been looking for.

The Gießen storm troopers were drunk that night with their own arrogance and more than a little beer. They were the least desirable audience: skeptical and inebriated. They enjoyed tripping Zabbatini as he clowned his way through the spectators. It was not just the usual amusement—they actually enjoyed his suffering. Their humor was cruelty, and they kicked him around like a soccer ball. Moshe, terrified and nearly in tears, felt as if they could see through his makeup, as if his face would give away his secret, his Jewishness.

Then he had a flash of insight.

He grabbed the arm of one of the Brownshirts, a stout ruddy fellow with a shorn head, and immediately became very still. His lips started to quiver, and his eyes bore into the other man's face.

"What?" asked the man, suddenly off guard. He looked uneasily at the others. Moshe prolonged his act as long as he could. Then he began shaking. The others started to back off.

Suddenly, Moshe flinched, as if he'd snapped out of a trance.

"What?" the man asked again.

Moshe became very calm, regarding the man with great pity, then leaned next to him and whispered, "In less than a year, you will die."

The man shrieked and took a step back. He was suddenly pale. Moshe turned on his heel and strode through the audience, making his exit. No one stopped him.

Outside the tent, Moshe felt jubilant. He'd done it! He'd scared the man off! Unbelievable that people should fall for such a stupid trick. His prediction was no more valid than that of the village idiot. And yet, the man had believed him. He, Moshe Goldenhirsch, had scared the Brownshirt!

He heard a voice behind him.

"What did you do to him?"

Julia emerged from the tent, a fur coat thrown over her white dress. These were the last days of winter, and the field was covered in snow. Her dress and skin shone in the pale moonlight. Her beauty was blinding. He could see her breath against the icy night, and he longed to feel it against his skin.

She lit a cigarette.

"I made a fake prediction," he said.

"All predictions are fake," she said.

Moshe nodded. "But he didn't know that."

"What did you tell him?"

"That he would soon die."

She laughed. "And he bought it?"

"Looks like it." He took a step toward her. Emboldened by his success, he made another daring prediction: "Before the night is over, you will be in love with me."

She smiled at him. "I've been in love with you from the first moment we met," she said.

It wasn't true, but she said it anyway. It sounded good.

"Oh," he responded, somewhat helpless. He was delighted, but also confused. Why hadn't she told him before? Why did she let him suffer all these months? "Well . . ." he stammered. "That's nice, isn't it?"

"Yes," she said. "It is nice."

He looked around. Dozens of rabbits were hopping about the nocturnal field. They had thick winter coats and seemed to be rather busy.

Julia glanced at him expectantly. Her eyes seemed larger and deeper than ever before. They were like an ocean, and he felt he couldn't swim. Any moment, he would go under.

Julia took the initiative. He felt something against his hand and looked down. Her slender fingers were resting on his.

Gradually, it dawned on him that he was supposed to kiss her.

He had never kissed anyone before. No one had taught him. His father had only ever talked about long-dead Talmudic scholars, and the Half-Moon Man was only interested in making pigeons vanish.

He was only seventeen, and he had no idea what to do. Julia, however, was twenty and had a very clear idea as to what should happen next. She took a drag off her cigarette and turned away, blowing out the smoke so it wouldn't get in his face. Then she ran her finger through his thick, black hair, pulled his head toward her, and kissed him.

When she was done, she wiped her mouth with the back of her hand.

"That was nice," Moshe said, somewhat helplessly. He could taste the tobacco on his lips.

She shrugged. "Could have been better."

"Oh." A devastating verdict, he felt.

"You're too tense," she said. "I'll show you how it works."

She threw away her cigarette and began her lessons.

MAX AND THE MAGICIAN

When Max came home that afternoon, he saw the Great Zabbatini snoring loudly in a deck chair on his front lawn. He was dressed in a Hawaiian shirt, and a suitcase was standing next to him. Max was surprised, to say the least. After school, he had gone on his bike to visit Mom at her shop and had spent two boring hours brooding over his homework. He didn't feel quite comfortable at Om Sweet Om, since it held nothing of interest to him. Just furniture, clothes, and tchotchkes from the Far East. Mom was dealing with some customers, and therefore had no time for him. When he finished with his homework, he biked home. And now this.

Max approached the old magician.

"Hello?"

No response. Max gently shook his shoulder. Perhaps he was dead again. Max shook harder, and Zabbatini flinched, then moaned as he opened his eyes.

"What is this nonsense?" he demanded indignantly.

"You were sleeping."

"So? Can't I sleep in peace?"

"What are you doing on our lawn?"

"Sleeping." With an elegant gesture, he brushed some imaginary dust off his shirt.

"How did you know where I live?" Max asked.

Zabbatini flashed him his trademark smile, which he had perfected during his many years onstage. A perfect blend of charm and mischief. "I am a magician, no?" he said, bowing with a flourish, and then groaned.

"Are you all right?" Max asked.

"My neck," Zabbatini said with clenched teeth. "A cramp. I can't move."

Max carefully guided the old man inside the house and helped him lie down on the sofa.

Zabbatini sighed with relief and rubbed his neck.

"Wonderful," he said. "What a beautiful couch. Give me now the remote control."

Max did as he was asked.

"I need more pillows," Zabbatini declared. "For my neck."

Max ran into Mom's bedroom to get pillows. When he came back, he saw Zabbatini agitatedly pressing buttons on the remote.

"How do I turn this thing on? I want the Playboy channel," Zabbatini proclaimed. "I want to see *nekkid* girls."

He looked around, as if he was hoping the *nekkid* girls he so desired were about to walk into the living room. Instead, his gaze fell upon a hideous painting that Deborah had hung next to the door, against her family's protests. The face of a clown was visible on a backdrop of black velvet. He had a tear on his cheek and a tortured smile on his lips. His white face seemed to float forward toward the viewer. Max found it creepy, but his mom was inexplicably attached to the thing. It wasn't so much its artistic value that she defended, but rather its emotional meaning for her. She'd had it since she was a child.

Zabbatini looked at it with disgust. Then a thought occurred to him. "Were you ever in Bongo's Clown Room?" he asked.

Max shook his head.

"On Hollywood Boulevard, at Winona. It is even better than the Playboy channel."

"Are there clowns?"

"Clowns, shmowns!" Zabbatini said. "It is a titty bar. There are *nekkid*, horny women with big breasts."

Max blushed.

"Paradise," Zabbatini said. "Women and whiskey." Then he added, "Why have I nothing to drink?"

Max rushed into the kitchen and poured a glass of tap water for his guest.

Zabbatini was indignant.

"Do I look like a shitty fish? I want something to drink. Whiskey!"

"We . . . we don't have whiskey . . ." Max said cautiously.

"No whiskey?" Zabbatini looked as if he'd just found out that the love of his life had married someone else.

Max shook his head.

"Shit," Zabbatini said. Then his face lit up. "I saw a liquor shop.

On the corner. They will have schnapps or something. In my wallet is my money. Give me pilsner or give me beer."

"They won't sell me beer," Max said.

"No beer? What is this nonsense?"

"I'm under twenty-one," Max explained.

"I can see that," Zabbatini said. "You are not drinking my beer, I am."

"We have iced tea," Max said.

"I shit on tea," Zabbatini said. "And why is the television working not?"

Max took the remote from him and switched it on.

A smile spread across Zabbatini's face. "Finally," he said.

After watching some quiz shows, Zabbatini felt hungry and demanded some lunch. Max went into the kitchen. He still had some leftover Indian food from when he and his mom had gone to India Sweets and Spices down the road. It was a grocery store and takeout restaurant, and one of his favorite places in town. Max and his mom would often get lunch at their buffet counter and sit in front of the huge flat-screen TV, watching dazzling dance sequences with Aishwarya Rai or Shah Rukh Khan. As it happened, he still had some vegetable korma and paneer masala left over from two days ago. He put it on a plate, placed the plate in the microwave, and then laid it down graciously on the coffee table in front of Zabbatini. The old magician began gobbling it up, all the while complaining that he was being fed leftovers. Max finally worked up the courage to ask the question that had been on his mind for the last hour: "Why are you here?"

Zabbatini lowered his fork and feigned surprise. "You invited me."

"Me?"

"Yes, you. Or see you anyone else here?"

"No."

"Aha!" said Zabbatini triumphantly, taking another bite of his paneer masala.

"But I didn't invite you."

"A beer would now be good," said Zabbatini accusingly.

Max sighed. The old man was driving him crazy. What was he doing here? More importantly, how could he get rid of him before Mom came home?

Zabbatini pushed the plate away and burped. Then he said, "You wanted me to perform love magic, no?"

Max looked at him, astonished. "What?"

"Eternal love. Like on my record."

"Is that why you're here?"

Zabbatini nodded, as much as his cramped neck would allow him to. "That is why I am here. Eternaaaaal loooooove," he said, sounding like Dracula. "The record, yes? It works not, no?"

"Yes," said Max. "I mean, no. It doesn't work."

"You see," Zabbatini said with a grin. "So I come here."

Max felt like jumping up and down with joy. "For real?"

"For real. To make your parents fall into the love."

Max rushed toward Zabbatini and gave him a hug. Zabbatini, who was never very good with children, looked as if he had just stepped in a dog pile. "All right already," he said. "Enough with the schmaltz."

"You're really going to help me?"

"As really as my name is Zabbatini."

This gave Max pause. "*Is* your name Zabbatini? The man in the retirement home said—"

"Firstly of all," Zabbatini declared, "it is not a retirement home. It is for the active seniors, a community."

"Okay."

"And secondly of all, this man, he is stupid, an ox. A nudnik also."

"Why?" Max asked. "What did he do?"

Zabbatini suddenly looked very nonchalant. He didn't dare tell Max that he had been kicked out of the King David Home for the Elderly as of this morning.

Ronnie, in his capacity as all-knowing manager, had simply marched into Bungalow 112, where Zabbatini was still passed out in his La-Z-Boy. He had awoken the great magician and repeated that he had to leave.

"But where will I stay?" Zabbatini said pleadingly.

"Not here," Ronnie replied.

Most of Zabbatini's personal effects were confiscated, because he hadn't paid his rent in a while. The incident with the gas valve had been the last straw. The *alte kaker* had to leave!

And so it came to pass that Zabbatini was, as of this morning, officially homeless. After he pensively sat on a bus bench for a few hours, flicking cigarette butts at pigeons, he hit upon an idea: the idiot kid from last night? The kid who wanted eternal love! An idiot kid must have idiot parents. With a roof over their heads.

He had gone back to the King David and peeked into the

lobby. Empty. Ronnie wasn't at the counter. Sneaking inside, he found that the idiot boy had indeed obediently written his name and address in the visitors' log.

And so, Zabbatini, who was all alone in the world, decided to visit Max Cohn of Atwater Village.

"You can really get them to fall in love again?" Max asked hopefully.

"Of course," Zabbatini said, his tone slightly offended. "I am the Great Zabbatini. I can work the mighty magic."

"But you said there is no magic."

He did? That had been, perhaps, a mistake. The first thing Zabbatini did was conjure up a charming smile. Then he said, "If you will it, it is not a dream."

THE BONES OF CHILDREN

In the fall of 1937, the Zauber-Zirkus was slowly moving north on muddy country roads. After a few appearances in Goslar—a terrible place, Moshe thought, and full of Nazis—followed by Brunswick—much better, the Paris of the North—they made their way to Hannover. Moshe didn't particularly like it here in Lower Saxony. The land was too flat, the sky too gray, and the buildings unbecoming. All that brick! There was none of the elegant architecture he had grown up with in Prague. The Czechs, he felt, constantly strived toward heaven. Not so much the folks in Lower Saxony. They clung to their muddy earth.

At least the boss was excited. The Half-Moon Man felt right at home in this dreary, rainy city. One evening, as he was joyfully sucking on a piece of candied sugar, he announced that they would spend the winter here. The Baron had a soft spot for all things aristocratic, and he hoped that some members of the House of Hannover might deign to honor the circus with their presence. Soon, a rumor spread that Ernest Augustus III, Duke of Brunswick, was going to attend one of their performances. And even though this rumor originated solely in the Baron's fervent wish, a "ducal loge" was installed in the circus tent.

But the duke never came, and the ducal loge remained empty.

Meanwhile, Moshe Goldenhirsch and Julia Klein carried on an affair behind the Half-Moon Man's back. Julia quickly took to Moshe. He was a pleasant diversion for her; he adored her, and she enjoyed being adored. They would exchange secret kisses behind the circus tent, and there were moments—brief, fleeting moments—when Julia was convinced that she was in love with him. Even though, deep down, she knew it wasn't true. Moshe, however, took their relationship much more seriously. Julia was his one and only. He felt drunk with happiness, and in the boundless optimism of youth, he was certain that it would never end. Everything around him tasted sweeter, the air, the water, and especially the stolen kisses.

This was, perhaps, the most dramatic change in Moshe's life. He learned the mysteries of love, both spiritual and physical. He especially enjoyed the latter. Up until that point, he'd had to rely on his feverish imagination and his left hand for relief. He still couldn't believe that an actual woman—and what a woman she was!—would voluntarily sleep with him.

Sometimes, however, the Half-Moon Man called Julia into

his wagon at night. Whenever that happened, Moshe would feel nauseous with jealousy. He would stand, shovel in hand, near the wagon and watch the warm glow inside the steamed-up windows. Thankfully, these visits didn't last long: the Baron was lacking in stamina, and after half an hour, at the most, Julia would emerge. She would walk briskly past him and go to the water pump to wash herself.

No one knew the secret Moshe and Julia shared. On Mondays, which was their day off, they would go their separate ways and then secretly meet some time later in a far-off café or a park. They would walk for hours on end. Sometimes, in the middle of the night, they would sneak into the circus tent and make love.

This was where he had lost his virginity.

Moshe had been cleaning out the lion cage when he suddenly felt someone staring at him. He looked up. Julia stood outside the cage. It was dark outside; the show had ended a while earlier. He saw a mischievous gleam in her eyes. She put her finger on her lips and smiled at him. He dropped the shovel and walked out of the cage.

She took him by the hand. "Come with me," she said. "I want to show you something."

He obediently followed. She led him to the ducal loge, which was, as usual, empty. Moshe looked around, confounded.

"There's nothing here," he said.

"Oh yes, there is," she replied and pulled him down into the sawdust.

When Julia saw him naked, she blushed, and said, "You really are a Jew."

Moshe nodded. He felt ashamed, but Julia merely smiled, leaned forward, and kissed him.

∿

The Baron's behavior had been growing more erratic in recent days. He drank too much, and whenever he was drunk, he was quick to anger. Maybe it was because Hannover's nobility ignored him. One day, Moshe saw Julia run past. Her cheek was red and she had tears in her eyes. He went after her.

"What happened?"

"Leave me alone," she whispered.

Moshe looked around helplessly The Half-Moon Man stood in the tent entrance, his mask sparkling in the light. He put a bottle to his lips and staggered off.

"Did he . . . ?" Moshe asked.

"Shut up!" Julia hissed. "It's none of your business."

But it was his business. The Baron had hit Julia, and not for the first time. When Julia finally told Moshe about it, they were lying in a meadow, far away from the circus tent, under a shimmering ceiling of stars. They looked into the endless night sky and began to wonder if a better life was possible, somewhere else. They talked about cities they wanted to visit: Madrid, Rome . . .

"Paris," Moshe said.

Julia stared at him. "I was just about to say that!"

He nodded. For a moment, he had felt as if he could read her thoughts. Maybe that was love, he thought. To know someone else better than yourself. Deep down, Moshe suspected that Julia's feelings for him were paper-thin. It was plain to see, in her many care-less gestures and words. Her heart wasn't his, it was hers alone. He felt it, and he suffered. He wished there was a magic spell he could perform to finally and forevermore win her love. But there wasn't.

"That's it," Julia said. "We'll get out of here and go to Paris."

"I'm not sure . . ." he replied.

"Why not?"

First of all, he didn't speak French. But in addition, it had become increasingly difficult lately to leave Germany. Maybe Berlin was a better option? They quickly agreed. They began to work out a plan. They would take the train from Hannover to Hamburg, then take another train to Berlin. Julia said that she could find them a place to stay, at Danziger Straße. The only issue was money. They had to save money. They had to be frugal, and very careful.

A few days later, Moshe was on his bicycle, headed back to the Hannover Zoo, where the circus had pitched its tent. He came by the Leine River, which ran through the city, and he saw a group of policemen standing around at the riverbank. There was a *Grüne Minna*, a police van, parked at the side of the road. A stocky man in a trench coat was wading around the swampy riverbank, cursing under his breath. He pointed in various directions, shouting orders. He was obviously in charge. Maybe he was a police inspector, Moshe thought. The odd scene had piqued his interest. He got off his bike, leaned it against a tree, and watched from a safe distance. This must be a crime scene, he thought. The inspector was grumpy. His officers were pale. As if they had seen something terrible.

Moshe returned to his bike, deep in thought. But he didn't get on it, for he had an idea. Crouching next to the tree, he simply waited.

He didn't have to wait long. Minutes later, the inspector and a colleague walked to their car and got in. The other officers got into their own cars and took off.

Moshe swung himself onto his bicycle and carefully followed the inspector.

It was good to be out, to feel the chill air against his face. He felt full of possibilities. His plan was insane, but Moshe was free and fearless.

The inspector's car stopped in front of a café.

Quickly, Moshe got off his bike, hid it behind a bush, and entered the café. The inspector was still sitting in his car, talking to his colleague. Moshe found a seat next to an empty table near the door. He quickly arranged two chairs by the table, so that they looked particularly inviting. He took a newspaper off the rack by the door and flipped through it. Thankfully, he had put on a clean suit that day. His face was freshly shaven, and he was wearing a fedora. When he looked up from his newspaper, he saw the police inspector enter the café alone. His colleague drove off in the car.

The inspector looked around for a place to sit, then saw the empty table next to Moshe and sat down there. He felt Moshe's gaze on him.

Moshe averted his eyes and whispered, "Sorry, didn't mean to bother you, Inspector."

"What did you say?" said the man.

"I said I'm sorry. I didn't mean to stare."

"How did you know that I'm an inspector?"

"You are, aren't you?" Moshe said innocently.

"Yes," said the inspector. "But how did you know?"

Moshe seemed to ponder this for a moment, looking at the inspector, examining his face.

"Your eyes," Moshe finally said. "It's in your eyes. You're a man who seeks justice."

The inspector was stunned. "How did you know that?"

Moshe smiled vaguely and went back to his newspaper. He remembered the Baron's words: The less you say, the better.

"Are you a medium?" the inspector asked.

Moshe shook his head.

"A spiritualist?"

"No, nothing of the sort. I'm just a . . ."

A what? What could he possibly say? The truth? That he was a circus clown dabbling in stage magic and fake premonitions? Out of the question.

"I'm a student," he said at last.

"Oh," said inspector. "What do you study?"

"This and that . . ." Moshe replied evasively. "I haven't really found my footing yet."

The inspector nodded. "Yes, I know what that's like. I was aimless and adrift, just like you, before I joined."

Moshe didn't get around to asking him what he meant by "before I joined," because the inspector kept pressing him to reveal his "secret." Moshe didn't. He played it shy, pretending there was nothing unusual about him, except that he sometimes had "feelings" and "just knew things."

"You're looking for a murderer, aren't you?" Moshe said innocently.

"Extraordinary!" proclaimed the inspector. "This is impossible."

Moshe held up the paper. "No, I read it in the paper."

The headline read: "The BUTCHER Strikes Again!"

The inspector laughed.

Then Moshe closed his eyes and held his hands up to his head. "You found something in the river today," he said breathlessly.

"That hasn't made the paper yet," the inspector said. "It just happened. Just now, today!"

"As I said . . . sometimes, I have these . . . feelings." He pretended to concentrate. "You were looking for something . . . something terrible. . . ." He continued to mumble, hoping the inspector would say something to help him along. He didn't have to wait long. The inspector was no different from other people. He wanted to be deceived.

"Bones!" the inspector said loudly.

"Yes!"

"We found bones! How did you . . . ?" He shook his head. "This is unbelievable!"

Moshe humbly averted his gaze.

Then the inspector stood up and held out his hand. "Leitner," he said. "Inspector Erich Leitner, Hannover Criminal Division. Pleased to meet you."

Moshe stood up as well. Only then did he see the NSDAP pin on the man's lapel.

He hesitated for only a moment then he took the man's hand and shook it.

Half an hour later, they were standing by the Leine River. It was cold and misty. The policemen were gone; only their footprints remained in the mud. The reeds had been trampled. The dreary landscape seemed to exist only in shades of gray. Cranes were flying majestically above, free of sorrow or guilt. Moshe felt a tugging at his heart. He thought of the song "The Eagle and the Lamb." He wondered if he had sealed his own fate just now, by shaking the inspector's hand. He wondered if he would soon be led to the slaughter, like his mother.

"Feel anything yet?" Leitner asked excitedly.

Moshe felt nothing. "What kind of bones did you find?" he asked with an air of expertise.

"The bones of children," the inspector said glumly.

"That explains it," said Moshe.

"Explains what?"

Moshe stared at the moist, sodden ground. Without looking at the inspector, he said, "The pain."

The inspector was deeply impressed. As was Moshe. It was all so effortless. He was giving a world-class performance for an audience of one.

"Help me," the inspector said. "Help me find the murderer."

Moshe pretended to think about it. Then he nodded.

THE BURGLAR

There seemed to be no end to the humiliations the Great Zabbatini was forced to endure. The kid had put out a few flattened cardboard boxes and old blankets in the garage for him. It was apparently important that Max's mother remained unaware of Zabbatini's presence. So this was what he was reduced to! Hiding in a cluttered garage like a stray dog! Unbelievable! He was an artist of worldwide renown, appearing in the finest cabarets of Berlin, then New York, Atlantic City, the whole West Coast. In Las Vegas, they had given him a private suite in one of the finest mob-owned hotels on the Strip. And now? Zabbatini tossed about, but he couldn't find a comfortable position on the cold concrete floor. At his age! Others spent their golden years in the lap of luxury, sleeping in feathered beds, eating the finest food, pinching the cheeks of grandkids and the asses of nurses. He didn't deserve to be in this dark, dusty place full of boxes and discarded furniture. That was how he felt, discarded. A cold wind blew in through the crack underneath the garage door.

He wondered if there were rats in the garage. Why not? It could always get worse, couldn't it? And it did. He saw no rats, at least there was that, but he had to pee. Zabbatini sighed and rubbed his tired eyes. There was no point, he knew, in delaying the inevitable. His bladder was not his friend of late; it had become unreliable. He laboriously lifted himself up and opened the door leading to the house. He shuffled into the bathroom next to the master bedroom, lifted the toilet seat, and relieved himself. When he was finished, he flushed and turned around. He saw a laundry basket standing in the corner, filled with clothes, the lid open. On top of the pile, he saw a pink lace slip. What have we here? he thought. He picked it up, pressed it against his face, and closed his eyes. Almost immediately, he was adrift in memories. The scent brought him back in time, to a small attic room in Berlin. When he opened his eyes again, he no longer saw the blue-and-pink-tiled bathroom, but the tiny, ramshackle garret. He saw Julia looking at him, seeing only him and nothing else, smiling for him, for him alone, her blond hair tousled, her green-gray eyes catching tiny sparks of sunlight, and her smile lighting up his heart. She took his hand into hers, her fingers so much smaller, so much more delicate, and she whispered a beautiful lie into his ear:

"I love you."

The memory was so strong, so powerful, that he forgot all else. And why not? He had nothing to look forward to. Friends and foes alike, they were all dead. He was the last survivor, the lone relic of a long-lost era. The train of life was slowly chugging toward its final destination, and the other passengers had already left. All that remained was the past. It was his refuge, his constant companion and constant torment.

\/

Ever since Harry had moved out, Deborah had difficulties sleeping. A recurring dream troubled her: she was sitting alone in a boat at dusk, in the middle of a lake. There was no sound and no sign of life around her, everything was perfectly still. She felt completely abandoned, and her boat was adrift, she had no power over it, the course could not be changed. As it floated by the shore, which was overgrown with wild plants, she saw the crumbling ruins of a long-lost civilization. There were square-hewn stones, fallen columns, and collapsed arches. Remnants of a once-great architecture, now abandoned to the wilderness. Deborah would reach out in an attempt to pull herself ashore, but whenever she did, there was a gust of wind, or a surging current, and she would be cast back toward the center of the lake, further adrift, more alone than ever.

Suddenly, she woke up. There was a noise coming from the hallway. She listened intently. There it was again. She couldn't place it. Was it Max? She looked around. He was lying next to her, snoring slightly. He, too, had been having difficulties sleeping lately and would sometimes come shuffling into her bedroom to snuggle up with her.

She heard a light rain, softly drumming against her window. Then the toilet flushed. Deborah shot up in bed. Suddenly, she was afraid. Was there a burglar? What else could it be? Maybe raccoons? Raccoons were always going through her trash at night. But they certainly didn't flush toilets. She peeked through the half-open door.

There was light and movement coming from the bathroom.

She groped blindly around in the dark until she found her cell phone, and dialed 911. A female voice answered.

"There's someone in my house," Deborah whispered.

The woman on the other end of the line asked for her name and address. Deborah gave her the information and impressed upon her that there was probably a burglar. Maybe even a rapist? She'd heard all kinds of stories. The operator asked her to remain calm and not do anything. Officers were on their way.

"Remain calm?" Deborah hissed indignantly. "There's someone in my house!"

"Don't do anything," said the operator.

"Don't tell me what to do," Deborah said, and hung up. She was furious now. All fear, all nervousness was gone. This was not unusual for her. She had always been prickly. When she was a young girl, one of the bigger kids in school had tried to take her lunch pail from her and she'd gotten so upset that she started attacking the boy, even though he was much stronger than she was. She had punched him in the nose, and he started bleeding. In the end, she and the boy were hauled into the principal's office and the boy was punished with detention, but the case against her was dismissed for lack of evidence. No one believed that such a small girl could hurt a much stronger boy. When Deborah got mad, it canceled out all other thoughts, including those of her own safety.

She went to the hall closet and armed herself with a broom; then she got a can of Mace, which she always carried in her purse.

I'll show you! she thought. Then, with steely determination, she sneaked down the hallway.

The bathroom door was half-open. Raising the broom with her right hand, she held the Mace in her left and got ready to attack. She inhaled deeply and closed her eyes for a second, then kicked the bathroom door wide open and lunged into the room, holding the broom before her like a lance. The moment she saw the old man sitting on the edge of the bathtub, she brought the broomstick down on his head, then sprayed a load of Mace at his face.

The man yelped in pain and fell backward into the empty tub. He lay there like a turtle on its back, his spindly arms and legs stretched out, gasping loudly as he rubbed his eyes. It would take a few minutes for the pain to subside. Mace was pretty strong stuff, that much she knew.

"Who are you?" Deborah demanded.

The old man moaned. Tears of pain ran down his face and he was shaking. His mouth was opening and closing, but he couldn't get a word out. Deborah could see that he was holding something in his left hand, which, she noted, was oddly disfigured. The thing he was holding was her lace slip.

"What are you doing with my slip, you pervert?" she asked. "How did you get in here?"

Zabbatini blinked, still fighting against his tears. Then he looked at her like a deer caught in the headlights. When the pain in his eyes and head started to recede, he began to realize how awkward the situation was. It didn't help that, from the moment he saw that angry beast with the broom, he was immensely attracted to her. And that fire in her eyes!

He moaned again—this time, it was a minor improvisation on his part—then he lifted himself up, so that he was now sitting in the tub. As if he were taking a bath. He reached into his pocket and removed a small pill bottle. He took out one of the pills—for his heart—and swallowed it dry. Deborah saw that he feebly tried to hold her slip behind his back. His other hand was rubbing his nearly bald head.

"And a lovely evening to you," he said quietly, and with an odd accent.

"What," growled Deborah, "are you doing here?"

"You hurt me," he said accusingly.

"Oh, it's going to hurt a hell of a lot more. I'm not through with you. Who are you?"

Zabbatini gave a slight bow. "They call me the Great Zabbatini," he said. "My kindest felicitations to you, too, young lady." He spread out his arms and gave her a look that had served him well over the course of his career, an innocent look that seemed to say, Would I lie to you?

"What are you doing with my slip?"

Zabbatini held out both hands. They were empty.

"Slip?" he asked innocently. "What slip?" Then, with a theatrical gesture, he pulled up the short sleeves of his Hawaiian shirt. "You see? Nothing hidden there."

Deborah was surprised. She could have sworn the old man had her slip. She had seen it, moments ago! Now all she could see were few faded numbers on his forearm, the remnants of a tattoo.

She knew what that meant.

"What are you doing in my bathroom, in the middle of the night?"

"Well . . ." Zabbatini began. He smiled helplessly. What was he going to say? That he had been kicked out of his old-age home? Deborah was still holding the broom in a rather threatening manner. His next words would be crucial.

"In each of our lives," he said, "there are moments that transform us." His accent was becoming thicker. He tried to climb out of the bathtub. Everything hurt. "This, young lady," he continued, "is such a moment." He managed to hoist one leg over the rim of the tub. "I am here," he declared grandiosely, "to transform your life."

"No tricks," said Deborah with a dangerous growl. "The cops are on their way."

Zabbatini, who had managed to pull himself up, looked at her pleadingly. "I am one of the greatest entertainers in the world," he said, but he didn't sound very convincing.

She suddenly heard a voice behind her. "Mom, don't!"

Deborah turned around and saw her son standing in the bathroom doorway, his hair and pajamas disheveled.

"It's all my fault," he said.

"What's going on here?" she asked him.

Max lowered his head and stared down at his feet. "He's a magician," Max said at last.

"A what?"

"The magician from Dad's record."

"That guy?" she asked incredulously.

"Hold on, I'll show you," Max said. He ran to his room to get the record. A few seconds later, he was back. "Look!" he said, holding the record up next to Zabbatini's face.

Zabbatini tried to smile like he did on the cover.

Max saw a glimmer of recognition in Mom's eyes.

"What's he doing here?" she asked.

"I met him last night," Max said. "He lives in an old-age home on Fairfax. He's the guy I went to Canter's with."

"I can everything explain," Zabbatini said. He cleared his throat. "This young Max here has visited me in my home. And so he wanted to find me." He carefully hoisted himself out of the tub, as fast as his age would allow him. His knees were shaking, but at last he was standing. Then he raised his withered hand in a grotesque parody of the gesture he had seen his father perform in the temple attic, so many years ago. With a creaky, feeble voice he said, "I am the Great Zabbatini!" Then he reached to Deborah's ear and said, "What have you there behind your ear?"

Deborah turned around. To her surprise, Zabbatini suddenly held her pink lace slip in his hand.

"Aha!" he proclaimed loudly. "It was there the whole time!"

Max applauded enthusiastically.

Zabbatini bowed. "Thank you, ladies and gentlemen."

At that moment, there was a loud banging at the door. A voice shouted, "Police! Open the door!"

All color drained from Zabbatini's face.

"Damn," Deborah hissed, and ran into the living room. Max followed her.

When Deborah opened the front door, she saw two uniformed officers standing outside, a young black woman with her hair in a bun, and an older, ruddy-faced white man with an enormous gut. "You called, ma'am," said the guy.

"Yes . . ." she said haltingly. "I thought there was a burglar."

"And?" the woman asked. "Is there?"

"No." Deborah shook her head. Then she said, "I mean, yes. There's a stranger in my bathtub."

The two cops looked at each other. They asked if they could come inside to take a look. Better safe than sorry.

Deborah nodded vaguely and stepped aside, letting them in. The cops looked around her house like tourists in a museum. Their hands rested on their leather belts. Deborah showed them the way to the bathroom. Zabbatini was sitting on the side of the tub, a beaming smile on his face.

Then the cop with the gut said to Deborah, "That the guy?" She nodded.

"He doesn't seem dangerous," he said.

"I just heard a noise. And . . . I was scared, you see. That's why I called you."

"I can everything explain," said Zabbatini.

"You better," said the cop.

Zabbatini told them how Max had shown up at his old-age home the previous night, how the boy had wanted to find him. Then his narrative began to take on some fictional elements, poetic even. He told them about the deep bond he and this fine young man had instantly shared, and that Max had asked him—what was he saying, *implored him!*—to come home with him, because, well . . .

Well . . . why?

The police officers were getting impatient. The woman asked to see Zabbatini's ID and took it out to the cruiser to run a check on him. Returning a few minutes later, she said that the geezer was apparently harmless. He wasn't even on their list of sexual predators, she said with an air of defeat. "No outstanding warrants. Nothing."

"He might still be a pedophile," Deborah offered helpfully.

The woman shrugged her shoulders. "Might be, but he's not in our system. Most of them are."

Deborah nodded. A ringing endorsement.

The two officers stood menacingly to the left and right side of Zabbatini. The cop with the gut placed his hairy paw on Zabbatini's shoulder.

"All right, then. Time to go, old man," the cop said.

They escorted him out, into the pouring rain, toward their cruiser.

"Where are you taking him?" Deborah asked.

"He'll spend the night in a holding tank," said the woman. "Unlawful entry. The rest is up to the judge."

Suddenly, Zabbatini tore away from them. He took a few feeble steps toward Deborah and did something unexpected: he sank to his knees.

"Please!" he cried. "I don't want going to the jail."

"Come on!" said the cop, the voice of reason. "You're making a scene. No point in that."

But there was a point. It was exactly what Zabbatini intended. Wrapping his arms around Deborah's legs, he began sobbing. "I am an old man, the jail I will not survive!"

Deborah blushed and looked around. She hoped that none of the neighbors were awake to witness this. She was mortified by the display, the feeble old man, clinging to her legs, sobbing uncontrollably.

"All right," she said, exasperatedly. "I won't press charges. You can stay. But for only one night."

"Thank you, Mom!" Max yelled and hugged her.

Deborah managed a smile.

The cops looked disappointed.

THIS COMING DARKNESS

At the banks of the Leine River, Moshe Goldenhirsch made a deal with Inspector Erich Leitner. Moshe would lend his expertise to the Hannover *Kripo*—the Criminal Police—as a "consulting detective," and in return he would be compensated thirty reichsmarks per week, for the duration of the investigation. That was a lot of money for him. Moshe hoped the investigation would continue indefinitely. He certainly would do everything in his power to make sure it did. They sealed their pact with a handshake. Then a police car brought them to the station.

"What's your name?" Leitner asked as they were driving.

"Zabbatini," said Moshe.

"What kind of name is that?"

"It's Persian. I was born in Tehran," said Moshe, who was well-prepared for just this question.

"Where?"

"Persia," Moshe said.

"Can you believe it!" The inspector slapped his own knee in delight. "Persia! You don't say!"

"Did you know," Moshe said, "that the Persians were the original Aryans?"

"That so? Well, you can't beat *that* for an Aryan certificate!" Leitner gave a choking laugh. "Don't take it the wrong way, but I'm not big on racial science."

"You're not?"

Leitner shook his head. "Politics. Not my thing. All that modern stuff, Aryans, Jewish question, what have you."

"But aren't you," Moshe said carefully, "a party member?"

"Got to be. Servant of the state and all that. And the Führer . . . what a guy! But folks like me . . ." He lifted his shoulders. "I just do my job. Let someone else worry about the rest."

Moshe nodded. It might be to his advantage that Leitner was not exactly a glowing admirer of the National Socialist movement. It might make him less distrustful.

"And how come you're in the Reich now?" the inspector asked.

"My parents had to leave Persia during the revolution," Moshe said.

"Revolution?"

"In the twenties. Bolsheviks."

Leitner nodded. "Of course. Those damn Bolsheviks," he said.

"The revolution failed, but my parents and I had already gone to Paris." The lies were coming to him with an almost frightening ease.

"And now you're here," Leitner said vaguely.

"Exactly."

They arrived at the police precinct. Even though he had claimed to be Persian, the swastika flags hanging from the windows of the police station made Moshe uncomfortably aware of what he truly was.

They entered the building and walked past gloomy offices with gloomy officers inside, smoking as they huddled over their typewriters. Moshe was to spend many joyless hours there. At least he got on well with Inspector Leitner, who was a small, cheerful man, and whose jolly disposition and lack of intelligence belied his chosen profession. Leitner quickly took a liking to Moshe and enjoyed talking to him. Moshe made sure it stayed that way. Then Leitner showed him the files: a child killer was on the loose in Hannover, and the bodies of the victims had been savagely mutilated. With an uneasy feeling, Moshe stared at the grainy, black-and-white photographs of tiny, abused corpses. The police had no leads. Moshe promised to help.

Now that he was earning money, Moshe rented a room in a house belonging to a retired schoolteacher, which he presented to Leitner as his current residence, and where he could inconspicuously fornicate with Julia. Moshe lived in a world of lies. He lied to the police and he lied to the Half-Moon Man. He lied to his colleagues at the circus. He certainly wasn't about to tell them about his arrangement with the police.

Instead, he invented an affair with a local woman. That was, he said, the reason he spent so much time away from the circus. It was a never-ending litany of lies. They came easily to him, but over time, there were too many made-up facts he had to keep straight. It was exhausting. Then there was the morgue, which was even more unpleasant than the police station. Leitner often asked him to come down there, and Moshe would have his hands hover over a small and pitiful gathering of human remains as he concocted an utterly useless clue. The morgue was cold and it smelled of formaldehyde, the sickeningly sweet odor reminding Moshe of rotting fruit.

He was naturally weary of human bodies, especially dead ones. He did not like to be reminded of his own mortality. The morgue depressed him, forcing him to think of his father, whom he had abandoned. His heart became heavy with his betrayal of both the living and the dead.

Also, it became increasingly difficult to make up clues. His stock phrases, such as "I sense a dark depravity" or "The killer is closer than you think," lost their appeal over time. If Moshe sensed anything, it was that the inspector was under increasing pressure. Six children had turned up dead so far, and the police had no clues to speak of. The more desperate Leitner became to produce the killer, the more he relied on Moshe.

Moshe had to attend interrogations and nightly raids of working-class neighborhoods. He would be asked to put the palm of his hand on the foreheads of dumbfounded workers who had been awoken in the middle of the night. At first, Moshe had been able to "feel their innocence," but as the pressure from the public increased, he began to sense a "dark sense of unease." It didn't take much for these men to be arrested. Moshe didn't want to know what happened to them.

One night, they led him to a small greengrocer's shop. Moshe knew it well, having often bought his vegetables there. The police had roused the merchant from his bed in the apartment above his shop. A new suspect! Luckily, the man didn't appear to recognize Moshe.

Leitner, who now had dark circles under his eyes, grinned at Moshe as he entered. He took him aside and asked him if he felt anything.

Moshe walked toward the merchant with heavy steps and put his hand on the man's forehead. The man looked at him, perplexed. Moshe had no idea what to say. He didn't want to use any of his normal phrases. It was important not to overdo it. But he had to offer something, anything. He closed his eyes.

"Well?" Leitner asked.

Moshe still couldn't think of anything. His thoughts were clouded. He removed his hand and looked at Leitner.

"So?" the Inspector asked.

Moshe remembered the Half-Moon Man's advice. If in doubt, better to say nothing. Moshe simply shook his head gravely and turned away.

Leitner, however, must have interpreted Moshe's silence as an indication of the suspect's guilt. "Arrest him," he said.

The grocer was dragged toward a car while his wife and kids stood crying by the upstairs window. Before they pushed him into the car, the man cast one last, desperate glance at Moshe. Moshe couldn't bear it, and stared at the ground. Then his conscience started to bother him, so he decided to put an end to the whole farce.

After all, where was he going to get his vegetables?

WHO WILL SAY KADDISH?

When Deborah Cohn got up the next morning, Zabbatini was already sitting at the breakfast table performing card tricks for Max.

"And there," Zabbatini concluded, "is the queen of hearts."

He winked at Deborah as he said it. She rolled her eyes. Max grinned broadly and applauded. The boy hadn't looked that happy in quite a while.

Zabbatini had to grudgingly admit that he'd begun to like the kid. A little bit. Not too much. He found most children insufferable, but this one had an air of melancholy that Zabbatini could relate to. And he wasn't too stupid for his age. A bit of a know-it-all, yes, but not an idiot after all. They had been chatting over breakfast, a careful rapprochement, Oh, you like Zagir Chicken? Me too! No wonder, it's right around the corner from Bongo's

Clown Room. And the garlic sauce? Heavenly, no? A life without garlic is no life at all. Stuff like that.

"Mom!" Max yelled. "Did you see that?"

Deborah shook her head, yawning. "Eat your cereal, honey,"
she said.

Zabbatini was staring brazenly at Deborah. Ah, he thought.
The heavenly one. The scented one. "Good morning, young
lady," he cooed.

"Mom!" Max said. "Do you know Bongo's Clown Room?
Zabbatini told me that—" He stopped when he saw the shocked
look on his mother's face.

She frowned at Zabbatini, who looked perfectly innocent. He
cleared his throat and decided to play it charming. "My dear," he
said, "do you offer coffee in this establishment?"

Deborah raised her eyebrows. "Coffee?" Really? Who did he
think he was?

"Yes," Zabbatini said. "A dark, hot liquid. They make it from
beans, you see. Black, please, and with sugar." He looked at Max
and winked again. "Dark as night and sweet as a stolen kiss."

Ever since the incident with the broom and the pepper spray,
Zabbatini had developed a healthy sense of respect toward Deborah, bordering on fear. But despite that—or maybe because of
it—she had featured prominently in his erotic dreams the night
before. With age, his pipes had become rusty, and as a result he
embraced all things sleazy with increasing gusto. Sometimes, his
feverish dreams woke him up at night, and his unfulfilled desires
kept him awake. He had spent last night on the sofa bed in the

spare bedroom, which used to be Harry's office. How generous! But he had mostly been awake, twisting and turning on the uncomfortable bed, tormented by his dirty thoughts. He had dozed off right around dawn.

"I am not your maid," said Deborah with quiet menace.

Max recognized that tone of voice. The calm before the storm. He had to act. "I can make coffee," he offered, jumping up from the kitchen table. "I know how."

Zabbatini could feel the turbulence in the atmosphere. After all, he was a mind reader. But in the bright morning sunlight, he felt confident and safe. She couldn't very well throw him out anymore, now that her son was under his spell. Her inner fire, her passion—Zabbatini was utterly enchanted by this angry goddess. It didn't matter to him that her hair wasn't brushed and her face was puffy from a lack of sleep. On the contrary, it was her domesticity that he found so appealing. He had always been a searcher, a vagabond, an outsider. The mundane had been out of reach for him. On top of that, Zabbatini had devoted his life to lying. To trickery. Now that the end was near, there was no one left to fool. His greatest regret was to have lived a life without regrets. He had only ever looked out for himself, never anyone else. And now he was alone.

"Let me get one thing straight," Deborah said. "I don't know who you are or what you're doing here. The only reason I let you spend the night was because it was raining, and you were embarrassing me in front of the cops."

"And for that I thank you. But now it is morning, the sun shines, and I wish for coffee."

That sounded like a command. Deborah didn't like being told what to do. This guy? This *alte kaker*? First he was sniffing her panties, and now he wanted the scent of coffee to titillate his nose?

"I think it's about time you left," Deborah said.

Max stared at her. His mouth opened, like that of a fish on land. Then he said, "Please don't."

"Why not?" she asked defiantly. "I said one night. Look outside. It's daylight now."

Zabbatini and Max exchanged a shocked glance. Zabbatini wasn't used to people resisting his manipulations. Apparently, he had overstepped his boundaries.

Max looked at his mom pleadingly, a look he had practiced on many occasions. "Remember you said I could have anything for my birthday that I want?"

Deborah nodded, the certainty gone from her face.

"I want him to perform at my birthday party in two weeks," Max said. "At Mickey's Pizza Palace."

Deborah's eyes wandered over the old magician mistrustfully as he sat there chewing his soggy cereal. He lowered the spoon and gave her a labored smile.

"You wouldn't rather have a *Tintin* book?" Deborah asked her son.

"Yes," Max admitted. "That, too, of course. But I also want Zabbatini to come to my birthday. He was really famous once."

"That's true," Zabbatini said with a sudden rush of vigor. "I was! I am!"

"So, what, you want him to fold balloons or something?" Deborah asked Max.

"The audience clamors," Zabbatini said.

Deborah's skeptical gaze wandered from the old man to her son, then back again. "Where on earth did you find him?" she asked Max.

"I went to the magic shop on Hollywood Boulevard, and the guy there told me where I could find him."

"And would you mind telling me why?"

Max lowered his gaze and stared at his cereal.

"Max?" Deborah said.

He crossed his arms. Then he said, "I want the Great Zabbatini to perform at my birthday!"

The wheels were turning in Deborah's head. First the drama with the record, then he'd run away . . . and now he'd dug up this old fossil. She had no idea what Max's reasoning was, but he seemed adamant. She could be adamant, too, but she didn't want to risk open warfare between her and her son. And if she relented?

She crouched down in front of Max and took his hands into hers. "Are you sure, honey?"

Max nodded. "Please let him stay. It's only two weeks."

He really is as stubborn as his dad, Deborah thought. At least the police had run a background check on the old man, and had found no prior convictions. Yay. Still, the idea of having a complete stranger in her house put her on high alert. But she had to admit: having the old geezer here seemed to make Max happy. She had no idea why.

She forced a smile, sighed, and announced her verdict. "All right. He can sleep in Dad's old office. But only until your birthday. That's it."

"Thank you, Mom," Max said effusively. He put his arms around her neck and gave her a kiss.

"Hurry up," Deborah said. "Or you'll be late."

Max grabbed his backpack and ran outside. He slammed the door and the walls shook. Deborah and Zabbatini looked at him through the window as he hurried into the yellow bus at the corner. The doors closed; the bus jolted, then rolled out of sight.

As soon as they were alone, Deborah turned to Zabbatini. She grabbed a kitchen knife and pointed it at his chest.

"Careful, dear lady," Zabbatini said with a nervous laugh.

Deborah impressed upon him that he could stay until the birthday party was over, and not a minute longer. Not one minute more! She explained to him the house rules, which, to his distress, included no more sniffing her clothes. She made it clear that the violation of any of these rules or even the slightest hint of improper behavior would result in this knife here being shoved up his ass. And one more thing: She didn't trust him.

"What is all this about? Why are you here?"

Zabbatini sighed. "What about the coffee?"

"Forget the coffee," said Deborah. "Why are you here? What did you tell my son?"

"I told nothing to your son," he said. "He came and troubled me."

The knife was making him exceedingly nervous, and his command of the English language was becoming shaky once again. He told her that one day, as he was enjoying his usual "active senior lifestyle," the kid showed up at the King David, which was, he assured her, a veritable palace, a Garden of Eden from which he had now been expelled because of the stupid slob in the front office. It would appear, Zabbatini surmised, that Max had become somewhat fixated on a certain record, which he, Zabbatini, had created so many years ago. The record in question was a promotional item from the early eighties, which his agent at the time, Benny Szimansky, may God rest his tiny soul, had asked him to produce in hopes of raising "audience awareness" and perhaps scoring a few children's birthday parties and bar mitzvahs. In those years, Zabbatini's star had begun to decline. His television stints had become increasingly rare, and even the bookers at Disneyland had not called him back, probably due to the fact that he had—after one particularly lackluster performance—been found with his pants around his ankles in a storage room, *shtupping* a female employee in a Minnie Mouse costume. Very awkward.

Following this debacle, he had gone back to the East Coast for a few months, performing in an Atlantic City casino, an un-rewarding but well-paid gig. Eventually, that dried up as well, and he settled in California for good. The weather was much more tolerable here. If he was going to be poor, at least he wanted some sunshine in his life. He liked the West Coast, especially the scent of jacaranda trees and lemons in the summer, and the ripe avocados he would steal from his neighbor's yard. Los Angeles seemed like an open, unending wasteland to him, but that was part of the appeal. At least there weren't any ruins. No burned-down synagogues or defaced graveyards. Nothing here reminded him of the past, those dark days before 1945.

And there was the Magic Castle, one of the oldest and finest magic clubs on the West Coast, renowned for its awesome acts and awful food. Zabbatini was friends with Milt Larsen, founder of the Castle and the "Academy of Magical Arts." It was a Boy Scout clubhouse for magicians—men-children who were stuck in adolescence. Amateurs, Zabbatini thought. Nonetheless, he had been delighted when they asked him to join. Milt's brother Bill had been an executive at CBS on Fairfax and Third, and had occasionally booked Zabbatini on programs such as *The Judy Garland Show*.

One night, a few months after his return to Los Angeles, Zabbatini, Milt, and Bill had gone out for dinner at Chasen's in Beverly Hills—the steaks were heavenly—and Milt had asked him if he would like to have tenure at the Magic Castle. Zabbatini, who had not been able to afford the aforementioned steak and who had been secretly hoping that the Larsens would pick up the tab, had, of course, been delighted.

The Magic Castle had been built in 1908, in the hills above Hollywood, an utterly absurd piece of pseudo-Victorian architecture that looked like a haunted house from a bad horror movie. In the early sixties, magician and businessman Milt Larsen had bought the run-down mansion and renovated it. The Castle was—and still is—a private club: only members and their guests were admitted. The food was a crime against humanity, but for magicians, the place was paradise. Zabbatini was among his peers—he knew everyone, he had friends here. The entrance was guarded by a fake owl, and if you uttered the words "Open, sesame!" a wooden bookshelf swung open, revealing a swank bar, abuzz with cocktail waitresses, drunk patrons, and the magicians who preyed on them. It was always dark inside the Magic Castle. The ambience was in itself an illusion, the illusion of stately, Victorian grandeur in Southern California, replete with plush red carpets and brass chandeliers. There was an intimate room for close-up magic, Zabbatini's favorite, as well as a larger parlor and a grand stage. But the true heart of the castle was its vast basement library filled with magical tomes from all over the globe. It was one of the world's most impressive collections of literature of the Unseen Art.

The Magic Castle was a place for kinship, rivalries, and petty drama. The corridors behind the kitchen, behind the parlor and the "Palace of Mystery," were hardly Victorian-looking at all. They had all the charm of a mental institution, with bright, greenish walls and neon bulbs. This was where the magicians sat around and ate the free food, got dressed for their shows, and tried to hit on the waitresses.

For many years, this was Zabbatini's true home. His own golden age of magic had long since faded, and he didn't make enough money to live. Other work was hard to come by. His agent, a squat man with a cigar who was always holding court in a wood-paneled, smoke-filled office on Sunset and La Cienega, had difficulties getting him gigs. Zabbatini was a relic. No one wanted to see guys like him anymore. And so, he had gone into a studio in North Hollywood to record *His Greatest Tricks*.

Sales were lackluster.

"It's your fucking Kraut accent," Szimansky had said. "You sound like a goddamn Nazi."

Indeed, Zabbatini's linguistic skills were rather limited. He had only shrugged and smiled. Apparently, there was nothing he could do to halt his decline, not even with *His Greatest Tricks*.

Zabbatini explained all this to Deborah Cohn. And now, more than twenty years later, Max had stumbled into his life and asked him to perform one of the spells on his record.

"What spell?" Deborah asked. In the course of Zabbatini's maudlin narrative, her anger had subsided. She began to see the larger picture. She felt pity for the old man. She even condescended to make coffee, not because she wanted to do the guy a favor, but because she, too, like every sensible human being, wanted coffee in the morning.

"The spell," Zabbatini said, "of eternal love."

Deborah was taken aback. "Isn't Max a little young for that?"

Zabbatini laughed. "The spell is not for him," he said. "The spell is for you."

"For me?" Deborah was thoroughly confounded. "Why me?"

"For you and your man," Zabbatini explained. "I understand you are parting, yes?"

Deborah nodded cautiously.

Zabbatini looked into his coffee mug. He could see the outline of his head reflecting in the cup. "Your son," he said, "is very unhappy. He wants you to be together again once more."

Deborah said nothing.

Zabbatini continued: "He believes that if I make my love spell, you and your man will fall back into the love again, and he will not be lonely no more."

Deborah stared at the kitchen floor. I should sweep, she realized. I haven't swept in a while.

"What about you?" she asked, without looking at him. "Why are you really here? It's not Max's fault, is it?"

Zabbatini sighed. "No. They threw me out. From the old age home. They want me not there. I met Max, so I come here. I have nowhere to go."

"You've got to admit," she said. "It's a little creepy. My boy shows up with an old man in tow."

Zabbatini nodded. "This thought had come to me also." He took a sip of his coffee. Then he said: "But I am not creepy. I am alone. Like Max."

When Deborah looked into his tired, washed-out eyes, she saw a little boy. Not the Great Zabbatini, but little Moshe Goldenhirsch.

"I have no family," he said. "No one."

He didn't want to choke up, so he looked away and stared into the kitchen. The clock was ticking, and a wedge of sunlight was on the floor. He could see the dust in the air.

"When I die," he quietly said, "there will be no one to say Kaddish for me."

THE END OF THE ZAUBER-ZIRKUS

T he search for the child-killer—the so-called Butcher of Hannover—was soon over, but not in the way Moshe had imagined. One day, after a particularity exhausting afternoon of interrogations and fake prophecies, he returned to the Zauber-Zirkus to slip back into his clown costume. He saw Horst the Artist waiting for him outside the tent. Night was falling and the performers were getting ready for the evening's show. Audience members were already filing in.

"The boss wants to see you," Horst said.

"Why?"

He received no answer. Horst silently led Moshe through the artists' entrance at the back of the tent. "Go in," he said. Then, with a curt nod, he vanished.

Not knowing what to expect, Moshe entered nervously and saw the Half-Moon Man sitting in front of a makeup mirror.

He wasn't wearing his mask.

His face was completely normal. There was nothing, no disfiguration, not even the tiniest scar.

"Well?" said the Half-Moon Man, who had become aware that Moshe was watching him.

"Your face . . ." Moshe said uncertainly.

"What about it?"

Moshe felt foolish and stared at the floor. "I thought it was disfigured. In the war."

"Did I ever claim such a thing?" the Half-Moon Man asked.

Moshe thought about it, then shook his head.

The Half-Moon Man turned back to the mirror and continued applying his makeup. "The best way to lie," he said, "is not to lie."

Moshe nodded.

"And speaking of lies," said the Half-Moon Man, "there is a matter that must be discussed."

He stood up and faced Moshe, swaying slightly. Moshe suspected that he was drunk. It was disconcerting to see him without his mask.

"What?" Moshe said timidly, but he already surmised what this was about. The Baron must have discovered their affair.

Quite unexpectedly, von Kröger struck Moshe across the face with his sword cane. Moshe felt a sharp and lingering pain. He went down on his knees, hot tears welling up in his eyes.

"Swine!" called the Half-Moon Man. "Did you really think I wouldn't find out?"

He raised his cane again.

"Baron," said a voice.

Both Moshe and his tormentor turned around.

Horst was standing in the entrance. "Baron," he said. "The show . . ."

The Half-Moon Man was breathing heavily. Then he lowered his arm and gathered himself. Horst helped him into his cape. The Half-Moon Man put his mask on, then his top hat.

"We will talk later," he said to Moshe, and went out into the circus arena.

Alone in the dressing room, Moshe rubbed his aching face. He could hear the Half-Moon Man giving his usual introduction. The audience was applauding.

It took Moshe quite some time to get back on his feet, and even longer to force himself into his clown costume. The others were in the middle of their performance. Löwitsch the Lion Tamer was taming Ludwig the Lion. Just as Moshe was about to leave the dressing room, he saw the second sword cane leaning against the makeup table. The sword that the Half-Moon Man was supposed to plunge into the crate. Startled, he picked it up and unsheathed it. With the palm of his hand, he pushed the blade in. No doubt: this was the retractable version. Which meant that the Half-Moon Man had failed to hide it in its proper place before the performance. He had gone out there with his real sword. Suddenly, Moshe felt nauseous. If the Baron didn't realize in time, he would risk injuring Julia.

Moshe walked up to the curtain and peeked out. The Half-Moon Man and Princess Aryana were performing their usual trick. Everything seemed normal.

Then, the time arrived and Julia, giving a slight bow, stepped inside the trunk. Moshe saw the audience, looking on in anticipation. When he saw the Baron's hand self-assuredly resting on the knob of the cane, he suddenly knew: the Half-Moon Man meant to plunge the real sword into the trunk.

The Baron closed the trunk and the orchestra gave a drum roll. As the Baron unsheathed his sword, Zabbatini the Clown suddenly pushed aside the curtain, emitted a feeble war cry, and came staggering out into the circus arena. The audience was puzzled. The Half-Moon Man turned around, his sword gleaming in the footlights.

"What are you doing?" he hissed.

Moshe didn't respond. In a moment of rare, if ill-advised, bravery, he suddenly flung himself onto the Baron.

Von Kröger squealed with surprise and both men fell into the sawdust.

The audience seemed uncertain. Some people applauded. Others laughed at the odd fight between the clown and the magician.

"You fucking shit!" yelled the Half-Moon Man. "I'll kill you! I'll kill you!"

He was quickly gaining the upper hand. He threw Moshe off, grabbed his sword, and swung it at Moshe, who barely managed to crawl away in time. When the Half-Moon Man began chasing Moshe around the circus ring, Moshe finally managed to regain his footing. Both men were impaired: the Half-Moon Man was drunk, and Moshe was wearing floppy clown shoes. When Moshe passed the trunk, he heard Julia banging on the inside. "What is going on?" she yelled.

The Baron was right behind him. Moshe climbed up a tent pole. The audience was laughing. A man in a clown suit being chased by a man with a sword was inherently funny. Moshe clumsily worked his way up the pole. The Half-Moon Man began hitting the pole with his sword, like a lumberjack. He accidentally severed one of the ropes.

"Crap," he muttered. At that moment, a sizable section of the circus tent slowly sank to the ground. Some of the smarter audience members began to realize that this wasn't part of the show. Several of their ranks were now covered by the canvas tent. Indignant voices rose from underneath and the laughter died out.

Moshe saw that one of the oil lamps illuminating the arena had been knocked over. The burning oil spilled over the sawdust with breathtaking speed. Within seconds, the sawdust caught fire, and the flames began to spread. Thick black smoke rose to the top of the tent. People began screaming. Benches were overturned as the audience members rose to their feet, their voices fraught with primal fear. It sounded like the deafening roar during a soccer match. The flames ate their way up the poles and ropes, and very soon, the canvas above began to burn.

Moshe fell from the pole and landed hard on his back. He rolled over. Flames were all around him, but he was unharmed, at least so far.

He got to his feet and looked around.

"Put it out, you idiot," the Half-Moon Man screamed. He began tearing down the curtains, which he threw over the flames in an attempt to stamp them out with his feet, with limited success. Moshe kicked off his floppy shoes, ran toward the trunk, and tore it open. Julia was cowering inside, covered in sweat, breathing heavily, her eyes bulging with fear.

"We have to go!" Moshe yelled. "Now!"

He pointed upward. She screamed as she saw the fire. The smoke was still rising, filling the tent, and it was getting increasingly difficult to breathe. Moshe's eyes were burning. In a mad panic, masses of people stormed toward the few exits like a blind trampling herd. Moshe could hear children crying, their voices shrill with fear. Women and men were shouting and the animals outside were howling in their cages. Siggy and Löwitsch came running in with buckets of water.

"We have to help," Julia said.

Moshe looked at her aghast. Help? All he wanted was to get out. Instead, he nodded weakly, realizing she was right. Even if he didn't like it. He looked around, but he couldn't see the Half-Moon Man anywhere. He saw the sword cane lying on the ground. He picked it up and dashed toward the canvas wall.

"Come on!" he called out to Julia.

She understood and followed him. They grabbed the sword and plunged it into the cloth. Using their combined strength, they managed to make a rent in the fabric. Some of the nearby audience members saw their chance. Dozens of hands reached for the opening and pulled it wider. More and more people streamed toward the hole in the tent. Some fell down, others simply trampled over them, while and more people managed to file through.

Moshe and Julia were among them.

From outside the tent, Moshe could hear the screams of those who burned.

※

They worked feverishly all through the night, forming a human chain from the well to the tent. Moshe handed down buckets of water and poured them onto the flames, but the fire seemed to only grow bigger. Horst managed to evacuate the animals before the firemen finally arrived. When dawn came, the last of the flames had been extinguished.

But there was not much left of the circus.

The tent had burned down completely, the benches and poles were smoldering, but all of the animals and almost all of the performers had survived. Only Hilde, the alcoholic acrobat, had perished. She probably had been too drunk to flee. Nine audience members had burned to death; their charred remains weren't found until late afternoon. The stiff corpses still had their hands raised, as if to protect themselves. Two children were among the dead.

There was no sign of the Half-Moon Man.

In the early light of morning, Moshe and Julia hastily threw some of their belongings into two suitcases and ran away from it all. The ground was warm. In some places, smoke was still rising. They ran into the woods, clutching each other's hands, never looking back, driven by guilt and shame and the sheer exuberant joy of having survived.

PUNCH AND JUDY

When Max Cohn got home from school, the Great Zabbatini was gone. Instead there was a middle-aged woman sitting at the kitchen table next to his parents. She was black, and her attire was specifically chosen to put her mostly white clientele at ease. She had perfectly coiffed flat-ironed hair, and she wore a beige pantsuit and a pearl necklace. Max, however, was not at ease.

As soon as he entered the room, their conversation ceased and they all looked at him.

"Hi, buddy," Dad said tentatively.

Max froze. He knew something was up. Why was Dad here? Who was that woman? "Hi, Dad," Max said quietly.

"My name is Susan," said the woman. "It's nice to meet you." She extended her hand.

Max didn't move. His fingers clutched the strap of his backpack tightly.

"Susan is here to help you," Mom said.

"All of us want to help you," added Susan.

"Help me how?" Max asked.

Dad cleared his throat and got up. He walked over to Max and went down on his knees. This was one of the things Susan had told him: always speak to kids at their eye level.

"Susan is a psychologist," Dad explained.

Dr. Susan Anderson nodded. She grinned at Max and also crouched down in front of him. Max was suspicious. He knew all about psychologists. They put other people in madhouses, like Myriam Hyung's aunt, who had run out into the street one night, dressed only in her underwear, right in the midst of the passing cars. She wasn't hurt, but it was the beginning of the end for her. A few days later, she was "institutionalized." Max now had the terrifying thought that he might be next. He could see it: strait-jackets, electroshock therapy, disgusting gruel served in wooden bowls. *One Flew Over the Cuckoo's Nest.* The strange woman kept talking to him, but Max was barely registering what she said. He looked at her icily. Then the woman turned to his parents with a demonstrative sigh. She went on to explain the concept of a child's "magical thinking." Every once in a while, she flashed a smile at Max. He knew it was nonsense.

"Imagine you're watching a puppet show. Like Punch and Judy," she said.

Max nodded vaguely.

"There are two boxes," she continued. "Punch comes on-stage."

Max nodded again. He'd heard of Punch and Judy. When he

was very little, his parents had taken him to a marionette theater downtown in a former warehouse underneath the 101 Freeway. Max had found the atmosphere distinctly depressing. He couldn't understand why grown-ups always brought him to such dreary places. Still, the funny marionettes in their colorful costumes had won him over quickly.

"Punch has a marble," Susan said. "He puts it into the first box. Then he leaves the stage. Judy comes on, opens the first box, takes out the marble, puts it in the second box and walks off. Punch comes back onstage."

At this point, Susan put both hands on his shoulders and looked deeply into his eyes. Max was getting a little creeped out.

"All right, Max. In which of the boxes should Punch look for the marble?'"

"In the second one," Max said. "Duh."

That must have been the wrong answer, because Susan took her hands off his shoulders and made a sad face. "A big boy like you should know that Punch would be looking in the first box. Because he didn't see Judy move the marble." Susan cast a condoling look toward his parents. "It's unusual for a boy his age," she said. "Usually, only children on the spectrum choose the second box."

"Spectrum?" Mom asked in dismay.

"Autism," Susan replied. "But don't worry. It's just—"

Mom interrupted her. "Max!" she said sternly. "Pay attention!"

"But Mom," grumbled Max, "the marble's in the second box."

"But Punch doesn't know that!" said Susan with forced cheer.

Her patience seemed strained. Max had assumed that psychologists were a little tougher than that.

"As far as Punch knows," Susan continued, "the marble has to be in the first box."

"But it's not!" Max insisted.

Susan gave a tortured smile. "Of course not. But that's where he should be looking."

"Why?" Max said.

"Because it makes sense!"

"How does that make sense?" Max said. "The marble isn't in there!"

"No, but—"

"Punch is a retard," Max yelled, and then added that he'd never seen a puppet show with such a stupid plot.

His parents looked distraught. This therapy session wasn't turning out quite as expected.

Susan looked at them. "Most children at Max's age understand that people can have false beliefs. They know that the marble is in the second box, but they also know that Punch believes it to be in the first one."

"But it's not!" Max interjected.

Deborah stood up and walked over to her son. "It's just an example, honey. Susan is here to help us cope with what's going on."

"With the marble?" Max asked.

"With the divorce," Mom said.

At that point, Max had had enough. "What's going on," he shrieked and pointed at Dad, "is that you left Mom and me! That's what's going on."

Mom tried to soothe the waves. She forced herself to smile.

"Your dad and I felt it would be good for all of us to get counseling. I know this is tough on you, and we all want to help you."

Susan was writing down notes on a yellow legal pad. Then she got up, which Max took as a bad sign. Suddenly, a thought occurred to him.

"Where is Zabbatini?" he asked.

Deborah and Harry exchanged a furtive glance.

"He's not around right now," Mom said vaguely.

"Why not?" Max was dismayed.

"Mom started a fight with him, and he left," Dad said, a bit sharply.

"Oh, now it's my fault? He tried to fondle me."

"You hit him with the frying pan."

Susan tried to intervene. "Remember what we talked about? Islands of calm. Islands of calm."

At that point, Mom looked at her and called her a name that Max was forbidden to use under penalty of death. Max blushed in shame. Susan blushed, too, but in rage. Dad was grinning. Once more, Max was reminded that for adults, the rules seemed to be different than for normal people.

"Enough!" Susan snapped. Her nostrils appeared to be quivering. "Take a deep breath! Both of you, right now!"

Mom opened her mouth and made a pitiful wheezing sound.

"Now hold your breath and count to ten," Susan said.

Mom nodded grudgingly and held her breath. She turned bright red. Then, after only a second or two, she opened her mouth again and gasped.

"I told you to quit smoking," Dad said spitefully.

Susan nodded in agreement. "Smoking decreases your lung capacity."

"That's none of your business," Mom snapped.

Max stomped his foot, shouting, "I want to know where he went!"

Dad shrugged, and Mom said, "I don't know. He just slammed the door and left. I figured he'd be back soon. I'm sorry, Max."

Susan chimed in, reprimanding Mom. It was unhealthy, she said, to be too indulgent toward her son. Deborah protested. How could she be too indulgent, when Max said she was much too stern. But Susan argued that in difficult times, children needed discipline and a firm hand. That was the only way to learn how to deal with change.

"Why did you let him leave?" Max said, interrupting the conversation. "Where is he?"

"That," Mom said, "is not our problem. He's a freeloader."

"And a fraud," added Dad.

"You're just pissed that he never came to your bar mitzvah," Mom said snidely.

"That's not true," Dad hissed, though he blushed. "I don't care about the stupid bar mitzvah or the stupid magician!"

"You're acting childish," Susan interjected. "Your son needs a father figure. He needs you to be in control," she said to him.

Mom laughed. "Yeah, right," she said.

"Shut up," Dad yelled.

"Childish," Susan said again. "What did I say about acting childish?"

Suddenly, Max turned his eyes toward the picture hanging next to the door. The black silk painting with the clown.

He quickly turned around and ran out of the kitchen. Throwing his backpack on the floor, he opened the front door and ran outside.

"Zabbatini!" he called. "Zabbatini!"

When he looked back over his shoulder, he saw Dad running after him, like a monster in a movie. Monster number two, Mom, was right behind him. Both seemed very, very angry.

"Come back here," Dad yelled.

But Max wouldn't dream of it. His bicycle was lying on the front lawn. He stepped up to it, pulled it upright, and swung himself onto the saddle.

Dad was only six feet behind him: "You stay where you are, young man!" he yelled.

Max leaned into the handlebars and lowered his weight onto the pedals. Within seconds, he had a sizable lead. Neither Mom nor Dad was in particularly good shape, despite all the yoga and extramarital sex. On his BMX bike, Max felt like a fish in water, swift and unbeatable. He bounced down the curb and onto the street.

"Max!" Mom called in despair.

Max had a goal in mind: Hollywood Boulevard, cross street Winona. He pedaled so hard that his heart was beating wildly in his chest. The wind ruffled his hair. Soon, he was out of sight.

When Deborah realized that she wasn't going to catch Max, she stopped, wheezing and out of breath. She ran her hands through her hair. "Not again," she whispered.

Deborah and Harry got into her Jeep Cherokee and drove through the neighborhood. Thousands of thoughts swirled unbidden though her head. Her shop, for example, was taking up so much of her time. Time she should be spending with Max. She couldn't balance it all: running a business, getting divorced, seeing after her son. It was too much. And she was neglecting her spirituality. She kept a statue of Buddha in her Jeep Cherokee that she always asked for help in finding parking spots. Even now she found herself asking for help. She hadn't meditated in, like, forever.

Harry also felt worn out. The office had been hell this morning. Then he'd had to take his mother to a doctor's appointment. She always wanted to go to the doctor's. He'd driven her all the way to Pasadena, where her favorite doctor had his practice, an elderly, talkative Israeli with hair growing out of his ears. On the way there, Harry had been forced to listen to a litany of his shortcomings and failures. No sooner had he dropped his mother off at the doctor's office than he had to drive back for the appointment with the psychiatrist. And now he was sitting in his future ex-wife's car and once again looking for his missing son. Could things get any worse? he wondered.

Suddenly, Deborah's face brightened.

"I think I know where he is," she said.

"Really?" said Harry sarcastically.

"Bongo's Clown Room."

"The strip club?"

Deborah nodded and turned the car around. They headed back toward Sunset Boulevard. Along the way, she told Harry about a breakfast conversation with Zabbatini, before the incident with the frying pan. He had mentioned Bongo's and that he longed to go back there. It was at least a possibility that Max might try to go there.

"We'll find him," Harry said to Deborah, and put his hand on hers.

She pulled back. "Don't touch me," she said.

WORLD-FAMOUS IN BERLIN

After a long and arduous journey, Moshe and Julia arrived in Berlin at the Anhalter Bahnhof station. The train ride had been a completely new experience for Moshe. He had looked out of the window with obvious delight, watching the world go by outside. Both of them were relieved to leave behind Hannover, the Half-Moon Man, and the charred remains of the Zauber-Zirkus. Moshe was thinking of the long nights he had spent in the morgue. Now, he would never have to look at dead children again. He had worked hard for his money, and now, he and Julia were ready to start their new life. As the train slowly rolled into the gigantic city, Moshe pressed his nose against the window like a child. The train came to a jerking halt and smoke from the locomotive obscured his view. The passengers got up and moved their bags and suitcases toward the exits. Moshe held Julia's hand. He felt reborn.

They got off the train and looked around. Making their way through the crowd, they passed a small kiosk and Moshe got a glimpse of the front page of *Der Stürmer*, the propaganda mouthpiece of the Nazi Party.

"Wait!" he said to Julia.

The headline read: "Butcher Caught!" Moshe reached for the newspaper and opened it. On page two was a picture of Inspector Leitner, shaking the hand of the gauleiter of Lower Saxony, the Nazi governor of the region. Both men were posing awkwardly and grinning into the camera. Moshe paid the woman at the kiosk a few coins and took the paper.

"What's this?" said Julia with a trace of impatience in her voice.

"Here," said Moshe, handing her the paper. The article said that the so-called Butcher had turned out to be an inconspicuous scrap dealer named Klaus K. According to *Der Stürmer*, a "suspected Communist and Israelite." Of course! Klaus K. had confessed to the crimes, and would no doubt be executed swiftly.

Moshe folded the newspaper and put it in his coat pocket. Then he reached for Julia's hand.

They took the tram to Danziger Straße, where Julia's friend Dagmar lived. Moshe was astonished at Berlin. He had never seen a city so vast. It was much larger than his native Prague, with swarms of people, carriages, horses, and automobiles. It was like a giant asphalt wasteland. There were electric streetlights, neon signs, and advertising billboards everywhere. The crowds were huge. People were packed onto double-decker buses, going up and down the congested, tree-lined promenades. There was a constant urban symphony of car horns, shouts, and whinnies.

At Danziger Straße, they entered an apartment building and trudged up the stairs. On the fourth floor, Julia rang the doorbell. The door opened and a stout young woman with short, dark, wavy hair stood before them.

"I don't believe it!" she called out.

The girls hugged and giggled joyfully. Dagmar was obviously happy to see Julia, but less so to meet Moshe. She looked him up and down before she deigned to shake his hand.

But she agreed to let Julia and her companion use the attic room above the apartment. She didn't seem all too pleased about it. She was sharing the apartment with her parents, who would not be informed about her visitors. "Only a few days," she said sternly.

Their new home was a tiny, dusty attic chamber with a mattress and a view over the roof across the courtyard. For Moshe, it was paradise. They used the money he'd made in Hannover to buy clothes, pots, and pans, as well as a small gas cooker for making coffee. They kept their milk on the windowsill. It was always cold outside.

Every day, Moshe went to the kiosk at the corner and bought the daily papers. He was riveted by the trial of Klaus K. Justice was swift. After a relatively brief trial, he was convicted and beheaded, and parents all over Lower Saxony could once again sleep peacefully. His skull was donated to the University of Göttingen, where students were allowed to study its cranial structures for indications of degeneracy. For the Nazi Party, the whole affair was a colossal propaganda victory. *Der Stürmer*, the party organ, wrote: "This, ladies and gentlemen, is JUSTICE in our New Germany. Criminals, Communists, and Jews: BEWARE!"

In one of the articles, Moshe was stunned to discover the following quote by Leitner:

"I doubt we would have made such a swift arrest if it hadn't been for the help of a renowned Persian psychic named Zabbatini. The general populace might scoff at such methods, but the authorities felt we should not be above pursuing any and every lead possible. Zabbatini provided us with uncannily accurate information as to the killer's identity. He had repeatedly warned us of his 'dark presence' and that the killer was closer than we thought. In light of the revelation that the murderer had actually worked with our department as an informer, Zabbatini's predictions turned out to be amazingly accurate."

Amazingly accurate indeed, Moshe thought. He was as surprised as the general public.

※

He would one day realize that his days with Julia in Berlin were the happiest of his life. They spent their first few weeks walking through the city, or staying in and making love. Occasionally, they would go down to the local pub for a beer and some food. Their stay in Dagmar's attic room stretched from a few days to three weeks. Dagmar had started to make cutting remarks, and they knew that they had to find their own place. But first, Moshe needed work.

One afternoon, Julia took him to Friedrichstraße, to the Wintergarten Cabaret.

"This is where I first met Rudi," Julia said. After the fire, she had never referred to him by his stage name again and simply called him "Rudi."

The manager of the Wintergarten was a corpulent man named Kowalcyk, who had a small dog that he liked to feed pralines to. When Julia and Moshe entered his narrow office behind the stage, the dog started yapping wildly.

"Stop it, you rascal," Kowalcyk admonished the dog, grinning as he laboriously lifted himself out of his squeaky chair. He hugged Julia a moment too long for Moshe's liking, then held out his hand halfheartedly to Moshe, without looking him in the eyes.

Julia explained to him that the man by her side, Zabbatini, was a great mentalist. And that she was his assistant, and they were looking for work. Kowalcyk wanted to see a few tricks. Moshe was prepared, and managed to win the man over with some card magic and mind reading. As proof of his psychic abilities, he brought the article about the captured killer. Since the Hannover police department had endorsed him, he suddenly had an air of legitimacy.

Zabbatini and his assistant were given a regular slot. When he said farewell, Kowalcyk patted Julia's butt, a bit too far south, and Moshe was forced once more to shake that hand of his.

＊

When the first night of their performance arrived, Moshe was almost sick with stage fright. But he and Julia had worked out what seemed like a solid routine, and thus his difficult apprenticeship and months of performing under humiliating circumstances finally paid off. Moshe had paid close attention and had a much better idea now what the audience would accept and what would be met with boos. Since the incident with the Brownshirts, he had come to realize that all of the magical arts, his favorite was mentalism. Looking back, much of what Kröger had taught him now seemed primitive. Silly card games, childish props. So instead, he and Julia decided to present a mind-reading act. Moshe bought himself a turban and pretended to be a deposed Persian prince.

The show was actually rather simple. Moshe remembered the Half-Moon Man's words, that magicians tend to hide their fears with talk, and he decided to go the opposite route. So he sat onstage in silence, his eyes covered with a blindfold, while Julia gathered personal items from the audience. She hardly said a word, and Moshe always managed to correctly identify each object. The act was a sensation. And so began the rise of the Great Zabbatini. He and Julia were a perfect team, onstage and off. They functioned in perfect harmony, during the day, at night, and throughout each performance.

Almost, at least.

One night before the show began, Julia and Moshe had an argument. Moshe had noticed that the announcer who appeared after them—a frighteningly good-looking man with dark, slicked-back hair—was flirting with Julia. And she had the audacity to smile at him! Moshe confronted her and she accused him of being vain and petty.

"I'm not allowed to smile at people, is that it?"

Yes, that was it, in a nutshell. Moshe didn't like it one bit. Sometimes, when he couldn't fall asleep, he imagined Julia leaving him. That was something he couldn't survive. Moshe wasn't at all sure if she loved him like he loved her. He had quickly learned that there is always one who loves and one who accepts that love. Julia was one of the latter, and it gnawed at him. On top of that, she knew his secret. She alone knew that he was a Jew, and if she ever betrayed him—whether intentionally or not—that would be the end. Not just of his heart, but of his life.

That night, she punished him for his jealousy. She held up a wallet from one of the audience members, a stout man in a tight suit, and deliberately gave Moshe the wrong code word. Moshe stood onstage and confidently declared that it was a handkerchief. The audience grew restless.

"No," said the man. "Not a handkerchief."

First there were just a few giggles; then laughter broke out. Moshe was humiliated.

After the show, in the dressing room, he made bitter accusations toward Julia. She sat across from him at her makeup table, taking a suggestive drag on her cigarette. Her eyes were cold. Then she stubbed out the cigarette and said, "That's what you get."

But they made up that very night. Julia felt a little flattered that Moshe was jealous. And it had been fun to pay him back during the show. But Moshe also profited from the incident, in a roundabout way. He had an idea. He realized that not only he, but every human being, lives for love. We need it, Moshe thought, like the air we breathe. On the drive home, he was pensive. A love spell, he thought. That might be interesting. It would lend a final touch to his act.

Later, in Dagmar's attic room, they made love, as if in a frantic rage, driven by lust and anger and fear. The country was going mad. There was a storm coming.

Afterward, when they were lying sweaty and exhausted in the moonlight, sharing a cigarette, Julia took her "little Jew" into her arms and told him that they would go to Spandau the next day, where she had grown up.

"Why?" he asked.

"You'll see."

Moshe was curious. But then his thoughts drifted off, far away from Julia, just as they had when he was a child. He felt her hand on his chest only from a distance, and when she whispered into his ear that she loved him, he barely heard her.

He was thinking of his love spell.

☀

In Spandau, Julia led Moshe through remote alleys and gray courtyards, to a small printing shop. She knocked on the door.

"I've known him since I was a little girl," she said.

The door opened. A haggard man with a long beard and un-kempt hair stood in front of them. A hand-rolled cigarette was dangling from his lips. He smelled of old sweat. Julia introduced him as "Friedhelm" and Moshe as "a friend."

In a long-winded speech, she explained that her friend needed papers. They both talked around it for a while, but Moshe soon realized what Friedhelm really was: a forger. Julia would later inform Moshe that Friedhelm was a Communist who forged documents for the left-wing underground.

Julia finally got down to business: "My friend needs an Aryan certificate, and a passport."

Friedhelm nodded. He had nervous eyes that were always moving toward the window. His fingers were long and graceful, exactly as Moshe had assumed the hands of a forger should look. They agreed on a price. It was too high, but what can you do?

A few days later, Julia went to get Moshe's new papers. Moshe was impressed and hugged Julia fiercely. Now that he had papers in the name of Zabbatini, he could start looking for an apartment. His previous place of residence was listed as Tehran, which explained why he hadn't been registered with the authorities as of yet. Soon, Julia and Moshe moved out of Dagmar's attic. Dagmar was relieved, not realizing of course that Moshe was Jewish, but nonetheless feeling that there was something odd about him. The mood had become tense in the last few days, and Dagmar was afraid that the neighbors might report her guests to the police. Every time the doorbell rang, she flinched. Moshe, too, breathed a sigh of relief when he and Julia finally moved into their own place on Fasanenstraße, in the west end of the city. It was a small but charming apartment near the fashionable

Kurfürstendamm promenade. When the contract was signed, Moshe took Julia into his arms and danced with her on the empty parquet floor.

Within a few months, the Great Zabbatini was what the locals called "world famous in Berlin." He managed to fill the Wintergarten's auditorium twice daily. Carefully crafting his persona as a Persian prince, he cultivated a foreign-sounding voice and what he assumed was a smoldering glance, which he practiced in front of a mirror. He even learned a few words of Farsi from a dictionary he purchased in a bookstore near Savignyplatz. And he always ended his act with the same flourish of the arm that he had seen his father make in the synagogue, so many years ago. Closing his eyes, he would bow deeply and intone, "*Istgahe Ghatar Kojast!*" It was his favorite phrase in Farsi. He relished the sound if it, and never ever told anyone what it really meant. Not even Julia.

After hundreds of successful performances, Moshe opened a private parlor in Uhlandstraße, just a few blocks away from the new apartment, on the fourth floor of a nineteenth-century office building that was otherwise occupied by respectable law firms. Moshe furnished it with imported Indian furniture and the finest Persian rugs, as well as a singing bowl from distant Tibet, which was in fact a colorfully painted former piss pot. His business hours, posted on a brass sign by the main door, ended prior to his nightly appearances at the Wintergarten.

He didn't have to wait long for his first clients. After about a week, a distraught housewife from Schmöckwitz stood at his door, a nervous, haggard woman in an apron dress. He drew her into his parlor like a fisherman reeling in a catch. The woman kept apologizing needlessly, as if her very existence were an inconvenience to others. Her cat, Adolf, had run away. Zabbatini was surprised when he heard the name; apparently, even pets had to make political statements nowadays. He soon surmised that the woman lived in an attic apartment, which led him to believe that Adolf the Cat was most likely wandering around on the rooftops of Schmöckwitz. Zabbatini closed his eyes and pretended to concentrate. Then, in a quavering voice, he proclaimed that Adolf would soon resume his rightful place once again. He felt quite certain of it, in fact. Zabbatini was hardly an expert on cats, but he knew a thing or two about hunger, realizing it would only be a matter of time until Adolf's stomach would start to growl. A few days later, the lady from Schmöckwitz rang his doorbell again, this time to thank him profusely and give him a handsome tip. Apparently, the furry Führer had been unable to resist the lure of her bowl of fish innards.

In time, more and more people came to him with their problems. Unfaithful wives, bankers with gambling debts, healthy hypochondriacs—they all wanted his advice. Zabbatini was able to play their emotions like a violin. Most of them became regulars. Soon, the first party members started to appear at his doorstep. The National Socialist German Workers' Party attracted the stupid and the gullible like a powerful magnet. So it was hardly surprising that many of its members turned into loyal customers for Zabbatini. After all, the party's leadership dealt heavily in occultism and mysticism, and on the top of the ladder stood a man whose talent for dazzling manipulation surpassed even Zabbatini's.

The Persian fortune-teller's reputation grew. Everyone came to him, even the random skeptic who sought to expose him. But Moshe had an eye for such people and he quickly sent them away, claiming they had a "negative energy." He noticed that over time, the party members who came to him were higher and higher in rank. Occasionally even a sturdy SA-Standartenführer would sit in his parlor, crying bitter tears in his silly brown uniform. It didn't take long before the crème de la crème of Berlin society beat down his door as well, for Moshe had a gift for telling people what they most wanted to hear, and what they were most afraid of.

Berlin was paradise for Zabbatini. After a long and dreary age of reason, the public had begun to turn once again to all things irrational. The city became a mecca of mysticism, a frolicking field for fortune-tellers and faith healers, hypnotists and hysterics alike. Looking back, Moshe was grateful that his father had made him learn the Torah and the Talmud: he used his understanding of Hebrew, numerology, and the Kabala in a completely different way, turning ancient scripture into easily digestible psychological mumbo jumbo with an uplifting message. He looked like a character from *A Thousand and One Nights*. With his ornate turban, flowing robes, and theatrical gestures, he managed to convince the public that he was a true Aryan, a prince of Persia. No one had the slightest inkling that he was, in actuality, a rabbi's son. Protected by his web of lies, he was seemingly unaffected by the hostilities toward the Jews.

Here, in the capital of the Third Reich, Moshe Goldenhirsch finally was able to thrive. Since money seemed not to be an issue for Berlin's upper crust, Moshe's fees became increasingly absurd. He realized that the more he asked for, the more people were willing to pay. Money suddenly came easy. It was lying in the streets. All he and Julia had to do was bend over and pick it up. They dined in the finest restaurants, they went to every lavish party and nightclub. Moshe soon discovered the joys of cocaine, and the illicit thrill of transvestite shows and burlesque dance acts. But despite all his cleverness, he could never fully shake the fear of being exposed. He remained dimly aware that he was far from being the greatest practitioner of the Unseen Art, but it didn't seem to matter. He was in fact a mediocre performer, who knew how to pull off his act well enough, but who never managed to take the last step on his journey—to deepen his art, to develop new ideas, to break new ground. He stuck with what worked. Why not? He had managed to become outrageously famous with just a handful of solid tricks. Why bother to go any further? His customers loved him still. What mattered was not his skills, but rather the audience's hunger for enchantment.

*

Moshe and Julia's apartment on Fasanenstraße was only a short walk away from a synagogue, which, like so many others, was burned down during the so-called Kristallnacht. Moshe would never forget that November night. He and Julia had been on their way back from another performance at the Wintergarten and were sitting in a taxi when they saw the fire. It reminded them of the night the Zauber-Zirkus burned to the ground.

A crowd of people had gathered in front of the temple, apparently having a good time. A lot of Brownshirts, but also entire families, even the elderly. Women were holding their small children up, so they could see better.

"Say good-bye to the Jews," a woman cooed to her daughter, as if she were reciting a children's rhyme. "Say good-bye."

"Good-bye, Jews," the daughter obediently said, laughing, an angelic and innocent sound.

Good-bye, Moshe thought glumly, feeling sick to his stomach. He was thinking about his father and the old synagogue where he had spent so much of his childhood. At least, he thought, Laibl was far away in Prague, safe and sound. Julia put her arm around him. "We still have champagne at home, don't we?" she asked with forced cheerfulness. Moshe nodded. His throat was dry and his face had turned pale. The taxi had difficulties making its way through the crowd. Outside the window, Moshe saw a young Brownshirt officer, whom he recognized as one of his clients.

Moshe smiled vaguely at him and waved. The man approached and knocked on the window. Moshe opened it.

"Didn't see that coming, did you?" the man said, laughing.

Moshe shook his head. "No," he said. "I certainly didn't."

Finally they arrived at home. They went upstairs, opened a bottle of champagne, and made love while Berlin, or parts thereof, was burning. That night, Moshe hardly slept. He tried in vain to ignore the calls and cries coming from the streets, the crashing glass, the scornful shouts. He felt that he belonged out there, down there, with those who suffered. When it was time to change into his costume at the Wintergarten the next day, Moshe was nervous and distracted. Even so, he thought, I am the Great Zabbatini. The show must go on.

No matter what.

THE CLOWN ROOM

The Great Zabbatini was dressed in shorts, his customary Hawaiian shirt, and a trench coat, in case it started to rain. Unlikely in Southern California, but you never know. He had a bruise on his forehead, where Deborah Cohn had hit him with the frying pan. He was sitting at the bar of Bongo's Clown Room, watching a young dark-skinned woman writhing in front of him. Edith Piaf was playing on the jukebox, and the girl seemed bored and distracted. Zabbatini didn't care. He was simply enjoying the sight of a human female. He was nursing a Heineken, mainly because he didn't have enough money for anything else. He had no idea what to do next, no place to go, and nothing to do. He was broke. But at the moment, it didn't bother him. He had a slight buzz, and he felt that he might stand a realistic chance with the girl onstage. A few charming lines, maybe a magic trick or two . . . who knew? He was suffering from the typically male delusion of having a chance. Like most men, he wasn't willing to blow it by opening his mouth. Nothing hurt as much as rejection, except perhaps a frying pan to the head.

The door to the strip club opened and a beam of bright sunlight briefly illuminated the inside of the room. Very unpleasant. The few lonely drunks that populated Bongo's in the afternoon flinched like vampires in a horror film.

Max Cohn entered the strip club.

The woman behind the bar, a large, severely tattooed blond lady who could have been a sailor or a wrestler, put the shot glasses that she had been scrubbing down and yelled at him: "Get out of here, kid. It's twenty-one and over."

Max threw her a pity-inducing look, which he called "the Starving Puppy."

"I'm looking for my grandpa," he said.

Zabbatini slammed down his beer bottle and gasped indignantly for air. He turned around to Max and yelled, "You heard the lady. Get out of here."

"Grandpa!" said Max.

The bartender looked accusingly at the old man.

"He is not my grandson," Zabbatini said. "I know the boy not."

The bartender put her dishrag down and walked over to Max. "Where are your parents?" she asked.

"They're fighting," Max said.

"Over what?"

"Over me. They're getting a divorce and now they hired a doctor to make me feel good about it, and I ran away."

The bar lady was moved by his plight. The dancer finished her set and carefully walked off the stage. She had on large, clunky, high-heeled shoes that made it difficult for her to move about. But the guys who frequented the place liked shoes like that. They liked a great many uncomfortable things.

Zabbatini applauded loudly. "Bravo!" he shouted. "Bravissimo!"

He was the only one.

The jukebox switched to the next song, "Dream Weaver" by Gary Wright. The dancer put on a bathrobe and approached Max.

"Hi, cutie," she said. "What are you doing?"

"He's looking for his grandpa," said the bar lady and pointed at Zabbatini with her thumb. "That old geezer over there."

"I'll get him for you," said the dancer.

Zabbatini saw her approaching and reached for a dollar bill to slip into her thong.

"I stick this in, yes?" he asked hopefully.

"You shut your mouth, old man," the dancer hissed at him. "Your grandson is here."

"He is not my grandson," Zabbatini insisted.

The bar lady glowered at him.

"You!" she hollered. "Take the kid and get out of here. I don't want any trouble."

"I am paying guest," Zabbatini declared, somewhat helplessly.

"Not anymore. Get out."

※

Outside, Zabbatini began griping at Max. "It is your fault they throw me out. It is paradise and they throw me out!" He started to walk away. "Leave me in peace already."

Max stood there for a minute, indecisive. Then he scrambled after the old man. He caught up with him at Sunset Boulevard. "Zabbatini!" he said.

Zabbatini turned around and pushed him. Max stumbled and fell on the pavement. "Hey!" he yelled.

He got up and charged at Zabbatini. Within seconds, the old man and the little boy were fighting. It wasn't a very graceful fight. It was like the final battle of *Godzilla vs. Mothra*. Zabbatini had Max in a feeble grip and started to spank his bottom.

"Bad boy!" he screeched.

"You left me!" Max was yelling. "Everybody leaves me!"

"Good!" Zabbatini hissed. "You *miesnik*!"

"Old fart!"

Max kicked the old man in the shin. Zabbatini moaned and began hopping about on one leg. When the pain subsided, he took a swing at Max with his crippled arm. Max dodged the blow, tipping over a metal trash can. It fell with a clanking sound, scattering papers, empty soda cans, used condoms, and discarded fragments of pizza over the sidewalk. Zabbatini stumbled over the trash can and fell. He attempted to leap to his feet, poised for the next attack, but Max was already coming at him.

Meanwhile, a group of five beefy Armenian men in Adidas tracksuits and gold jewelry, who had been smoking cigarettes outside of Zagir Chicken, rushed to join the fight. They descended on Zabbatini and Max with an agility that belied their substantial bellies. They were the last of a tribe of battle-hardened warriors, a force to be reckoned with, whether by the banks of the Tigris and Euphrates in their ancient kingdom, or today, in "Little Armenia."

"Yo, asshole! Leave boy alone!" one of them shouted.

Another man struggled to subdue the raging eighty-eight-year-old magician. He didn't have to struggle very hard. A third man held Max at bay.

"The fuck are you doing?" he said.

Zabbatini and Max exchanged bitter words. Then, suddenly, the Armenians looked toward the fast food store. The glass doors opened and a short, squat, hairy man with a stubbly beard stepped out. He was wearing stained khakis, an undershirt, and a beret. He lit a cigarette.

"What goes on?" he demanded.

The men began to explain the situation in Armenian. Neither Max nor Zabbatini knew it, but the man was Aram Iskander, son of an Armenian immigrant, owner of Zagir Chicken, and no less than the highest authority of Solomonic justice in East Hollywood. Having listened to the report, Iskander decided that violence in front of the hallowed doors of Zagir Chicken—home of the famous chicken in garlic sauce—was unacceptable. Both Zabbatini and Max seemed to instinctively grasp the power of this man and became very quiet.

Iskander rendered his verdict.

"You," he said to Zabbatini. "No more hitting boys, unless they are assholes."

"But he is—" Zabbatini began.

Iskander raised his hand.

"This boy no asshole. I can see. He is idiot. There is difference."

Zabbatini lowered his head. He had to concede the man's point.

"And you," he said, pointing at Max. "Leave your elders alone. Show respect."

Zabbatini nodded in agreement. Max stared at his feet.

"Now hug!" commanded Iskander.

Zabbatini and Max glared at each other in mild disgust.

"Hug! Or no more chicken. Never again."

Both Zabbatini and Max had been to Zagir Chicken before. It was a Los Angeles institution. And neither of them wanted to live out their remaining days without its renowned grilled chicken dish. So, reluctantly, they hugged.

"Good," said Iskander, and he went back inside to supervise an order of shawarma.

A few minutes later, Zabbatini and Max were sitting next to each other on the bus bench at Sunset and Normandie.

"I'm sorry I called you an old fart," Max said.

"And I'm sorry also," Zabbatini said. "I had an important meeting. Not even my beer they would let me keep."

"Why did you just leave us?" Max asked.

Zabbatini sighed. "Your mother hit me. I love her, you see."

"You love my mom?" Max asked incredulously. He couldn't

understand how anyone could possibly love his mom. Except his dad, of course.

"Ach," Zabbatini said. "What is the love? It is only a crazy."

Max nodded. He was thinking of Myriam Hyung. What Zabbatini said had the ring of truth to it. Zabbatini leaned closer to Max. "Your mother said I am bad influence. I make you unhappy." And then he added, "I don't want to make you unhappy. So I left."

"But you don't," Max said. "You make me happy."

Something vaguely unpleasant happened to Zabbatini at that moment, something that hardly ever happened to him: he was touched. After a life on the stage, he found it hard to believe that there were people who actually meant what they said.

Max reached for Zabbatini's hand. And Zabbatini took it. Neither of them spoke.

※

This is how Max's parents found them, sitting side by side on a bus bench, holding hands. Deborah and Harry saw them and looked at each other.

"You're jealous," Deborah said. "You're jealous of the guy."

"No, I'm not," Harry said. "Why should I be jealous?"

"He's there for your son, which is more than can be said about you."

"That's ridiculous," Harry said, but left it at that.

For months, they had fought and argued so much that all that was left now was a feeling of inner weariness and quiet despair.

During the search for their son, they had rehashed all the reasons for their breakup, which could pretty much be summed up in two words: yoga instructor.

Deborah felt justified in throwing her worthless, no-good husband out after discovering his affair with the yoga instructor.

Harry accused her of sexual and emotional neglect and explained that his affair with the yoga instructor was in fact Deborah's fault for not being nicer to him. "There's a reason I was vulnerable to this," he said.

"Yes," Deborah replied. "Because you're an asshole."

Deborah had met Eleanor fleetingly, because she had posted her business card on the bulletin board of Om Sweet Om, advertising her services. Never in Deborah's life would she have imagined that her own husband would fall under the sway of that slut. She herself had suggested to Harry that he try yoga, for his health! God! For weeks she had been clueless; then one night he'd come home smelling of a sweet, unfamiliar perfume. Unable to withstand her inquisitorial gaze and subsequent interrogation, he had made a full confession. Deborah felt as if she had been hit by a car. A sudden impact, a moment of weightlessness, then the hard landing on the asphalt.

That was months ago. Now Deborah and Harry were just plain tired; they had fought their war, and both had lost. There was nothing left to say.

They pulled up by the bus stop. Zabbatini was sitting there blinking like a lizard in the sun. When he saw Harry, he asked Max, "Who is that schmuck?"

A VISITOR

In January of 1939, Julia and Moshe ordered a new vanishing trunk at Conradi-Horster. Their show at the Wintergarten needed some spice. Moshe's love spell wasn't quite worked out yet, so they decided to include the "Vanishing Princess" instead. It had taken Zabbatini quite some effort to convince Julia to do it, since she was still deeply unsettled by their final experience at the Zauber-Zirkus. But in the end, she relented, if only to keep Moshe happy.

Conradi-Horster was one of Moshe's favorite places, an old, musty store filled with leather-bound books and magic equipment. Afternoon sunlight filtered in lazily through the dirty yellow-tinted shopwindows. Friedrich Wilhelm Conrad Horster, who went by the name Conradi-Horster, was a shining personality in magician circles. Born to a family of Prussian bureaucrats, he had transformed himself into an accomplished magician and inventor of countless illusions and magical apparatuses. His career had begun in the retail business. As a co-owner of the Hamburg department store Borwig and Horster, he had begun including magic items in the store's catalogue in the late nineteenth century, shortly before an outbreak of cholera ravaged Hamburg. To escape from the dreaded illness, Conradi-Horster moved to Berlin, where he opened his own shop in the area of Schöneberg, the first "factory of magical machines on the continent." His beguiling shop was soon considered the "mecca of magic."

The Great Zabbatini was delighted when the owner himself showed him and Julia a marvelous handcrafted trunk. This trunk, Moshe was told, was unique, its design superior, for the illusion was not created by a mirror. Moshe had quickly realized that mirrors had a fatal flaw—they reflected everything, including the audience, if you weren't careful. When Julia stepped into the trunk, she instead vanished beneath a false bottom. The difference between the trunk's outside height and inside volume was carefully masked by the lining, which consisted of design patterns meant to fool the eye. The illusion was perfect. Foolproof. Moshe was satisfied.

"What's happening?" Julia asked from underneath the false bottom. "Can I come out?"

"It works. But only if you hold your tongue. If you talk, the illusion is ruined."

He heard murmurs of protest from inside.

"Also," Moshe said, "you should be able to open the false bottom from the inside. A safety feature. Feel around, you should find a button near the top."

A few seconds later there was a click and the false bottom opened up. Julia crawled out of the suitcase. He took her into his arms.

"I'll take it," he told Conradi-Horster.

The old man simply smiled and nodded, his face revealing no emotion.

❋

A few weeks later, in the middle of the night, there was a knock at Moshe's door. He flinched awake, feeling dazed. The sound continued, a sharp, rhythmic rapping that shattered the silence. Cursing, Moshe crawled out of bed, put on his robe and slippers. Julia murmured in her sleep. Moshe went to the door, looked through the peephole, and called out, "For God's sake, what? Who is it?"

The knocking stopped abruptly, and a muffled voice replied, "Shouldn't you know that?"

"How the hell should I know? What kind of idiot would make such a racket in the middle of the night?"

He opened the door. His face went pale, and he instinctively took a step back. Two tall and rather intimidating-looking SS officers were standing there in the darkness.

One of them politely lifted his cap. "Are you Zabbatini?"

Moshe nodded, frozen with fear.

The second SS man wagged his finger reproachfully and said, "Wouldn't a psychic know who knocks at his door?"

"No." Moshe vigorously shook his head. "It doesn't work like that."

"How does it work?"

Zabbatini had talked to the gentleman of the SS for less than a minute and he was already fed up. Rolling his eyes, he said, "Gentlemen, surely you have not come in the middle of the night to discuss the finer points of mentalism?"

"Not us, no," said the first man. "But there is someone downstairs who wants to talk to you."

Moshe went to his hallway table, removed one of his business cards from a small silver case, and handed it to the men.

"There," he said. "Tell your friend he can visit me anytime during business hours."

The SS men, however, remained there, frozen and silent.

What the hell do they want from me? Moshe thought. They made no attempt to accept his card. An awkward moment passed and Moshe cleared his throat, lowered his hand and, finally, his gaze. It probably isn't wise, he thought, to look men like this in the eye for too long. He was afraid they might be able to see his secret.

"We need you to come with us," said the man closest to him.

"Right now," added the other.

Zabbatini was shivering, and it wasn't just from the cold. "Let me put some clothes on," he whispered hoarsely. He'd heard rumors about people being taken in the middle of the night and shipped off to work camps.

The SS men escorted Moshe down the staircase and then outside. A cold wind was blowing. Outside, a black limousine was waiting. A Mercedes. One of the men opened the rear door and Moshe could feel his heart thumping wildly in his chest. This is it! he thought. They're going to take me away, to some dark cell, and then . . . He shuddered.

"Get in, please," the man said.

Moshe nodded, but didn't move. He felt as if his feet were glued to the ground.

"Nothing is going to happen to you," said the other one.

He gently but firmly pushed Moshe forward. With shaking fingers, Moshe reached for the car door, then reluctantly got in.

The door was then closed and his eyes darted around, but he couldn't make out anything in the darkness.

Suddenly he was aware that someone was sitting across from him. The man bent forward a little and Moshe could see his face illuminated by the streetlight falling into the car.

At first, he couldn't believe it. Then he took a deep breath and put on his best smile. He was a professional, after all. There was no need for fear. He had to rise above that if he was to survive the night.

"Good evening," Moshe said with a smile.

"Good evening," said the other man in a strained voice.

There was an awkward silence.

"I hope you understand that I cannot visit you in your parlor," said Adolf Hitler. "The chancellor and Führer of the German people cannot be seen frequenting such places."

"Why not?" Moshe brazenly began, but then held his tongue.

One careless word could cost him his life. But he'd already asked the question, so there was no backing off now. Forward, then, into the breach. "Even the kings of old Persia sought the wisdom of the seers." That was better. His thoughts were whirling around inside his head. What exactly did the Führer want from a second-rate psychic?

"I cannot allow rumors," Hitler said. He seemed embarrassed by the whole thing.

Moshe decided to press on. "Mein Führer," he said, the words tumbling from his mouth, "it is a sign of greatness when a man opens his heart to the mysteries of the world."

"How right you are!" Hitler said enthusiastically. "But the people wouldn't understand."

Moshe nodded. "How can I be of service?"

"I have a question," Hitler said with slight hesitation.

Moshe had embraced his role completely by now. He was a wise man. A seer. He knew all. He knew the future. He stood above the world. That ridiculous little man across from him was no different than any other fool who came to him. At least he hoped so.

"Yes?" Moshe said.

"Is it true that you can see the future?"

Moshe went out on a limb. "The future," he said, "is in a state of constant change. It's a mistake to speak of only *one* future, fixed in stone. Think of it as the strings of fate, intricate and eternal, stretching through time. But to answer your question, yes, I am— through some mercy of the gods—indeed blessed with the ability to occasionally glance at certain fragments."

"Really?" Hitler said, flabbergasted.

"Yes. We are only allowed brief glimpses at the contours of our world."

"Do you think you might be able to make a prediction for me?"

Moshe pretended to think about it. Then he sharply inhaled and said with a commanding voice, "Ask your question!"

"International Jewry is trying to drive our nation to the brink of war," Hitler said. "Surely you know this."

No, Moshe hadn't known this. There had been rumors of war, yes, but he hadn't paid much attention. He allowed an air of impatience to sneak into his body language.

"A war on two fronts would be difficult," Hitler said.

"The history of our race," Moshe replied, "is the history of gallantry caught between two fronts, two choices."

"I knew it!" Hitler said. "Gallantry! Two fronts!"

"Thus spoke Zabbatini," Moshe added grandiosely.

"Well, what I would like to know . . ." stammered Hitler. "Will the Jews succeed in this?"

Moshe was confused. What the hell was this guy talking about? "In what, exactly?" he carefully asked.

"In driving our nation to war, of course!"

"Right. Of course."

Moshe stared blankly at the Führer. It was never a mistake to allow a few seconds to pass in silence. Then he reached for Hitler's hand. "Allow me," he whispered.

"What are you doing?" Hitler asked indignantly.

"I need to feel you," Moshe explained. "To answer your question, mein Führer."

Hitler seemed appeased, at least for the time being. He smiled slightly.

"Well, why didn't you say so?" He held out both his hands.

They felt cold and limp, and oddly clammy. Moshe closed his eyes. His lips began to tremble. Then he said, "You will bring a great peace into the world. A peace such as the world has never known. Your name will never be forgotten, mein Führer."

Hitler smiled.

THE LAST MAGIC SHOW

Zabbatini moved back into Deborah's house. Peace, or at least some kind of truce, had been achieved. It was decided that he could stay until he had made more permanent arrangements. Deborah and Harry had reconciled themselves to the strange old man's presence, even though they weren't exactly thrilled. Deborah especially continued to cast a critical eye on him, and who could blame her? Harry called Dr. Susan Anderson, the child psychologist, and told her, after some stuttering awkwardness, that her services would no longer be needed, thank you very much.

Dr. Anderson was miffed. "This is not healthy for your child," she said. "He is almost eleven. Most children at that age have abandoned the magical thinking of their early childhood."

But Max wasn't like other children. Max neurotically clung to his beliefs.

"Is it so terrible to believe in magic a little bit longer?" Harry asked.

"Yes and no," Dr. Anderson said. "You don't want your child's emotional life ruled by superstitions. One day, Max will realize that there is no such thing as magic, and that you have lied to him all this time. What happens when he realizes that it's all a trick?" she asked.

Harry hung up the phone and told Deborah, who had been nervously pacing the kitchen, what Dr. Anderson had said. Deborah naturally didn't want to shatter Max's few remaining moments of happiness. Just a few years ago, they had had a similar debate regarding Santa Claus. An enchanted childhood, was that really so bad? Was it a mistake to try and protect Max a little while longer from the inevitable disappointments of adult life? Is it harder to wake up from a long sleep than from a short nap? If Deborah had her way, Max would remain a small child forever. She would never forget what it had been like when he was cradled in her arms right after birth, so small and pink, oddly foreign and yet intimately familiar. She wished she could have preserved that moment, like a photograph, untouched by time. But time always had the last word. At some point, Max Cohn would grow up. He would get his driver's license, he'd drink and go to college and sleep with women, or—God forbid!—with men.

"What happens when he realizes that the love spell doesn't work?" she asked Harry. "He thinks the old man's mumbo jumbo can bring us back together. What do we do when he sees that it won't?"

Harry, who on some level hoped the mumbo jumbo would work, merely shrugged.

They looked at each other, with no idea what to do.

※

Harry Cohn had always been enamored of noise. Even as a child he had felt the need to fill any void with sounds. He was distrustful of silence. As a young man he had dreamed of a career as a rock musician. All that stood between him and fame was a lack of talent and discipline. Deep down, he just wasn't the type of guy to hop around on a stage, sweating and grunting. His mother, Rosl, had pressured him to "do something real." Harry had acquiesced and put his electric guitar away. It had since gathered dust. Every once in a while, after a few glasses of red wine, he took it out and played a few bars. Once upon a time, its sounds meant endless freedom; now they only reminded him all too bitterly of his abandoned dreams. His overbearing mother seemed to have taught him only to be a weakling. Harry had changed careers and gotten into law, telling himself that being a music licensing attorney was a pretty good compromise: after all, he was still surrounded by noise. But it was the noise of others, of more successful people.

His inner child had not been silenced completely. Whenever things in his life were too calm, too steady, there was something in him, some instinct that sought to make noise, to create drama, to disturb the peace. That was probably why he went for the yoga instructor. That, and her nimble stretchiness. He tried to feel ashamed, but when he was honest with himself, he had to admit that making love to her was one of the sweetest times of his otherwise uneventful life. He liked how she surrendered, how she let herself go. So unlike Deborah, who was very controlled, even in bed. He loved the way Eleanor would walk around nude, the way her sweat tasted, the way she kissed him, so hungry, so angry. He missed her. It had been fun having an affair. In her arms he felt like a kid again, stealing cookies from his mother's jar. He loved the secret meetings in her apartment, and he loved taking Eleanor out to dinner, the titillating risk of getting seen by someone he knew.

But, eventually, all things must end.

For Eleanor, Harry had only been a distraction. He had entered her life during a time of great upheaval. Her heart had just been broken. Her fiancé, a muscular, tattooed, aspiring rock musician who worked as a bartender downtown in the Arts District, had broken up with her via text message. Women were always throwing themselves at him, and he had realized that it was a mistake to commit to only one of them. He wanted to enjoy the buffet a while longer.

Eleanor had been hurt and humiliated. And she suddenly had an enormous appetite for men. She needed to prove to herself that she was an attractive and desirable woman. Then came Harry. He, too, had been vulnerable. The years of an uneventful marriage had taken their toll. He was depressed, he felt stuck in his life. One thing led to another.

Soon, however, a lightbulb went off in Eleanor's head. What the hell am I doing here? she thought. Have I gone mad? She couldn't see a future with Harry. Around that time, Harry had become careless. After going home one night, he had neglected to shower before going to bed. And that's how Deborah smelled the perfume on him.

Harry had never really trusted the concept of familial stability. His mother had taught him that the natural state was tension and anxiety. His father had died young, and Harry had been the sole focus of his mother's attentions. The only stable families he knew were on TV. He didn't quite believe that something like that could exist in real life.

And now he missed it all. He missed his family, his home, his wife.

It gradually dawned on him that he loved Deborah. Still. Again.

But it was too late.

Zabbatini, meanwhile, was happier than he had been in years. He grudgingly had to admit that meeting the brat had, in a way, turned his life around. Hardly something you could take for granted at age eighty-eight. He was ready to make a comeback! God, how he had missed the stage, the applause, the adoring crowds. But there was a lot to prepare. Deborah took him on some errands. Among other things, they were going to stop by her store on Glendale Boulevard to pick out a costume for him. His big show was scheduled for tomorrow, at Mickey's Pizza Palace in Burbank. In the car, Zabbatini voiced his concern that a pizza parlor might not be the ideal venue for an artist of his caliber.

"It's Max's favorite fast food place," Deborah said. "He insists."

She explained to him that Mickey's Pizza Palace was a themed chain restaurant, very popular for kids' birthday parties. Mickey's Pizza Palace was specifically designed for exhausted parents and overeager kids. The concept was brilliant. The little ones could eat greasy pizza and romp around an indoor playground. And there was a small stage, where costumed employees—mice, squirrels, and bears—performed silly slapstick shows. For the childless, Mickey's Pizza Palace was hell: The room echoed with the shrill cries of kids, the food was an affront, and the college-age employees in their furry costumes seemed creepy rather than cuddly. For children, however, it was paradise. For parents, too, because after only a few hours, the little ones were exhausted and ready for bed. Plus, you didn't have to clean up. You could just get up and leave the battlefield.

Zabbatini grew increasingly concerned when he heard all this. But Deborah wouldn't take no for an answer. "You're living with us," she clarified. "So you do what I tell you."

Zabbatini was disgruntled. People dressed as squirrels? Really?

Deborah took him to Baller Hardware in Silver Lake.

Zabbatini needed a padlock; then he asked to talk to the owner in private. They vanished into the back of the store. The man was, as Zabbatini realized with a tinge of nostalgia, a trained locksmith.

"What a coincidence," the old magician said. "I knew a locksmith once."

The store owner, a hefty man with a gray moustache and a comb-over, merely nodded vaguely.

"Each lock is a mystery," Zabbatini said.

"I don't have all day," said the man. "What do you need?"

Zabbatini explained it to him and the man listened in astonishment. Then he said it was doable, but that it would take one or two hours.

"The lady pays for all," Zabbatini said with a glance toward Deborah, who stood by the front register. She frowned at him.

Next, Zabbatini dragged her into a Kinko's. He asked to use a computer. He surfed the internet for a while, looking for images of cities. He printed them out and made colorful postcards.

Deborah watched all this, puzzled. She had no idea what any of this had to do with love.

When Zabbatini was done at Kinko's, they went to two or three other stores. Traffic was heavy. Zabbatini was hungry, and the hungrier he got, the grumpier he became. Deborah stopped at a taco truck and bought him a burrito, which he practically inhaled. Then the old man looked at his watch and said it was time to pick up the keys.

All that was left was the costume. As they drove to Glendale Boulevard, headed for Deborah's store, Zabbatini began acting more and more curmudgeonly, complaining that the burrito had been too heavy for his delicate stomach.

As soon as they entered Om Sweet Om, Zabbatini's mood lifted. He was delighted at the place, which was full of Asian-inspired tchotchkes that reminded him of his days as a Persian prince in Berlin. He had always longed to go to Persia, or better yet, India, the land of fakirs and elephants, but he had never had the chance. Now it was too late. At his age, he couldn't afford to get diarrhea. Still, his fascination with all things Asian remained, and though Deborah's shop wasn't India, it was as close as he would ever get. He wandered around her store with a bittersweet feeling of gratitude and regret.

He saw a flowing white robe, much like the one he had once seen Julia wear, floating in the air, back in Prague, when he was a youth and had visited the Zauber-Zirkus for the first time. He let the fabric run through his fingers, and the memories came flooding back. He asked himself, as he often did, what had become of Julia. Was she still alive? Had she survived the war? Did she have children? Grandchildren? Did she sometimes think of him? He felt transported back in time, to the moment when his fingertips had touched the fringes of her white dress. His sudden desire for her was like a physical pain. He had never forgotten that moment. This was why he loved to smell women's clothes, to feel again. He was searching for a scent, *her* scent. He longed to return to a time when he still had illusions. A time when he was still little Moshe Goldenhirsch and not the wreck of a man he now saw whenever he looked in the mirror.

He took a deep breath, stepped back, and asked, "Can I try this on?"

"Uhm," said Deborah, "that's for women."

He looked at her like a beaten dog.

"Fine." She sighed.

When Zabbatini emerged from the changing room, he felt like a shining angel. The costume was perfect. No one would know that it was a ladies' dress. And he would, in his own way, feel close to Julia. *His* Julia. He looked at himself in the mirror. He was pleased. His age, he felt, worked to his advantage for once, bestowing on him a certain gravitas, as befitted a mentalist. As he began to search for a turban, he came to a realization. The time for colorful charades was over. He was too old for silly tricks and games. What he was looking for was a deeper truth, a return to the essential. He decided that his new act would be no act at all. He would not play any tricks. Not as such. He would simply be. He imagined himself in his clean, white robe, standing once more in front of an adoring audience. While this didn't exactly compare to his appearances on *The Tonight Show*, or even to his stint at Disneyland, he felt, at last, that he was close to achieving what he had always longed for: the fundamental purity of his art.

Who knows? he thought. Perhaps I can even make Harry and Deborah fall in love.

TWO POUNDS OF SUGAR

In 1943, the Allies began bombing Berlin. Come November, Moshe and Julia were awakened almost every night by sirens. Together with their neighbors, they had to go downstairs and hide in the cold basement, listening to the distant thunder of falling shells. Old Mrs. Rettenbacher from next door seemed to enjoy these nightly interruptions. The war brought out her maternal side, and she always brought cookies she had made, insisting that everyone eat.

Moshe took his own precautions. The constant bombings, the news from the Eastern Front, the endless suspicion and denunciations, the rumors about deportations. For once, you didn't need to be a psychic to see what the future held in store. He bought a tiny summer house outside of Berlin, in Grunewald, no more than a shack. This was where he and Julia would escape to, just in case. They brought some furniture, blankets, and canned food.

If things got too dangerous in their neighborhood of Charlottenburg, if one of them ran into trouble or didn't return home or if they were separated for some reason—this was where they would meet and hide.

When the hard winter gave way to spring, the bombing took on a new intensity. The Americans dropped their bombs by day, the British by night.

In August, a remarkable incident occurred during one of Moshe's performances at the Wintergarten. He didn't like being interrupted onstage, much less by bombs. In the middle of his mind-reading act, he heard the shrill whistle of a falling shell. He knew from experience that he was safe, for the higher the sound of the falling bomb, the farther away it would hit. The ones you had to worry about where the ones that made a low, droning noise. He reacted to the high-pitched screech by standing up and announcing: "Ladies and gentlemen, I feel a dark thunder approaching." As the audience got restless, he raised his hands, closed his eyes and whispered, "None of us will be harmed."

He was right, of course. The bomb fell far away—they heard the impact. It was as if the air itself was torn apart. The ground shook. The lights went out, and dust engulfed the room. People screamed and the audience threw themselves on the floor. When the lights came back on, everyone was huddled there except Moshe, who stood heroically on the stage, motionless. Slowly, people rose to their feet. Seeing that his prediction had been correct, that no one was hurt, a few people started to applaud. The relief was palpable. Moshe stood silently as the applause rose to a deafening roar.

It was to be his last triumph. The nightly curfews and black-outs made it impossible for him to continue his performances. All public performances were forbidden, except for those by the Berlin Philharmonic. The Wintergarten closed down and the windows were boarded up. The time of magic, it seemed, was over. Moshe and Julia came to pick up his equipment, his costumes, and his vanishing trunk. Sunlight fell through the cracks of the boards on the windows, and Moshe walked through the auditorium, feeling infinitely sad. Julia put her hand on his shoulder. Neither of them spoke.

As they left the Wintergarten, Moshe looked at the ruins of nearby buildings. Berlin was covered with scars. The war had come home. He noticed a young girl, maybe fifteen years old, sitting in the midst of a bombed-out apartment building, surrounded by dust and rubble, on a wooden chair, playing a cello. Her eyes were closed and the wind tousled her red hair. The music was so beautiful that it gave him pause. He reached for Julia's hand, and together, they stood and listened in silence:

> *Though like the wanderer, the sun gone down,*
> *Darkness be over me, my rest a stone;*
> *Yet in my dreams I'd be nearer, my God, to Thee*

※

It happened on a cold, gray morning. "I'm just going for a walk," he said to Julia. "I'll be back in an hour." Julia was still in bed, half-asleep. He kissed her head. For a while now, he had been lying awake and brooding. Perhaps a walk would clear his mind. Moshe heard Julia murmur something; then she turned over in bed and pulled the blanket around herself. He went outside and carefully pulled the door shut.

When he left his apartment on Fasanenstraße, he passed a man in a black overcoat on the sidewalk. Moshe was on his way to the Café Kranzler for a malt coffee, and when he looked over his shoulder, he saw that the man was following him. He quickened his pace and turned at a corner. The man was still behind him. Nervously, Moshe broke into a trot.

In the grotesque and distorted wasteland that was Berlin, the real and the surreal lived side by side. People tried to go about their daily business as best they could. Everyone chose to ignore the obvious: that each night, when the sirens howled, more and more of the city and its people were bleeding and dying. Things that had previously seemed solid—bricks and walls, stone and steel—were now revealed to be feeble, no more solid than the illusions Moshe had been performing for all these years. It was the most awesome and awful magic Moshe had ever witnessed: now you see it, now you don't! Entire buildings disappeared, streets even. Bodies were floating in the canals. And still, the audience acted as though none of it was true. Now, Moshe found himself chased through a nightmarish landscape. Nothing felt real anymore. He was terrified. He ran faster and faster, but the man—like a demon—never let up.

Moshe kept running until he was out of breath. His forehead was covered in sweat. By now, he was tired of running. He was tired of this game, and he decided on a different tactic. He turned around and called out, "Who are you? Show yourself!"

The man stopped and lifted his hat.

Moshe gasped. This isn't possible, he thought.

The man slowly approached, limping slightly, his heels clicking on the broken asphalt, holding his hat in his left hand.

Despite his nervousness, Moshe stood his ground, his feet planted firmly on the pavement. He felt like a gunfighter in an American movie.

"Good morning," said Moshe with a cool smile.

"Good morning," said the Half-Moon Man.

❧

Several minutes later, Moshe Goldenhirsch and Rudi Kröger were sitting in the Café Kranzler on Ku'Damm, drinking malt coffee, like two gentlemen of the world. Pretending the world wasn't ending. The café had escaped the bombings so far. The windows were boarded up—some of them were even still intact.

The Baron was dressed in a ragged, shabby suit. He looked much older, and haggard, and he was no longer wearing his mask. Moshe could see scars peeking out from his shirt collar. He wondered what his body looked like.

"How did you get out?" Moshe asked. "Out of the tent, I mean."

"A burning pole fell on me," Kröger told him. "Smashed my leg. At least I'm unable to serve in combat." He stirred his coffee and looked around. "I wish there was sugar," he suddenly said.

The Half-Moon Man had always had a weakness for sugar.

Moshe shrugged. "Rationing," he replied. "What can you do? I'm sure final victory is just around the corner."

"I was in terrible pain," said the Half-Moon Man. "I've never experienced anything like it. I thought I would die."

"But you didn't."

"I didn't," said the Half-Moon Man. He knocked on the wooden table with his black-gloved hand. "Two men lifted the pole before the flames could devour me. They put their coats on me, choking the fire. Then they carried me outside."

Moshe didn't know what to say. He looked the Baron in the eyes. "The fire was your own fault."

Rudi Kröger smiled humorlessly and sipped his coffee. "I don't think so," he said. He explained to Moshe that he had lived only for one reason: revenge.

Moshe felt a cold chill run down his spine.

The Half-Moon Man continued speaking in the calmest of tones. He had waited for years. He wanted to enjoy his revenge. It had to come at exactly the right moment. "I made it out, and I saw my life's work go up in flames. Thanks to you."

"You tried to kill Julia with your sword," Moshe said with some indignation.

"She was unfaithful," explained the Baron. "She had to be punished."

"I was only trying to protect her."

"As any true knight would." Kröger leaned forward and stirred some milk powder into his coffee. "But even worse, you stole my act."

"Only parts of it," Moshe said weakly.

"Only parts of it," the Half-Moon Man repeated, mocking his voice. Then he said, "For this, I'll destroy you."

"How?" Moshe asked lightly. But the fear was rising within him, strangling his throat.

"Oh, it's quite simple, really," said the Half-Moon Man. "You know the law." He leaned back in his chair. "Anyone who reveals the identity of a Jew in hiding receives an extra ration of two pounds of sugar."

Moshe thought about running away. He could catch a subway nearby. The subways were still running. At least sometimes.

The Half-Moon Man gave a short wave to someone outside the window. Moshe turned to look. Two men entered the café. They politely lifted their hats, smiling at him.

"Heil Hitler!" one of them said.

"Heil Hitler!" echoed the other.

They introduced themselves as Breinholm and Francke of the Gestapo.

"Are you the man they call Zabbatini?" asked Breinholm, a tall, lanky fellow in an ill-fitting suit.

"Yes," Moshe replied.

"You are under arrest."

"For what, if I may ask?"

"Race defilement," said Francke with obvious pleasure. "We'll have to ask you to come with us." He was shorter than Breinholm, well-dressed and athletic-looking. He had red hair.

"What?" Moshe said.

"According to our information, you are having an affair with an Aryan woman."

"So? I am Aryan. I am from Persia. I can show you my race certificate." Moshe started rummaging through his coat pocket, his fingers shaking. He found the piece of paper, unfolded it laboriously, and held it out.

Breinholm and Francke studied it very carefully. Then Francke said, "This is a forgery. We've been informed that you are a Jew named . . ." He took out a notepad and leafed through it. "Moses Israel Goldenhirsch."

"Just Moshe," he said. His throat felt dry. "Everyone calls me Moshe."

"One last question," said the Half-Moon Man.

Moshe looked at him.

"Your silent act at the Wintergarten," he said. "How did you do it?"

Moshe looked at him. He said nothing. He thought of Julia, hoping she would make it to their shack in Grunewald in time.

"Please follow us," said Francke.

Moshe got up.

"Don't worry, old fellow," said the Half-Moon Man. "I'll settle the bill."

※

In the car, Moshe felt it prudent to inform the gentlemen of the Gestapo that he was acquainted with the Führer himself.

"Oh, are you?" asked Francke sarcastically. "The Führer?"

"Yes," Moshe replied.

Breinholm and Francke exchanged amused glances. Of all the brazen Jewish lies they'd ever heard, this was by far the worst.

"Please," Moshe pleaded. He could feel tears coming to his eyes. "Please let me call the Reich Chancellery."

They arrived at the Gestapo-Headquarters at Prinz-Albrecht-Straße. After much begging and pleading, Breinholm and Francke finally agreed to let him use the phone. They thought it might be amusing. His fingers still shaking, Moshe dialed the number of the Reich Chancellery, which was written on a small piece of paper. Moshe was surprised that the call went through. That didn't happen too often anymore, not these days. He asked to speak to the Führer. "Tell him it's the Great Zabbatini." Breinholm and Francke were listening with big grins on their faces. The operator refused to put him through. He begged, he insisted, but she would not be swayed. Then, Francke put his finger on the phone's cradle and took the receiver from him.

"That's enough," he said.

Moshe sank to his knees. Tears were flowing freely down his cheeks. "Oh God," he begged them. "Please, please, please, please . . ."

Breinholm and Francke lifted him up by his arms. Then they took him out of the office. The people in the corridor looked the other way. His fate didn't concern them.

They took him to the basement and tortured him for two days. They wanted to know the identity of his lover, even though Moshe suspected that they already knew. They knew, and still they asked. There was a reason, of course. They wanted him to betray the only person he'd ever truly loved. That, too, was amusing.

Finally, Moshe gave them what they wanted. "Julia," he screamed in pain. "Her name is Julia Klein." He tried to rationalize his betrayal. What difference does it make? he thought. They already know. But they still didn't stop torturing him. Breaking his will was only the beginning. "Where is she?" they yelled at him. "Where?" It didn't take long for him to talk. He couldn't bear pain, any pain, really. He gave them the location of the shack in Grunewald.

When they were finished with him, his left arm was grotesquely distorted. And Moshe was forever broken.

On the way out, Francke asked him for an autograph. He had seen his show at Wintergarten, he explained. "This," he explained cheerfully, "is why we only did it to your left arm."

Moshe took the pen. He didn't speak.

"Please write, 'Zabbatini,'" said Francke. "There is no more Moses Goldenhirsch."

Moshe nodded and signed his name.

Breinholm and Francke brought him to a car. "We'll bring you to your train," said Francke. "But before we do, there is something you have to see."

They drove to Moshe's apartment on Fasanenstraße. "Where is Julia?" he asked when Breinholm opened the apartment door.

"Don't worry," said Francke. "You'll see her soon enough."

He was allowed to pack a few things: his robes, his turban, his deck of cards and magic books. And his vanishing trunk. Moshe felt as if he was wandering through a dream. After two days of torture they brought him home and allowed him to pack? He didn't realize at the time that the man who was expecting him, Siegfried Seidl, had specifically impressed upon the Gestapo that the magician was to arrive with all his equipment.

"Come on, now," said Breinholm.

Moshe took one last look around his apartment, his life, all of which he would now leave behind. He had felt so safe. Untouchable.

"Where is Julia?" he asked again, but received no response.

As they were leaving, the building manager and next-door neighbor, old Mrs. Rettenbacher, opened her door. She had always been kind to him. Whenever she had baked cookies or cake, she and her husband had shared them with him and Julia.

"Are you leaving us?" she asked Moshe.

He merely nodded silently.

"He won't be coming back," said Francke. "He's a Jew."

Mrs. Rettenbacher put her hands over her mouth. "Oh," she said with a sudden note of disgust. "I had no idea! Honestly. I thought he was Persian."

Francke made a generous gesture with his hand. "Don't worry about it. The Jews make fools of us all."

"I'm glad you caught him," she said. "I always knew there was something odd about him. I just thought he was Persian."

"Good-bye," said Moshe.

Mrs. Rettenbacher said nothing. As soon as Moshe and the

two officers had left the building, she and her husband opened the door to his apartment with their master key and began looting it. No point letting all those nice things go to waste. All those suits and linens and whatnot.

☀

They brought Moshe to Ku'Damm. A sizable crowd had gathered. They got out of the car and Moshe was forced to watch as Julia stood naked in the middle of the crowd.

"A German cunt," Francke explained, "once defiled by a Jew, can never be cleansed again, not even with an Aryan broom."

Julia's petite body was covered with welts and purple bruises. She was shivering in the cold, and her face was a mask of horror and humiliation.

There was a throng of people around her, laughing at her and throwing dirt at her. She had a sign around her neck that said:

I AM THE BIGGEST SWINE IN TOWN,

A JEWBOY I CALL MY OWN.

Suddenly, Julia lifted her head and their eyes met. Moshe, who had given up her name just a short while ago, felt a sudden surge of shame.

But Julia steadfastly held his gaze. Her mouth twitched and she raised herself up, defiant and proud. Then she indicated a bow, as if she were still Princess Aryana, standing next to the Great Zabbatini on the stage of the Wintergarten.

They grabbed his shoulders. "Let's go," said Breinholm. "The train is leaving soon."

Moshe was brought to track 17 of the Grunewald train station. When the train arrived, Breinholm and Francke escorted him to his seat. Everything looked normal. As a German Jew, he was allowed to travel with a modicum of comfort. The train was headed toward Terezín.

He never saw Julia Klein again.

MICKEY'S PIZZA PALACE

When Deborah, Max, and Zabbatini arrived at the venue where he was supposed to perform, Zabbatini realized that his doubts had been well-founded. Mickey's Pizza Palace was located in a slightly shabby strip mall on San Fernando Road in Burbank, nestled in between a Kmart and a Korean nail salon.

"Where is the artists' entrance?" he demanded to know.

"We all go in through the front," Deborah said firmly.

Zabbatini frowned. He briefly toyed with the idea of throwing a tantrum, playing the diva for a bit, but then thought better of it. Deborah was a force to be reckoned with. When he had attempted to negotiate an appropriate fee for his appearance, she'd pointed out that, for now, he had a roof over his head, a condition that was likely to change if he didn't shut up. So he shut up.

Deborah marched ahead; Max followed her. Zabbatini straggled after them, carrying a large brown paper bag that contained his props for tonight. Next to the entrance sat a sullen-looking teenage girl wearing a baseball cap and a purple T-shirt with the company logo. She placed a stamp on the back of Max's hand, and his mom's as well. Then she pointed the stamp toward Zabbatini, who flinched away from it, as if it were a cattle prod.

"What is this?" he demanded to know.

The girl rolled her eyes demonstratively. "It's so we know which kid belongs to which family," she crabbily explained.

"Why must we know this?" Zabbatini was highly suspicious of the whole stamping business.

"We check the stamps on the way out so that your child isn't taken by a stranger."

Zabbatini looked at Max, then at the girl. "So? If someone wants to take a child, take the child. There are enough, no?"

Zabbatini couldn't, for the life of him, imagine anyone voluntarily wanting to take a child. What would you do with it? You'd have to feed it and take it to the playground and all sorts of things. But he graciously condescended to have his arm stamped.

"The last time someone put numbers on me," he cheerfully informed the girl, "was at Auschwitz."

The girl gave him a bored smile and simply said, "Wow. That's great." Then, under her breath, she muttered, "*Pendejo.*"

The inside of Mickey's Pizza Palace was loud, garish, and much too brightly lit. It smelled vaguely like old gym socks. The worst thing was the children. They were everywhere, like an alien species poised to take over our planet. They were running, screaming, crying, and squealing. Zabbatini had often felt it to be a curse that he, an entertainer at birthday parties and bar mitzvahs, didn't like children. Many moons ago he had gotten a girl pregnant. It happened in the course of a short and generally pleasant affair with a showgirl he met in Vegas. Zabbatini had just gotten used to the idea of being a father when she suffered a miscarriage. He would never forget the dead look in her eyes when he visited her in the hospital. And so, he resigned himself to being childless for the rest of his life. Maybe it was better that way.

In the middle of the restaurant was a contraption of bright plastic tubes and ladders, for the children to crawl around in, like rats in a maze. There were loud video games and large, fuzzy toy animals that seemed to spring from a psychedelic nightmare. Essentially, Zabbatini realized, this place was just like a fun fair or a circus, only indoors. Wherever he looked, there were blinking lights, screaming brats, or monitors showing music videos with people dancing to rap music, dressed up as oversize rodents. A man in a mouse costume was jiving around a garbage truck, singing loudly.

This is hell, Zabbatini thought. I'm in hell.

Zabbatini was reminded of the only time he had taken LSD, back in 1969. He had just finished an appearance at the CBS studios on Fairfax and Third, and was invited to a party afterward. The party was in a house in the Hollywood Hills, and there were long-haired men and women with impossibly colored shirts, who were passing various drugs around. Zabbatini, being somewhat older than the rest of them, had felt rather misplaced, and when someone offered him a small, white pill, he gladly accepted. Perhaps it would make him feel like he belonged. "Acid," that was what they called it. He was suspicious, but also curious. So he tried it. At first he felt nothing. But after about twenty minutes or so, he came to realize that the green shag carpet they were all sitting on was, in fact, an alien intelligence. The strands of carpet were tentacles. They were trying to reach for him and the other guests. Funny that he hadn't noticed that before. He shared his newfound knowledge with the others. Some started screaming and leapt to their feet. The shag carpet was declared a forbidden zone. From that point on, everyone was careful to avoid it. Zabbatini didn't understand all the commotion. Then he discovered a Jacuzzi in front of the house. He undressed down to his underwear and took a seat in the hot, bubbly water, next to all the handsome naked men with their big-bosomed girlfriends. He was beginning to enjoy his acid trip. The others enjoyed it less. Zabbatini regaled everyone with stories from the Nazi death camp. What a relief, to be able to finally talk about all that pent-up pain. And in such a setting, on acid, in a Jacuzzi full of beautiful women, with a view over the city. He started remembering vivid details that had been dormant for years. He didn't notice that the others were looking increasingly distraught. When he started describing the smell from the mass graves, a penetrating and sickly sweet scent, a young woman climbed out of the water and started crying. "The bugs!" she shouted, rubbing her arms vigorously. "The bugs! Get them off me!"

"What is the matter, dear?" Zabbatini innocently asked. One young man, a pale-skinned redhead with a fake Afro, threw up into the hot tub. The chunky vomit was sucked into the side nozzles of the Jacuzzi, where it was turned into a fine mist and sprayed back into the water. Panic erupted. It was like the sinking of the *Titanic*. Everyone fought to get out of the hot tub. When Zabbatini had made it out, he said to the red-haired fellow that he wouldn't have survived a single day in the camps.

"Fuck you!" a total stranger said to him.

Zabbatini felt as if someone had slapped him. The beautiful people all stared at him with disgust and contempt. He suddenly felt ashamed. He wasn't like other people. His experiences, in the war and the preceding years, made him an outcast. He had no place among mankind.

Zabbatini slipped into a bathrobe he found lying by the Jacuzzi and staggered off. He fought his way through the bushes by the side of the house and went to pee. Below him, he could see the skyline of Los Angeles, shimmering in the night, like strings of pearls stretched out on black satin. He felt better already. He swore to himself not to do any more LSD, not ever. All kinds of things could happen.

Engulfed now by the blinking lights and shrill music of Mickey's Pizza Palace, Zabbatini felt reminded of that night, of the view over the lights of the city, his feeling of euphoria. He didn't realize that the Cohns had gone ahead and left him behind. Deborah came stomping back and guided him gently but firmly to the tables that had been reserved for Max's birthday party. It was a row of long plastic tables, covered with a colorful paper tablecloth. Cardboard plates in the shape of cartoon characters were everywhere. A large, rectangular brown birthday cake—it looked like a giant brick—stood at one end of the tables. On it were the words HAPPY BIRTHDAY, the only indication of its actual nature.

Max's many relatives were already there, Uncle Bernie and Heidi the shiksa, accompanied by Max's cousins Esther, Mike, and Lucas. Some of his classmates were also present, including Joey Shapiro and Myriam Hyung.

"Is this him?" Joey asked.

Max nodded proudly.

The old man gave a slight bow. "It is I, the Great Zabbatini," he said. He smiled and reached out to touch Myriam Hyung's ear with his left hand. "You must wash your ears, little girl," he said and pretended to pull a coin from her ear.

Myriam giggled enthusiastically.

Zabbatini felt young again. He was performing. And he could tell that this was an easy audience.

"Where is Dad?" Max asked his mom.

"I don't know," she said. "He went to pick up Grandma."

"When shall I begin the magic?" Zabbatini asked.

"Wait until Dad gets here," Max said.

Zabbatini nodded. Time to prepare. He walked through the room toward the stage, hoping to inspect it. It was fairly small. To the right and the left, animatronic mice were waving mechanically in rhythm to the awful music. This, Zabbatini thought, is the first time I'm upstaged by rodents. He was pleased to see, however, that a small side table had already been arranged. Good. He was going to need it. He pulled it toward the middle. Then he unpacked his paper bag, carefully arranging his various props and tools. A candle, a pad of paper, a deck of cards, several small wooden boxes, and many other things.

When everything was arranged to his satisfaction, he climbed down from the stage and sat down at one of the plastic tables. "I will now eat the pizza," he announced. No one seemed interested. He helped himself to several slices of pizza, piling them onto a mouse-shaped paper plate. Joey Shapiro was watching him with a melancholic look in his eyes. Then he took a plate of pasta for himself.

Myriam Hyung noticed Zabbatini's withered arm and asked: "What happened to your arm?"

"I was tortured by the Gestapo," Zabbatini said, chewing. "Hand me the Parmesan."

"Why?" Myriam asked.

"Because," Zabbatini said, "the pizza is better with the cheese."

"No, why were you tortured?"

Zabbatini looked at her and shrugged. "The Nazis wanted to."

Myriam handed him the glass shaker with the Parmesan. "For no reason?" she asked incredulously. "They just tortured you?"

"Yes," Zabbatini said. "Just like so. Do you want to see it?"

Myriam nodded. Zabbatini glanced around furtively to make sure no one else was looking. Then he pulled up the white sleeve of his robe.

Myriam gasped with disgust and fascination. The Gestapo had broken his arm in several places, at the forearm and the elbow. It had healed over time, but since his arm had never been properly splinted, it now looked like a gnarled and twisted tree branch. Myriam stared at it. Then she pointed at a white, scarred spot on the forearm and said, "What is that?"

"There they poured on me some gasoline and held to it a lighter," Zabbatini said in between bites of his pizza.

"Like when you're grilling!" Myriam said, happy to contribute to the conversation.

"Yes, like when you're grilling," Zabbatini said.

"Gross," Myriam said.

Zabbatini nodded proudly. Then his arm suddenly lurched forward, as if trying to grab her. Myriam emitted a shrill scream and flinched back.

Zabbatini laughed. "Worry not," he said. "I will not hurt you."

Myriam looked at his arm with growing curiosity.

"Can I touch it?"

"If you want," Zabbatini said.

Carefully, Myriam ran her fingers over the scarred flesh, the knobs and gristles, as if she was trying to read a map.

"Did it hurt?" she asked.

"Of course it hurt," Zabbatini said with a sigh. He was getting tired of this discussion. He just wanted to eat his pizza in peace. "That is why they call it torture."

Myriam, however, was still fascinated. "But, really, why did they do it?" she asked. "Be honest!"

"They wanted from me that I betray someone who I loved very much."

Myriam looked very indignant when she heard this. She looked at him with big eyes. "And? Did you?"

Zabbatini became very still. He was holding the Parmesan shaker. For a moment, he seemed frozen in time. Then he set the shaker down. He stared at the table.

Then, very slowly, he lifted his gaze toward Myriam and looked at her with infinite sadness. "I did," he said, and there was something in his voice, a hollowness that scared Myriam more than his twisted flesh.

✳︎

Meanwhile, Max's mom was trying to reach Harry. There was no reception inside the restaurant, so she went outside into the parking lot and tried again. It was cold, and she pulled her coat tighter. She lit a Marlboro Light, and finally, Harry answered.

"Hello?" he said. His voice was hurried.

"Your son," Deborah said icily, "is waiting for you. Everyone is waiting for you."

"I know, I know," said Harry, exasperated. "I'll be there shortly. Traffic on the freeway."

"Just get here," Deborah hissed. With that, she hung up. She paced back and forth for a few minutes, taking angry drags of her cigarette; then she threw it to the ground, stepped on it, and went inside.

The audience was clamoring to see the Great Zabbatini. Several of the kids were clapping and shouting rhythmically: "Magic, magic, magic."

Max looked at Deborah with a hint of sadness. "Where is Dad?" he asked in a small voice.

She gave him a hug. "He'll be here shortly," she said. "He's stuck in traffic." She attempted a smile and said, "Maybe we should get started."

"But I want Dad to be here," he said with a trace of panic in his voice.

"I know," Deborah said. "He's on his way."

Max sighed and walked up to Zabbatini. "Will the love spell work without Dad being here?" he whispered.

Zabbatini was slurping on the straw of his soda. "This," he said indignantly, "is Seven-Up. I wanted cola. Why is nothing in life ever as it should be?" Then he turned to Max and said, "The love spell will work only when both are there."

"But he's not here!" Max said, sounding shrill.

"Worry not," Zabbatini declared. "I do my show, I play for time, and then, when your dad comes, I do the love spell then."

That seemed like a good plan. "Okay," Max said.

Zabbatini took one last slurp of his soda, adjusted his turban, and stood up. Raising his hands, he looked around imperiously.

"Dear children," he said. Something happened when he spoke: a change came over him. He was no longer a frail old man—he became the Great Zabbatini, seasoned performer. The noise slowly stopped and all eyes turned to him.

He stood between the tables and chairs, in his flowing white robe. Under any other circumstances he might have been taken for a madman. But right here, right now, he seemed like an Old Testament prophet.

Zabbatini walked with heavy steps through the room toward the small stage, which was now illuminated by colorful spotlights. His arms and palms were raised upward as he parted the sea of children before him. Everyone reverently moved aside to let him through.

With a groan, he lifted himself onto the stage and turned toward the audience. "What you are about to see," he said, "is not magic."

The kids looked surprised at this announcement. They looked at each other. What? No magic?

Zabbatini gave them a reassuring smile. "There is no magic," he went on, "except the magic that is in your hearts. What I am about to show you is the art of mentalism. It is the power of thinking."

The children were listening attentively. So far, his speech was going over well.

"The powers of your mind," Zabbatini went on, "are not some hocus-pocus. They are for you to use. And you should do this! You should always think!"

The kids applauded. The overachievers in Max's class clapped especially hard. Zabbatini remembered how he had felt, as a child, at the circus in Prague. As he stood here, looking at the expectant faces of his young audience, he remembered why he was here in the first place: to see on their faces the wonder he had felt so many years ago.

He waved his arms about in what he knew was an appropriately mysterious manner. He had learned early on in his career that a substantial part of a magic show consisted of waving one's arms around convincingly.

Then he started. At first, he was a little rusty, but he slowly warmed up. He asked a little girl to think of a vegetable, "any vegetable"; he did various card tricks and interspersed his performance with philosophical ramblings. It was, so far, a mediocre performance, but the audience seemed quite forgiving. Twenty minutes passed.

Then the front door opened and more guests filed into

Mickey's Pizza Palace. Max turned around anxiously. It was Dad and Grandma. He was immensely relieved. Max turned to Zabbatini and wondered how he was going to signal him that the second victim had arrived.

"He's here!" Max mouthed with great exaggeration, and pointed toward his dad.

Zabbatini nodded and winked at him, ever so slightly.

Dad and Grandma hurried toward Max and hugged him.

"*Bubala,*" Grandma said, much too loudly. "Happy birthday."

"Not so loud!" Max shushed her.

They took their seats, making even more noise. Zabbatini glared impatiently at the latecomers. When they were finally settled, he continued. Grandma glanced at his arm. Something about it struck her as odd.

"For the following trick," Zabbatini said, "I will need two volunteers from the audience. You!" He pointed at Harry.

Harry groaned, but Max looked at him imploringly, so he got up and went onstage. He stood to the left of the giant animatronic mouse.

"What is your name, young man?" Zabbatini asked.

"Harry Cohn," said Harry Cohn.

Zabbatini asked him for a personal item.

"I'm sorry?" said Harry.

"Any item you might have on you, please," said Zabbatini and extended his hand. "No matter what. But it has to come from the heart."

Harry patted his pockets. "Is my cell phone okay?"

Zabbatini nodded patronizingly, even though he would have

preferred something more romantic. When he had first premiered the trick in Berlin, the personal items people had given him had been much more, well, special. In those days, people had pocket watches with engraved declarations of love that he would later read out loud. The gentlemen had cuff links and tie clips with their initials; the ladies often carried intricately embroidered handkerchiefs. The world was much more personal. But today? Today, everyone had the same phone with the same corporate logo, and yet everyone thought themself an individualist.

Harry reluctantly handed over his phone.

Zabbatini held it up for all to see. "Look carefully at this thing," he said to the audience. "We will see it again soon." Then he put the phone into a small wooden box.

Zabbatini began looking around for another volunteer. Most of Max's friends had their hands up in the air. Myriam Hyung even bopped up and down on her chair, biting her lip, like she did in class when she knew the right answer, which happened way too often, in Max's opinion.

Zabbatini took his time, steadfastly ignoring the imploring looks of the eager children. Then he pointed at Deborah, who was standing in the back of the audience, typing a text message.

"You!" Zabbatini said sharply.

Deborah flinched. Oh no! she thought. The damn love spell! It's all over now! She was terrified of disappointing Max again. But she had no choice but to play along.

"Yes, you!" Zabbatini repeated. "Come here! The fate has chosen you."

Mom sighed heavily, put her phone in her purse, put it down

onto a chair, and clumped onto the stage. She stood as far away from her soon-to-be ex-husband as possible.

"And what is your name, young lady?" intoned Zabbatini.

"You know my name," she replied curtly.

"Yes," Zabbatini replied. "But can you tell the audience?"

"Everyone here knows me," she said. "I'm Max's Mom. Deborah Cohn. Is this really necessary?"

"Oh yes," Zabbatini said gravely. "It is important that a thing is named like the thing it is."

"I'm not a thing," Deborah snapped.

"No," Zabbatini cooed. "You are the divine Deborah."

"How long is this going to take?" Grandma interrupted loudly and impatiently.

"It will take how long it takes," Zabbatini said. He was beginning to sound somewhat agitated. He had never appreciated interference from the audience.

"Hurry up," Grandma insisted. "I don't have all day."

"Worry not, dear lady," Zabbatini murmured grudgingly.

"What's your name?" Grandma asked.

"This is not important," Zabbatini said with a dismissive gesture.

"Oh? It was pretty important when you asked me," Deborah replied, her voice dripping with sarcasm.

"Yes," Zabbatini said, as if explaining the facts of life to an idiot child. "*Your* name is important, since *you* are about to be the magic."

He waved his hand once more and suddenly held a lit match. The audience whispered excitedly. There was applause. Zabbatini held the match up to a large candle, which he had gotten at the 99-cent store on Sunset and Lucile.

"Dear children, in all our lives, there are moments that we never forget. Moments that change us, that are burned into our memory. This, boy and girls, is such a moment."

Breathless anticipation spread amongst the audience.

"Now comes the spell of eternal love." He held his arms up high. "Eternaaal loooove!"

Max sat up straight in his chair. He had gotten no farther on the record. Oh boy, he thought. This is it!

"What is this . . . the love?" Zabbatini asked and stared at his audience. No one said anything. No one moved. Idiots, Zabbatini thought. This was the problem with magic. It made you lose all respect for people. They were so easy to manipulate. No one had a more acute sense of disillusionment than an illusionist. Zabbatini waited another moment; then he said, "We all know the answer. Love—that is when you can feel the thoughts of the man you love, or the woman you desire. When you know the secrets of their heart." Zabbatini waved. "Love is when you know their soul better than your own. But the love is no illusion. It is the most true thing in the world. It is the reason to live." He spread his hands. "We cannot make it so, the love. It is or it is not. We can only show it. If," he said, gesturing first at Deborah and then at Harry, "if there is still a little bit of love with you, then we are about to know it."

He walked toward Deborah. "Allow me," he said and pulled a silver necklace from his sleeve. With a sweeping gesture, he put it on Deborah. A small padlock was attached to the chain. Deborah looked at it, confused.

Max was chewing his fingernails. The suspense was unbearable.

Zabbatini picked up a wooden box from his table at the back of the stage and opened it in front of the audience. In it were dozens of identical-looking keys. They sparkled in the spotlights.

"Will the man find the key to the heart of the woman?" Zabbatini asked. "It must be the right one!"

He randomly reached into the box, took out three keys, and tried them on the padlock, one after the other. None of them fit.

"I fear I have it not, the key to your lovely heart," Zabbatini said with a wink at Deborah.

"No," she said dryly. "You don't."

Then he approached Harry and held the box in front of him. "Pick one! The right one!" he suddenly shouted.

Harry seemed embarrassed and looked at the floor. Then he reached into the box. He rummaged around for what seemed like an eternity. At last, he pulled out a key.

"Good!" Zabbatini said. He was annoyed that Harry had taken so long to decide. Perhaps he was trying to upstage him? That sometimes happened when you allowed civilians on the stage. The moment they looked into the spotlights, they felt the call of stardom. And then they thought they could outfox him. Him! The Great Zabbatini! As if it made the slightest difference which key they chose or which card they pulled from the deck. Zabbatini's act had been prepared down to the last detail. There was no room for error. Nor for obnoxious know-it-alls who thought they could humiliate him in front of his audience. "Please give me the key, so that I can show the children."

Harry handed Zabbatini the key. The magician held it up, marching up and down the stage with the key held high and a grim look on his face. Then he turned to Harry and handed it back.

"Do not lose it," Zabbatini said. "You have already lost so much."

"Oh, really?" Harry snapped back, putting the key in his jacket pocket. "Says an old geezer who's sleeping on my sofa!"

"Wait," Deborah interjected. "It's still *my* sofa. *I* paid for it when we went to IKEA—"

Zabbatini clapped his hands loudly. "Silence!" he shouted. "The love works better if you do not fight!"

Harry rolled his eyes.

Zabbatini turned toward Deborah. "I want you to think of a city," he said. "A city that has meaning to you. A city of big meaning, big feeling."

"Sure," Deborah said lightly. "It's P—"

"Silence!" Zabbatini shouted and took a step back from her. "No more word! Say nothing!"

Deborah seemed embarrassed. Her mouth closed.

"That's a pretty neat trick," Harry said appreciatively. "I could never get her to do that."

"Be silent!" Zabbatini shouted again. He was sick of it. He had appeared at hundreds of children's birthday parties, but no one had ever acted as childish as those two adults. "Are you ready?" he asked Deborah.

"Oh, so now I'm allowed to talk again?" she said.

"If you must." Zabbatini said. "But do not tell me the name of the city." He handed her a notepad and pen. "Write it down. Big letters, so that everyone in the audience can see."

Deborah took the pen and wrote something. Just as Zabbatini had anticipated, she pressed down quite hard. That always happened when he said "big letters." When she was finished, she looked up at Zabbatini.

He put his hand on his forehead and looked up. His face was strained. He rolled his eyes. His voice became unsteady. "Tear off the paper and show it to the audience. But do not show it to me! And not him either, the schmuck."

"I'm sorry?" said Harry indignantly.

"Nothing," Zabbatini murmured. "I said nothing."

Deborah tore off the page and held it up for the kids to see. Max could make out the word very well: PARIS.

Max knew that his parents had spent their honeymoon in Paris. In the middle of a sweltering summer, in a "romantic" hotel without air-conditioning. They had schlepped back and forth through the vast city, covered in sweat, from one museum to the next, stopping only to eat overpriced food in lousy bistros. This was where they'd had their first fight as a married couple. Ah, Paris!

"Did you all see it?" Zabbatini asked the audience.

"Yes!" the children shouted. They murmured excitedly. Max could feel his heart beating in his chest. He couldn't tear his gaze from the old magician. Zabbatini no longer seemed like an old, frail man. He was a magus, a high priest, a descendant of the princes of Persia.

"Can I have the pad?" he asked Deborah. "Keep the sheet." Zabbatini took the pad away from her and cast an inconspicuous glance at it. Then he put it away. He went to a small filing box for index cards and opened it. Inside were postcards. With a well-rehearsed gesture, Zabbatini took out three postcards and showed them to the audience. Not the fronts, only the backs. Large numbers were written on the back, from one to three.

Then he put the cards facedown on the table.

He glared at Harry. A few seconds passed. Zabbatini knew well how dramatically effective silence could be.

Then he said, "Pick one!"

Harry nodded. He pointed at card number two.

Aha, Zabbatini thought. Why am I not surprised? Normally, people chose number one. A number one is more magical than a number two. But no, not Harry, the nonconformist. No wonder she left him. But the expression on Zabbatini's face didn't change. He was a seasoned pro.

"Number two!" he proclaimed. "Very well! Take the card, look at it, and show it to the audience."

Harry did. He gasped when he saw the picture. Deborah looked at him, concerned. His hand trembled a bit as he held the card up for all to see.

The audience saw a picture of the Eiffel Tower, and the word PARIS.

The children inhaled sharply, then burst into applause. Max

was louder than the rest. The adults, too, were surprised, especially Deborah. She seemed shocked.

"I want to know the guy's name!" Grandma said.

Zabbatini ignored her and bowed slightly. Then he pretended to have an idea. "The love goes both directions, no?" he said. He nodded and turned to Harry. "If the divine Deborah loves you truly, she can also read your thoughts. She can feel your very substance. Your *galemi*."

"His what?" Deborah asked with a trace of suspicion in her voice. She wasn't sure that *galemi* wasn't a dirty word.

"Your eyes beheld my unformed substance," Zabbatini said. "All the days ordained for me were written in your book before they came to be."

That went over pretty good. The kids clapped. Deborah still looked at Harry, frowning. Max, however, was beaming.

Zabbatini led Deborah to the small table at the back of the stage. She now stood directly across from Harry. Only two feet or so separated them. The tension between them was palpable. Zabbatini put the postcards away and laid three identical-looking wooden boxes on the table.

"In one of the boxes is the item that belongs to the man." Zabbatini indicated Harry. "Pick the right one!"

Deborah pointed at box number one.

"Very well!" Zabbatini said loudly and clapped his hands. "You're excluding this one, are you not? This is not it, no?" He pushed the box aside, unopened. "Only two are left."

Deborah nodded uncertainly. Fifty-fifty.

Deborah pointed at box number two.

Zabbatini pushed that box aside as well. He didn't have to say anything. The audience understood. Only box number three was left.

Both Deborah and Zabbatini stared at it.

In a deep voice, the magician said, "So this is it. The box you chose."

Deborah didn't move. She was tense.

"Open the box!" Zabbatini yelled.

Deborah flinched and clumsily opened it. With shaking hands, she took out Harry's cell phone and showed it to the kids.

Applause. Max's hands hurt from all the clapping. He was completely enchanted by what he saw.

But it wasn't over yet. Zabbatini pulled a deck of tarot cards from his sleeve, making it appear out of thin air. The children whispered loudly. He had bought this deck years ago in Brooklyn. The drawings were in the art-nouveau style. He showed some of the cards to the audience: the devil, the sun, the fool, the wheel of fortune, and so on. Then he put the deck facedown on the table.

He launched into a monologue about the magical power of tarot cards. Ancient wisdom, knowledge of the future, glimpses into the hearts of men, blah blah blah. As he spoke, he walked around the table a few times, putting his hand on the cards here and there. His speech was a bit long-winded, but effective nonetheless.

"I want you to both pull a card together at the same time," he said to Deborah and Harry. "The card will tell us if there is still the love." Then, menacingly, he added, "Or not."

Deborah and Harry exchanged a nervous glance.

"Together, please," Zabbatini said. "At the same time. Both of you."

Deborah reached for one of the cards. Harry followed her gesture and touched the other corner.

"Turn over the card!" Zabbatini demanded. "And hold it high."

Together, they held up the card, revealing the image of two lovers in an intimate embrace.

The figures on the card were both naked, but their genitals were discreetly obscured by the woman's flowing hair. The show was supposed to be PG, after all. Despite that, the woman on the card had abnormally large breasts. It was the reason Zabbatini had bought the deck.

"The lovers," Zabbatini said.

The audience erupted. Max fought against tears of joy.

Zabbatini raised his hands to calm the waves. "One thing still," he said. "The key!" With measured steps he walked toward Harry. "Do you have it?"

Harry nodded. Zabbatini glowered at him. Clumsily, Harry began digging around in his pocket. He pulled out the key, and it dropped to the floor.

Max yelped and leapt to his feet.

"It's all right!" Harry said, trying to placate his son. Max stood there, breathing heavily, looking accusingly at his father. Harry went down on his knees and felt around the stage until he finally found the key. He held it up triumphantly. Then he walked toward Deborah with it. She stood there, frozen like a statue.

His hand approached the chain around her neck.

"Well? Does it fit?" Zabbatini asked.

"Hang on . . ." Harry mumbled. He gently reached for the lock. He put the key in and turned it. It made a slight clicking noise.

The lock opened.

"Eternaaal loooove!" Zabbatini yelled and waved his arms around.

Max stood there cheering loudly. Most of the kids leapt off their chairs and applauded.

"Those two people," Zabbatini said, "are destined for each other. Their souls are forever intertwined. Even if in life they should become apart, they will still be always one. Their love is eternal. It is predestined in the book of days. They belong to each other, since the dawn of time."

As a final flourish, he pulled a rose from his sleeve and handed it to Harry. Harry gave it to Deborah, who was fighting against tears.

Max couldn't believe it! It worked! It really worked! He hopped up and down, applauding all the time.

Then he heard someone clearing her throat impatiently.

"What's your name?" Grandma asked sternly. "I want to know!" She was not used to being ignored.

Zabbatini sighed and bowed. "I am the Great Zabbatini."

"Nonsense!" Grandma said. "I meant your real name."

Zabbatini smiled vaguely. He had no intention of telling her. Onstage, he was the Great Zabbatini, and no one else. He bowed and spread his arms. Then he loudly proclaimed, *"Istgahe Ghatar Kojast!"*

Suddenly, there was a noise from the audience. A loud yelp

and a clattering. All eyes turned toward Grandma. She had risen from her chair and knocked it over.

Rosl Cohn stood there pale as a sheet. She was gasping, her mouth opening and closing. She held out her hand and pointed at the old magician. "Where is the train station?" she said.

Zabbatini suddenly froze and stared at her with astonishment. *"Du bist es!"* she went on. "It's you!"

He blinked at her a few times, utterly puzzled. He didn't move.

"Goldenhirsch," Grandma said. "You're Moshe Goldenhirsch!"

Grandma slowly approached to get a better look at him. Max looked back and forth between Zabbatini and his grandmother, wondering what was going on.

"Du bist es!" Grandma said again. *"Ist das zu fassen?"* She was almost at the stage now, looking entirely amazed. *"Ich bin's! Das Mädchen aus dem Zug!* The girl from the train!"

All color drained from Zabbatini's face. He placed both his hands over his heart and emitted a pained gargling sound. Then he sank to the floor.

Max stared at him, alarmed. Mom and Dad simply stood on-stage, looking dumbfounded.

"Helft mir!" Zabbatini gasped. His eyes were bulging and his hands were clasping his chest, digging into the cloth of his white robe, like the gnarly feet of a bird clutching a tree branch.

"Ich sterb!" he said. *"Mir tut's so vay!* I'm dying!"

Grandma reached him and knelt down next to him. Max's parents suddenly came alive, as if a spell had been broken. Deborah pointed at her purse on the chair in the back of the room. "My phone! Call 911!"

Harry took out his cell phone and started dialing.

Max stumbled onto the stage. He reached Zabbatini, whose face had turned into a white mask of pain. His eyes were bloodshot. He grabbed Max's hand.

"Hold my hand," he whispered. "I'm scared."

He knew that this was it. The final curtain.

"The ambulance is on its way," Dad said.

Grandma was holding Zabbatini's head in her lap. He turned to look at her, ever so slightly.

"Rosl. *Du bist es*," he said.

Grandma was suddenly struggling against tears. She stared at the old man and nodded.

"A miracle . . ." Zabbatini said in a whisper.

Then he flinched and emitted a sharp cry of pain, and his body went limp. His fingers stopped grasping Max's hand and sank to the carpeted floor. Max felt a surge of panic. Next to him, the giant animatronic mouse was still waving.

SCHEHERAZADE'S
LAST TALE

Terezín, also called Theresienstadt, was known as the "city of the Jews." It was the most beautiful concentration camp the Nazis had to offer, with walls and barracks freshly painted after the recent Red Cross inspection to make sure the Third Reich was treating its Jews no worse than commonly accepted. But as soon as the foreign visitors were gone, Terezín's true face emerged.

Moshe arrived after an arduous train journey, and all he wanted was to get some rest. The camp had once been a garrison, very near his native Prague. He and the hundreds of other new arrivals stood in the drizzling rain, uncertain and afraid.

At first glance, it didn't seem too bad. The buildings looked nice, the inmates were not too skinny, and there were no outward signs of violence.

"Maybe it won't be so bad," whispered one of the arrivals as they waited on the platform.

"Maybe," Moshe echoed, but he was doubtful. All he had to do was look down and peek at his mangled left arm to get a glimpse of the Nazis' true intentions. Hope was dangerous. An illusion, no different from the ones Moshe had used to earn his daily bread. An illusion that allowed men and women to march to their deaths. And even as they drew their final breath, they would be thinking, Maybe it won't be so bad.

To Moshe's surprise, he was given a warm welcome at Terezín. As he and the others of his "unit" stood on the platform, he saw a tall, handsome man in a freshly pressed uniform stride toward him. After exchanging a few whispered words with some other officers, he turned to Moshe with a broad smile and an out-stretched hand.

"The Great Zabbatini," said the officer. "A pleasure to make your acquaintance."

Moshe, always the consummate professional, gave a slight bow. "The pleasure is all mine, Commandant," he said.

Nudging one of the other officers with his elbow, the man said: "I told you he was a psychic."

The other man nodded and rubbed his ribs.

Then the officer turned to Moshe and said, "How did you know I was the commandant?"

Moshe hadn't actually known. He had surmised it from the way the man moved, his self-assuredness. And even if he had been wrong, in his experience, no Nazi would object to being called "Commandant."

Moshe simply shrugged and smiled. "Forgive me," he said. "But the inner workings of my mind are a mystery, even to myself."

The inner workings of his mind were actually rather simple: he was so terrified that he thought he might faint. But the camp commander, Siegfried Seidl, was in a cheerful mood. Taking Moshe aside, he proceeded to show him the camp. But the more gentlemanly and gracious he tried to appear, the more uneasy Moshe became. He had learned to be aware of smiling men in uniforms. After so many nights onstage, he had become a hardened performer and knew never to let the audience see his feelings. Also, he suspected that it might be to his advantage to humor the camp commander. Seidl had seen one of Moshe's performances at the Wintergarten, and had been very impressed. He had since followed the magician's career closely, being something of an amateur of the art himself, and had been delighted when he learned that Zabbatini was actually a Jew and was to be deported to Terezín—his kingdom. He had called Gestapo headquarters and requested that the artist should not arrive here without his equipment.

And now it was his turn to impress his idol.

Seidl was very proud of his camp, like a child showing off his new toy. He explained to Moshe that Terezín had been built by Emperor Joseph II, in 1780, and that it was a completely self-sufficient city-fortress. He showed Moshe the Magdeburg Casern, where the "Judenrat," the Jewish council, was situated; he showed him the courtyard, the barracks and, as a not-so-subtle warning, the "death chambers" in the catacombs of the fortress, where the "unfortunate few who succumbed to typhoid" were buried in mass graves, thirty-five to a pit.

Inside an underground tunnel, Seidl and Moshe witnessed a

group of haggard-looking inmates pushing a wagon laden with corpses toward a vast open pit. Other prisoners began unloading the wagon, throwing the emaciated bodies into the gaping mouth. A rabbi was standing against the rough stone wall of the underground chamber, mechanically saying Kaddish, rocking back and forth.

Moshe immediately felt ill. His knees were weak and there was a knot in his stomach. He was reminded of his nights at the Hannover morgue. With each breath the stench of decay entered his body, like a rancid gas. It drove tears into his eyes. The bodies seemed like puppets with broken strings. Their skin was as pale as ash, their limbs were hanging down at grotesque angles, and Moshe thought: That must hurt. But then he reminded himself that they were beyond hurt. He began to feel a sense of awe. And shame. Each of these human deaths made him feel ashamed to be alive. He was ashamed at the thought of transience, at the immeasurable loss of everything each of these men and women ever was and ever could be. Who were they? Who would they have been if he had met them on the street? He felt rage against the thieves who had robbed them of their futures.

Seidl gently put his arm on Moshe's shoulder and turned him away from the pit. "Maybe," he said, "you can teach me a few of your tricks."

Moshe nodded weakly and said, "It would be my pleasure, Commandant."

Seidl considered himself a patron of the arts. The majority of the Jews sent to Terezín were scholars, artists, and musicians. They were encouraged to lead seemingly creative lives. Within the camp, the Nazis had installed parks, flower beds, concert venues, and statues, all to hide the truth—that Terezín was a way station on the road to extinction. Most of the intellectuals here were going to be sent to extermination camps. Sooner or later. Places without parks or concert halls, where the regime showed its true intentions. Moshe had heard rumors back in Berlin, but he had closed his eyes, like so many others, refusing to see. The truth was too bitter. It couldn't be so.

Over the next few days, Moshe slowly got used to daily life in the camp, which held no pleasures, despite the flower beds. It was all unworthy of him, an artist of the highest order. The soup, if you could call it that, gave him the runs. The nights in the barracks were terrible. Moshe had always hated sleeping in the presence of strangers. He constantly woke up from the coughing, the fleas, and the stench of others. All night long, there were sniffles and whispers, cries and prayers. And fear, constant fear.

Roughly one week after his arrival, in the soup line, there was a miracle.

The person in front of him was old and haggard, like so many of the others. He seemed frail, weighed down by the burden of his years and the many injustices of the world. His beard was white. Moshe stared at him. Could it be true?

"Papa?" Moshe said tentatively.

The old man seemed not to recognize him. Was he wrong?

"Papa," Moshe said again, this time louder. "Don't you know me?"

Slowly, the old man turned around. And as recognition lit up his weary, lined face, Moshe could feel hot tears well up in his own eyes.

He took his father into his arms.

Laibl told Moshe how the Nazis had kicked in his door one day and dragged him out of the apartment. Moshe asked what had happened to the Locksmith. He hung himself, his father said, since all his locks had proved useless. Laibl's friend Dr. Ginsky had been forced to wear a pink triangle, which had been his undoing. He was stomped to death by a group of SS men.

As Laibl told him this, he began weeping.

He didn't cry for my mother, Moshe thought bitterly. But he's crying for this doctor.

Laibl took hold of Moshe's maimed arm with both hands and said: "I'm so sorry. . . ."

⚜

Occasionally, Seidl invited Moshe into his luxurious office. After sitting down with a brandy and discussing the finer points of magic, Moshe would perform a few simple tricks for him. One day, Moshe made Seidl's party pin disappear, a small but satisfying act of insubordination. Seidl merely laughed and applauded like an obedient child. Moshe started to teach him, but was careful not to divulge too many tricks at a time, because he quickly realized that his survival depended on how amusing he was to Seidl.

He was Scheherazade, the Persian princess from *A Thousand and One Nights*. And Seidl was the evil King Sharyâr, who married a different woman each night, only to have her killed in the morning. Except, of course, for Scheherazade, who stayed alive as long as she entertained the king with a new story each night.

And so, in Seidl's office in Terezín, Moshe converted all the tricks of the trade he had learned from the Half-Moon Man into his currency for survival. Over time, he taught the commandant about production, the vanish, teleportation, legerdemain, and the art of mentalism. He found himself constantly performing, laughing at stupid jokes, in exchange for another day of life. Another day with his father.

☀

Several weeks passed. Cold, hard, dreary weeks. One day, Laibl contracted typhoid, like so many others. Moshe tended to his father as best he could. It was as if, in the face of death, father and son were making up for lost time.

Like Rifka before him, Laibl was granted the mercy of dying in his son's arms. But his death was neither easy nor painless. It happened at night, in the barracks. Moshe held the frail shape that was once a man.

Laibl was shivering. "Moshe," he said, "it hurts."

Moshe put a finger to his lips and shushed his father, as if the old man was a child.

"I'm scared," Laibl cried out.

"There's nothing to be scared of," Moshe said.

"Where's Rifka?"

After a moment, Moshe said, "She's home. Waiting for you."

He saw that his father was weeping. Is he weeping for her? he thought, or for himself? For all these wasted years?

"When can I see her?" Laibl asked.

"Soon," Moshe said. "Very soon. Tomorrow, maybe."

There was no more tomorrow. At sunrise, Moshe carried his father's body into the death chambers and watched as the man who had raised him was swallowed by the abyss.

He was an orphan now.

※

Moshe continued with his lessons. As long as he did, he was still breathing. His student was not particularly gifted, but he was slowly making progress. Seidl reminded Moshe of an idiot child, grinning, laughing, clapping, delighted and surprised at the obvious. But if he didn't master a trick quickly, he would lose his patience and turn moody. Moshe was a seemingly calm teacher. He had taught himself not to feel. That was a luxury he could ill afford. He was neither happy nor unhappy. He simply was.

That was his true art: living in the shadow of the slaughterhouse and pretending not to notice the slaughter.

It came as no great surprise to him one day when he was told that he would be boarding a train to "the East."

He knew what that meant. Seidl had grown tired of him. The last time Moshe had been in his office, the commandant had seemed listless. Moshe had tried his best, he had joked and fooled around, but Seidl remained distracted, flipping through the papers on his desk.

Moshe had no more secrets left to reveal, having taught Seidl every trick he knew. Scheherazade had told her final tale. Moshe packed his few meager possessions into his trunk, his vanishing trunk, and, together with several hundreds other lost souls, waited for the train that would usher him away from this world.

HIS LAST FIGHT

Several hours later, there was still no news. Max and his family sat around the waiting room at Glendale Memorial. Zabbatini had been brought from the emergency room straight to the operating room, but Max was not allowed to go with him. The doctor, a large Armenian woman with a mane of thick, black hair, named Dr. Arakelian, had told Max in no uncertain terms to stay out. The doctors were doing everything they could.

Zabbatini was in critical condition. Every once in a while, as the giant double doors leading from the waiting room to the operating room swung open, Max could see glimpses of hectic activity. Doctors and nurses were standing around the old man. A machine emitted a drawn-out beeping noise, which didn't sound promising, Max thought. One of the doctors looked as if he was about to climb onto Zabbatini's chest. He placed metal paddles on the old man's chest, gave a signal, and the body jerked upward like a puppet on jangled strings. Then the doors swung shut again. It was like a commercial break on television, when the story is brought to an abrupt stop. Max paced nervously up and down, passing his grandma, who was sitting stiffly on one of the visitors' benches staring at the linoleum floor. Finally he sat down next to her, something he had not done in a long time.

"Grandma?"

She turned to him.

Max cleared his throat and said, "How come you know him?"

Mom and Dad looked up. Dad moved closer to Grandma.

"Yeah," he said. "I'd like to know."

Grandma waved her hand dismissively. *"Ach . . ."* she muttered.

"Mommy!" Dad said in a whiny voice, a voice Max normally couldn't stand. Grandma raised her head and looked at them with an expression of wonder, as if she were seeing the world for the first time.

"He saved my life," she said.

While the doctors and nurses rushed in and out of the operating room, Max and his parents gathered around Grandma.

"Water," she said to Harry. "Give me water. I'm thirsty."

Dad got up and went to the water cooler, filled a paper cup, and brought it over to Grandma, who put it on the table next to her and proceeded to ignore it.

"When the war broke out," she said, "I had only just been born."

"I know," Dad said. "You told me. You were born in Zirndorf—"

"Yes," Grandma said. "In Bavaria."

Max stretched his legs. He had heard all this before. But usually, Grandma's memories were all mixed up, like scrambled eggs. He had never heard her talk like this before. Her voice was clear and calm and steady.

"The war had been going on for a few years, but we didn't notice. Not in Zirndorf. In Zirndorf, there was peace."

"Mommy," Dad said, "don't you want your water?"

"Don't interrupt," Grandma snapped at him. "I'm talking. You never let me finish!"

"Sorry," Dad said. "Go on."

Grandma huffed and continued: "Everything was very peaceful, Mama used to say. We were lucky. We had very nice neighbors, who let my mama and papa stay in their barn. All of a sudden you weren't allowed to be a Jew anymore."

"Not allowed?" Max asked.

"No," Grandma said. "There were laws, and you could break most of them just by being a Jew."

"How is that possible?" Max wanted to know. "How can it be wrong to just be?"

Grandma shrugged. She finally reached for her water, which allowed her to make a dramatic pause.

"The Germans," she said, "made the impossible possible."

She drank; then she put her cup down.

"At the time," Grandma continued, "the Germans were very poor. And Hitler said, 'We will simply take from the Jews.' So they elected him. They stole everything from us. And when there was nothing left to steal, they locked us in ghettos and camps. And they went to other countries, to France and Poland and Russia, to steal everything there, too. The Germans were like magpies—they grabbed everything they wanted."

"What happened next?" Max asked.

"Then they had to kill everyone. It is no good to steal from people and let them live."

"But you said you were all right?"

"Yes," Grandma said. "At first. Our neighbors were decent people: they hid us. Not for free, mind you. My papa paid them money so that they would hide us."

"Ah," said Max.

"After a while, my papa, your great-grandfather, ran out of money to pay our nice neighbors."

"And then?"

"Then they went to the Gestapo. And the Gestapo paid them for my mama and papa."

"What's a Gestapo?" Max asked.

"It was Hitler's secret police," Dad explained.

"You mean, like secret agents?" Max was puzzled. As far as he could tell, secret agents were good. And Hitler was evil. James Bond was good. James Bond would never work for Hitler.

"These were evil agents," Mom explained with a forced smile.

All right, Max thought. I can see that. Even Bond runs into enemy agents once in a while.

"So," Grandma continued, "the Gestapo came to our barn."

"And they wanted you to come out?"

Grandma shook her head. "No," she said. "They wanted us to stay inside."

"But I thought they wanted to steal from you?" Max asked. He was confused.

"They already had," Grandma said. "My papa said that they already took his shop and his money. He was a clockmaker."

"Then what happened?" Max asked.

"They knocked on the barn door. My mama hid me and pressed my mouth shut, so that I couldn't say anything. No one said anything. And they kept knocking and said, 'Come out, Jews!'"

"But you didn't come out?"

"No," Grandma said. "We did not come out. We thought if we just hid under the hay, they would go away."

"And did they?"

"No. They locked the barn from the outside and set fire to it."

Max was shocked. He thought about it for a few moments, then said, "But you survived."

Grandma nodded. "When the fire almost reached us, my papa jumped up and yelled, 'Let us out, let us out!'"

"And did they?"

"They opened the door, and we all came out. Oh, they were laughing! It was very funny," Grandma said, and she herself was smiling at the memory. "Only the neighbors were upset. Their barn burned down."

"Oh no," Max said. He felt almost bad for them, those decent people. They were just trying to make a living.

"What did they do?"

"They complained to the officer who was there, and he wrote them a receipt. The Germans love things like that, receipts. But the neighbors were very upset, very angry."

"And you?"

Grandma shrugged. "My parents were scared, so I was also scared. The whole time, I kept clutching my teddy bear. They put us on the back of a van and brought us to Fürth, to a police precinct. And there we waited."

"What happened then?"

"After a few hours, we were brought with other Jews onto a bigger bus and brought to Munich, to the train station. It was a long ride. And then, from Munich, we were sent to the East."

THE TRICK

I t had been a long and arduous journey for Rosl Feldmann and her parents. First, they had to wait for hours at the train station in the sweltering heat, along with thousands of other people. At first they spoke to one another, but gradually, the talking gave way to exhaustion and heat. Finally, the train arrived. It was a first-class carriage, complete with curtains at the windows and plush seats.

At Dachau, the train slowed down, which was puzzling to Rosl's parents. Dachau? They had been there many times, going to the market or visiting friends. It was strange to them that the train would pass such familiar places. Rosl let her teddy bear look out the window. They stopped at an encampment surrounded by barbed wire. A bad sign. Rosl's father insisted that things couldn't get any worse, not yet realizing that things can always get worse. The world had an infinite capacity for getting worse.

But Dachau was only a short stop along the way. They were headed to a small town in Poland, a place called Oświęcim. The journey took several days, and they were the most uncomfortable days that the Feldmanns had ever endured. The time for plush seats was definitely over. At a station in Poland, they had to board a different train. Along with hundreds of others, Rosl and her parents were herded onto a cattle car. Everyone was unwashed, sweating; many were crying. The air smelled of fear. The only place to relieve yourself was a small bucket in the corner of the compartment. The passengers sarcastically called it "the most beautiful toilet in Poland." The stench was unbearable.

Several hours later, the bucket was overflowing. But Rosl absolutely had to go, and she made her way through the thicket of legs, pressing her teddy bear to her chest. When she finally arrived at the bucket, she began to have doubts. Here? Like this? Perhaps she could hover above the bucket. No easy feat in a moving train. But where was the toilet paper? Looking around, Rosl saw a young man near the bucket, with an arrogant and disdainful look on his face. He was sitting on a large suitcase and was wearing a torn black cape over his striped inmate's uniform. He noticed her gaze.

"What do you want?" he asked harshly.

Rosl stared at the floor. "Nothing," she whispered.

But the man saw her glancing at the bucket, and he understood. He stood up.

"Come here, your highness," he said. "Your throne awaits."

Rosl carefully approached the bucket. Disgusting puddles had formed around it. She could hear flies buzzing, and she fought against nausea. When she was close enough, the man lifted his cape, shielding her from the others.

"Come on," he said. "I won't look."

She held her teddy bear out to him. He sighed, took the bear, and spread his cape again.

"Thank you," Rosl murmured. She tiptoed close to the stinking bucket and carefully pulled down her underwear. Then she squatted down, not too deep, and closed her eyes.

"Hurry up," hissed the man. "I haven't got all day."

"Oh," replied Rosl, who did not appreciate being rushed. "Why, do you have plans? Maybe a walk in the countryside?"

"No," replied the stranger with forced patience. "But my arm is getting tired."

"Ah," Rosl said. This made sense. She noticed that his left arm was deformed. She did her best to hurry.

"Do you have toilet paper?" she asked.

"Of course," said the man. "The rose-scented kind?"

"I'm sorry," Rosl mumbled, feeling stupid. She was surprised when the man suddenly rummaged around in his pocket and handed her a piece of paper. It was an advertisement of some kind. A woman in a white dress appeared to be flying in the air. There were big and colorful letters splashed across the picture, but Rosl was too young to be able to read. She murmured a quick thank-you.

"I'm done," she declared.

"That was my life," the man suddenly said.

"I beg your pardon?" Rosl asked politely, the way her mama had taught her.

"The paper. My life. Everything I ever was. And now . . ." He suddenly sounded sad.

She didn't know what to respond. Hoping to distract him, she said, "What's in your suitcase?"

He managed a smile. "The path to freedom."

Rosl pressed her fists against her waist and said, "That's not true. That would never fit in a suitcase."

"It's magic," he said. "If you crawl into the suitcase, you can get out of here."

She was briefly tempted to believe that.

"Then why don't you just do it?" she asked.

"Because I'm too big. I don't fit into the trunk."

She nodded. That made perfect sense.

"How about you?" he asked with a smile. "Would you like to get out of here?"

She thought about it, but then she shook her head. "I can't," she replied. "I have to stay here and look after my mama and papa." She nodded toward the corner where her parents were leaning against the wall of the train, half-asleep, their mouths open like those of fish in a dry tank.

"And you?" Rosl asked the man. "Where are your parents?"

"They're dead," he replied.

"I'm sorry."

"Don't be," said the man. "They're better off. All of us are trapped here, and only the dead are free."

"And anyone who fits in your suitcase."

"Yes. Of course." Then he said to her, "Would you like me to set your bear free?"

She looked at the bear, and then at the man. Finally she nodded. "Yes, please."

Rosl knew that this was a very serious moment in her life. She would be separated from her bear, perhaps forever. Her whole life he had been with her, protecting her. And now she would have to get on without him. But it was better that way. She hugged her bear one last time, then handed him to the man.

"You should kiss him good-bye," the man said.

She kissed the bear on his furry forehead. Then she put on a brave face and said, "He says he's ready now."

The man opened the suitcase. As far as Rosl could tell, it was completely empty. All she saw was the lining. She peeked inside. It smelled vaguely of old sweat.

"There's no freedom here," she said.

"Watch," the man replied.

The conversation between the little girl and the man in the cape had attracted the attention of the people around them, who craned their necks to see what was going on. The man gently took her teddy bear and placed it in the suitcase. Then he closed it and began mumbling something. His eyes were shut. Suddenly, they snapped open, as if he were awakening from a trance.

"Look closely now," he said.

When he opened the suitcase, the bear was gone. Rosl didn't know whether to laugh or cry. She had never seen anything like it!

But then the man suddenly closed his eyes again. He frowned and began mumbling again.

"What's wrong?" Rosl asked.

The man opened his eyes and said, "He wants to be with you."

With that, he closed the suitcase, only to open it again, moments later. The bear was back! Rosl squealed with delight. She grabbed her bear and hugged it tightly.

The man smiled, and this time, the smile had no trace of sadness. *"Istgahe Ghatar Kojast!"* he said with a slight bow.

"Istgahe Ghatar Kojast," Rosl repeated. "What does it mean?"

"It's Persian."

"But what does it mean?"

"Do you really want to know?"

She nodded.

The man seemed to think for a moment. Then he leaned over and whispered into her ear. "I've never told this to anyone before," he said.

"Really?"

"I read it in a dictionary. It means 'Where is the train station?'"

Rosl laughed. *"Istgahe Ghatar Kojast! Istgahe Ghatar Kojast!"* she cried out in delight. She looked at the man. He was still smiling. "What's your name?" she asked.

He was about to introduce himself by his stage name, but then thought better of it.

"My name is Moshe," he said. "Moshe Goldenhirsch, from Prague."

"My name is Rosl," she said. "Rosl Feldmann, from Zirndorf."

"It is a pleasure to make your acquaintance, young lady." He bowed deeply and pretended to kiss the back of her hand.

Rosl giggled and blushed. "I should get back to my parents," she said.

Moshe Goldenhirsch nodded.

˅ǀ˅

Two days later, they arrived at Oświęcim, that godforsaken place the Germans called "Auschwitz." As the train slowed down, people started peeking anxiously through the small cracks in the boards, trying to gauge what awaited them at their destination.

In the middle of the crowd, a ragged-looking woman with a bulky overcoat struggled to reach Moshe.

"Sir!" cried the woman. "You!"

Moshe looked at her questioningly.

"Help me, please!" the woman said.

Moshe gave a sharp, fake laugh. "Help you?" he asked dismissively. "How can I? I can't even help myself."

The rhythmic stomping of the locomotive was putting him on edge. He was in a bad mood. Irritable. He had the distinct feeling that whatever awaited them at the end of their journey, it wouldn't be good.

The woman came closer, uncomfortably close. "Save my daughter," she said imploringly. "I beg you!"

A little girl was standing behind her. Rosl Feldmann.

Moshe looked at the woman. "Why, what do I get out of it?" he asked coldly.

The woman fell silent. "I have nothing left," she finally said, her voice cracking. "Nothing I could give you . . ."

And then she did something that was utterly mortifying. She fell on her knees. Right next to the bucket. She clutched Moshe's legs and began to sob. "Please save my daughter. . . . Please . . . Your trunk . . ."

Moshe looked around helplessly. The other passengers made a point not to notice. Everyone's mind was on their own survival, their own despair. Wherever Moshe looked, he saw nothing but dull eyes, tears, whispered prayers. And the sobbing woman was still clutching his legs. "I have nothing left in this world. Please. Please save my child."

Moshe just wanted to get out of this awkward situation. "All right," he said. "I'll try."

The woman began kissing his hand, which was even worse than her tears.

"Thank you," she gasped.

Moshe withdrew his hand. The woman got up and ushered her daughter over.

"Hello," Rosl said timidly.

"Hello, Rosl," said Moshe. "Your mother says I should try to set you free."

The girl shook her head. "I want to stay with Mama."

The train suddenly lurched forward. Rosl and her mother almost fell over. Cries were heard all over the compartment. The locomotive was hissing and aching like a dying animal.

Moshe knew that the doors would open at any moment.

So he opened the suitcase. "Now or never," he said.

"Please, Rosl," said the mother. "Do it for me."

But Rosl slung her skinny arms around her mother's neck. Tears were streaming down her face. "No!" she cried. "I want to be with you!"

Moshe noticed a man standing next to them. Probably the father. "Rosl!" he bellowed. "Do what your mother says!"

"No!" Rosl stamped her foot.

Suddenly, Rosl's father slapped her. The girl was astonished. Her cheek turned red. She started sobbing, trying to control her tears and her breathing.

"Go!" her mother hissed.

Rosl, frightened and hurt, nodded and complied. She turned around and crawled into the trunk. She had to struggle. She was still clutching her teddy bear.

Moshe bent down toward her and showed her the button that opened the trunk from the inside. Then he said, "Rosl, listen to me very carefully. Don't move. No matter what happens, no matter what you hear, do not make a sound, and do not come out. You should only come out once everything is quiet."

The girl looked at him, frightened. She nodded. Then she looked at her parents, her eyes filling with tears.

In her father's face, all traces of rage had vanished. Her mother said, "I love you."

Moshe shut the trunk. Not a second too soon. At that moment, the train doors were pushed open. Fresh air blew into the cart. It smelled of ash, and a sweetness that Moshe recognized at once. He heard shouts outside, the barking of dogs. Soldiers started pulling people out of the train. Bit by bit, the cart emptied. Rosl's parents looked at Moshe one last time; then they stepped outside.

None of the people in here paid any attention to the girl in the trunk. A few had seen what happened, but what business was it of theirs? An older man, haggard, Orthodox, looked Moshe in the eyes and allowed himself a brief smile and a nod. Moshe breathed a sigh of relief. The audience knew the trick, but wouldn't betray it. They didn't want to ruin the show.

As the cart emptied, Moshe saw that there were bodies lying on the wooden planks, mainly those of old people. They must have died during the journey. All around him, people were simply walking over them.

Moshe grabbed his trunk and stepped out of the train car. The girl was skinny and didn't weigh much, but Moshe was weakened. The suitcase felt heavy.

It was getting dark outside. Possibly an advantage for Rosl. Too much light could ruin any illusion. Moshe stood, along with thousands of other lost souls, on a vast concrete platform. SS guards were marching up and down, pestering the new arrivals. In front of him, he saw dogs, guns, and barbed wire. The guards were herding the men, women, and children into two lines. Moshe understood what that meant. The last few months had taught him how the Nazis operated. He noticed that all those who looked weak, or were either very young or very old, were in one line. The other line contained people who still looked healthy enough to work. That meant they might still have a chance. Moshe put the trunk down so they wouldn't notice his exhaustion. The SS men were yelling out orders. Moshe saw the girl's mother, who had already looked alarmingly frail on the journey here, being pulled by a black-gloved guard into the line with the old and the weak. Her husband was just about to follow her, but the guard pushed him back.

"Not you!" he yelled.

"Please," said the girl's father. "Let me be with my wife."

"Not you," the SS man repeated.

Very quietly, the man looked the guard in the eyes and said, "Wherever she goes . . . I want to follow her."

The SS man averted his eyes and lowered his hand.

"Thank you," whispered Rosl's father. Then he stepped past the guard into the line on the left, where his wife was. She looked at him as if he'd lost his mind.

Moshe saw the SS man reach for a flask in his uniform pocket and take a deep sip. The look in his eyes seemed haunted, irrational. Then he moved down the line of people to continue the selection. He fought his way forward, yelling, pushing, beating.

Moshe held his breath when the guard approached him.

"To the right," the SS man said. Then he glanced down at the trunk that was standing beside Moshe's feet. "The luggage goes there," he said, pointing toward a large collection of bags, purses, and suitcases about fifteen feet away, at the side of the platform. "Make sure to label it, so we can return it to you after."

A skinny inmate in an ill-fitting uniform handed Moshe a piece of chalk. Moshe wrote "Zabbatini" on the trunk. He wrote with a flourish, as if giving an autograph.

"Zabbatini?" the SS man asked. "What kind of name is that?"

"I'm Persian," Moshe said.

"You're a Jew."

"I'm of Persian descent," Moshe insisted. "The Persians are Aryans."

"You're a Jew," said the SS man. "A piece of shit is what you are, remember that."

Moshe nodded.

"Say it," the guard insisted.

"I'm a piece of shit," Moshe said.

"You have no right to live."

"I have no right to live."

"Very good," said the guard, like a proud teacher who'd just taught his student something useful. Then he nodded and the inmate took the trunk from him. He wanted to put it with the rest of the luggage, but it was heavier than he had expected, and his legs nearly gave out. He moaned.

Moshe looked around. He could see the girl's parents anxiously watching from the left line. The guard noticed that the prisoner was struggling with the trunk.

"What's in the suitcase?" he suddenly bellowed.

"Nothing," Moshe said. "They took everything from me. It's an old model, they're heavy."

The SS man peered at him, unconvinced. "Open it!" he instructed the inmate.

Moshe prayed that the Conradi-Horster's mechanism would not fail him. He forced himself not to look at the girl's parents.

The inmate was struggling with the lock. His fingers were stiff from the cold.

"Open it!" said the SS man with a dangerous tone of annoyance in his voice.

"Yes," said the inmate. He was shivering with fear now as he kept struggling with the lock. And still the trunk wouldn't open.

Growing tired of this sorry spectacle, the SS man drew his gun and shot the inmate in the head. The bang was barely audible over the noise on the platform. A fine spray of blood and yellow tissue blew out of the hole in the man's skull. He crumpled to the ground, his head an open wound. Blood stuck to the trunk.

The SS man walked toward it and pulled it open.

Moshe closed his eyes.

Oh God, he thought. Oh God. Please, God.

His heart was pounding. If the girl was found, they would both be dead.

Then he opened his eyes again.

The SS man was peering into the suitcase. It was dark, and the man was a little drunk, which was good. The guard shook his head.

"Empty," he said. He sounded a tad disappointed.

He waved another two inmates over, who picked up the body of their dead comrade and put it onto a handcart with corpses. The guard carelessly closed the trunk and pushed Moshe forward.

Only then did Moshe dare look at the girl's parents. For a brief moment, he could see the relief in their eyes.

The SS man blew into a whistle. Selection was over. The new arrivals were now neatly lined up in two columns. They started marching. Moshe could see the girl's parents holding hands, then they vanished around a corner.

Before Moshe left the ramp, he cast one last glance at the trunk. It stood unnoticed among the rest of the luggage.

THE LIVING

The door to the operating room opened, and Dr. Arakelian came out. She quickly glanced at a clipboard she had with her; then she looked up.

The Cohns were staring at her. Except for Grandma, who was snoring, her head leaning against the wall. Dad was lying on one of the benches, and Mom was holding Max's hand.

Fifteen minutes ago, mother and son had finally, and for the first time, talked about the argument that had led to Max's escape through the window. About all the nasty things they had said. Up until that point, they had both avoided the subject. Deborah had taken her son into her arms and whispered, "I'm sorry about what I said the other night."

And Max had pressed against her and said, "I'm sorry, too."

Dad looked on, annoyed at the display of family closeness that was happening without him. He tried to move closer to Mom, but she squirmed away.

Dr. Arakelian cleared her throat.

"Are you his family?" she asked.

Max and Mom exchanged nervous glances.

"No," Mom finally admitted. "Not as such. He's more of a houseguest. He has no living relatives."

"I see," Dr. Arakelian replied.

"Is he okay?" Max asked.

Dr. Arakelian shrugged. "We're not sure. He's fine for now, he's stabilized, but his condition could worsen. We're putting him in intensive care. At his age . . ."

"Can we see him?" Deborah asked.

"I don't think it's a good idea," said Dr. Arakelian. "He needs rest."

"Rest?" Grandma said. She had just woken up. "What are you talking about, rest? He's done nothing but lie around." She got up and reached for her purse. "Let's go," she said.

"Intensive care, where is that?" Mom asked.

Dr. Arakelian pointed to an elevator. "Second floor. But visiting hours are over. The man needs rest."

"Nonsense," Grandma said. "He'll be delighted to see me."

"The last time he saw you," Dad carefully interjected, "he had a heart attack."

After some back-and-forth, Dr. Arakelian relented and agreed to a five-minute visit. Even a hardened physician was no match for Grandma's iron will. She said that the patient should not get upset under any circumstances. But she understood that it might do Zabbatini good to not feel abandoned at a time such as this.

The elevator brought them to the second floor. When the doors opened, the Cohns stepped out into a light-green corridor with Monet prints in gilded frames. Dr. Arakelian showed them to Zabbatini's room.

Zabbatini was lying in bed, attached to various tubes and cables. He looked like a dying turtle. A monitor was beeping at regular intervals, and when the Cohns entered the room, he turned his head and smiled weakly.

"Moshe Goldenhirsch," Grandma said, "I never had the chance to thank you."

He gave a dismissive wave of his hand. "Oh," he said, "it was nothing."

"Without this man," she said, "I would not be alive." She pointed to Harry and Max. "And neither of you would have been born."

It sounded almost like a threat to Max. He nodded and said, "Yes, Grandma."

Zabbatini waved Grandma over to his bed. "Could you . . ." he began, but then he coughed. "Could you fluff my pillows?"

Grandma sighed and reached for his pillows. "Men . . ." she muttered under her breath. She carefully took the pillow out from under Zabbatini's head, then shook it vigorously. Then she put it back, gently helping him place his head on it. "You would all be lost without us," she said, but Max could tell she was happy to mother him a little.

She pulled up a chair and sat down beside Zabbatini's bed. They both looked at each other with utter amazement. He still saw in her the little girl from the train, and she saw the haggard, handsome young man.

"That you're alive . . ." Zabbatini whispered, sounding awed.

Grandma nodded; then she reached for her handkerchief and sneakily dabbed at a tear. "I didn't think you made it out of the camps," she said.

"The act of living," Zabbatini said, "is in itself the purest prayer."

"Where did you hear this?"

"My father used to say it," Zabbatini quietly said.

She gently took his hand. He allowed it.

"Tell me how you got out," he said.

Grandma took a deep breath and adjusted her glasses. "So I crawled into the suitcase . . ." she began.

"Yes, the suitcase," Zabbatini said with a smile.

"The path to freedom," Grandma said.

THE SUITCASE FACTORY

Rosl Feldmann didn't feel free at all. She had thought that the trunk would open a magic passageway, leading her somewhere with fresh air and sunshine. But instead, she found herself stuck in a cold, dark, stuffy suitcase. It was like being in a coffin. The false bottom was right above her head. The mechanism now became clear to her. She made herself as small as possible. She tried to control her breathing. It was just like playing hide-and-seek. But this was no game. She knew that if she was found, she would pay for it with her life. From outside, she heard agitated voices, barking dogs, chaos. She felt the trunk being lifted and then carried a few steps. She pressed against the sides with her arms and legs, hoping to avoid being bumped around. The trunk was put down hard on the ground, and then nothing happened for a while. She heard voices talking outside.

She heard someone struggling with the lock. She was gripped

by sudden panic, and she almost screamed. She pressed her hands over her mouth and bit her tongue so that no sound would escape her lips. Moshe Goldenhirsch had told her to be quiet, no matter what. Then she heard voices again, and then a bang. She flinched at the sound, but at the same moment, she regained control over her body. She forced herself to be still with a willpower she never knew she had. Something collapsed next to the trunk. A person?

Suddenly, the suitcase was opened. The false bottom remained in place, but she could feel the air from outside. A terrifying chill came over her. She squeezed her eyes shut and reminded herself that she was invisible. At least, she hoped she was invisible. And apparently, she was. A few moments later, the trunk was closed again. She slowly exhaled with relief. Then, nothing happened. Someone blew a whistle, and, very slowly, the voices and sounds moved away. It seemed to take forever. Her limbs were stiff. Her arms and legs were starting to tingle. Her back ached. She tried to shut out all feelings. She tried to think of something else—the fairy tales her father used to tell her before bedtime, back in Zirndorf. Stories of evil goblins and friendly dwarves. She had to distract herself, because she knew that any false move carried the risk of being found out. At some point, overcome by fear and exhaustion, she fell asleep. It was a brief respite, a short, thin slumber.

Suddenly, the trunk started moving again. She awoke with a start. She was trying to control her breathing. There was sweat on her forehead, cold and clammy sweat. Her arms and legs were numb by now. The suitcase was pulled along roughly. Then it was lifted onto something, perhaps a pushcart. It was lying sideways now. Rosl felt dizzy and increasingly uncomfortable. She moaned, and immediately regretted it.

The girl didn't know it, but she was no longer in immediate danger. The SS guards were otherwise occupied by now. The men who were moving the trunk were camp inmates. With a loud squeaking noise, the pushcart began to move. Rosl wondered where her parents were, and if she would ever see them again. The thought drove tears to her eyes, but she forced herself to stay calm and quiet. She had to keep playing hide-and-seek, no matter what!

Soon the suitcase and its precious cargo were lifted once more, and then they came slamming down on the ground. This time, Rosl was prepared and preventively pushed against the movement, making it easier to absorb the blows. She didn't moan. She didn't make a sound. Distant voices were audible, if only barely. Again, her eyes closed and an uneasy sleep came over her. She drifted away with a feeling of relief.

She had no idea how long she'd been asleep, but at some point, the aching in her arms and legs got so bad that it woke her up. She heard nothing from outside, and she made a decision. She was sick of this uncomfortable hiding place. Moshe Goldenhirsch had told her to come out only when everything was quiet. Well, now it was quiet. She opted to open the trunk and risk a brief glance. Raising her right hand, she pushed the false bottom up. Then, with her other hand, she reached upward and felt around until she found the release button. She gently pressed it. The trunk clicked and the lid opened slightly. Rosl pushed against the top and peeked outside.

She was lying on a large pile of luggage. A mountain of luggage. She had never seen so many bags and suitcases in one place. Each had a name and a few numbers written on it with chalk. She was in a large warehouse of some sort.

What is this place? she thought. It looked like a factory. A suitcase factory.

She could see brick walls and a wooden ceiling. Lights were hanging from the ceiling, illuminating the room. In the middle of it were large tables, with some open suitcases on them.

Rosl heard sounds, and quickly pulled the trunk shut.

She didn't see the group of inmates enter the warehouse, escorted by two SS men. The inmates began dragging pieces of luggage from the pile toward the tables. The men in uniform watched as the inmates opened the cases and started digging through them. Clothes and personal items were carelessly tossed aside. Money, gold, and jewelry were brought to another man in uniform, who had come in a little later and had taken a seat at a small table. He examined the valuables, noting them in a huge ledger in front of him. The two guards were chatting with each other, even as they kept their eyes on the inmates.

They were standing near Rosl's trunk. Rosl heard snatches of their conversation, something about the results of a soccer match. She had heard the clattering of the luggage, and she was trying to guess what was happening outside. One thing, however, was clear: she couldn't risk crawling out, not now. She had to wait. But she wasn't sure how much longer she could endure it.

When the trunk was picked up, her heart started thumping.

What will they do to me? she wondered. Will they kill me? Or send me back to my mama and papa? That would be nice, but it seemed unlikely.

They would probably kill her. She closed her eyes and tried to imagine what being dead would be like. She had no idea. Maybe it was like sleeping, except that you didn't wake up again. That wouldn't be so bad. She'd probably find out soon enough.

She was carried a few feet and then put back down. And then, a moment later, the latch was opened. Bony fingers reached inside and touched the false bottom. Rosl found herself staring into a haggard face. The man's eyes widened with surprise. The face was so thin it reminded her of a skull. She felt sorry for the man. She raised one finger up to her lips.

The prisoner reacted quickly. He moved his skinny body slightly in front of the open trunk, to block the view. Then he quickly picked up an old blanket and threw it over her. Rosl understood. She made herself as small as possible and curled herself up into the dirty wool blanket. Suddenly, she heard footsteps.

"What do you have there?" the voice asked.

"Nothing," the inmate replied with terror in his voice.

"Let me see."

"Nothing but old clothes."

After a few seconds of silence, she heard the voice saying, "Get on with your work."

She could feel the inmate's hands reach for her, as if she were nothing but a bundle of rags. The man pulled her out of the trunk and placed her on something soft. A pile of clothes. More clothes were thrown on top of her, and soon she was completely covered. She slowly and carefully stretched out her aching limbs, hoping that no one would see her move.

Then she fell asleep again. This time, lying in the midst of all these soft clothes, her sleep was deep and restful.

She felt a movement, and it woke her up. She was still lying in the middle of the pile of clothing, but now she seemed to be on a pushcart. She could hear the wheels squeaking. She could smell fresh air, and she felt the cold night around her. Suddenly, the cart was raised up at one end and the pile slid off. She let out a scream, unable to stop herself, as she felt herself dizzily falling. But she landed softly.

She tried to control her breathing and the wild beating of her heart. She waited a few minutes before digging her way to the top, toward the fresh air.

She was in the middle of a garbage pile, surrounded by clothes, pieces of luggage, shoes, glasses, and personal items, as well as human excrement. The smell was awful. She looked around, but saw no one. As far as she could tell, she was alone in a desert of waste, outside the camp. In the distance, she saw barbed wired fences and spotlights. Then she passed out.

※

When Rosl Feldmann woke up again, the sun was rising. It was much warmer now, and the sweet sunlight brought hope to her heart. She could see the world again. Then she heard sounds. Someone was rummaging through the garbage. Her heart skipped a beat.

She curled up and dug as deep as she could into the blanket she had been wrapped in, hoping that no one would see her. Suddenly, before she could react, the blanket was torn off her, and she lay shivering and exposed in the glaring light.

It was a man. He was dressed in dirty rags. He flinched back when he saw her. Then, suddenly, he lurched forward and grabbed her. His grip was hard. She couldn't make out his face; he seemed like a shadow to her. He lifted her up and carried her away.

A short while later, they reached the edge of a forest. He roughly put her down on the ground. Then he crouched in front of her. He said something to her, but she couldn't understand his language.

She did understand one thing, however: his outstretched hand. She reached for it. He led her into the forest.

They walked like this, hand in hand, for about half an hour. Then they reached a path in the forest, and the man followed it. Soon, they left the woods behind and came upon a small village. It was early morning, and everything here seemed peacefully asleep.

The man had put his smelly cloak over her shoulders. He pulled her close and walked with her toward a small church. Next to the church was a white two-story house. The man knocked at the door. No one answered. He knocked again and again, until, at last, the door opened.

When Rosl looked up, she saw a black shape looming in the doorway. The man and the black shape exchanged a few hurried words in their odd language. Then Rosl was pushed into the house, and the door closed behind her. The man was gone. Rosl looked at the black shape. It looked like a ghost, wrapped entirely in black cloth. Rosl's gaze went up and down, and then she noticed a pair of feet sticking out from under the dark clothing. She saw leather shoes. Women's shoes.

The ghost began talking to her, but she couldn't understand a single word. When the black shape bent down, Rosl was finally able to make out a human face. It was an old woman. There was a kind glimmer in her eyes, and she wore a crucifix around her neck. She smiled at Rosl, and Rosl smiled back.

THE FINAL CURTAIN

Grandma paused for a moment and glanced around the hospital room. Her family and the old magician were looking at her.

Zabbatini nodded. "She was a nun?"

"Yes," Grandma said. "There was a monastery in the village. The ragpicker had found me in the trash and brought me there. The nuns hid me until the war was over. They taught me Polish, and they taught me about their faith."

She looked at Zabbatini. The man to whom Rosl Cohn, née Feldmann, owed her survival looked exhausted. He leaned back in his hospital bed.

"What happened to my mama and papa?" she asked him, and her voice was suddenly that of a child again.

Zabbatini shook his head slowly. "They were in the left line," he said.

She nodded, knowing what that meant.

"The last I saw, they were being marched off." He looked at Rosl. "They were holding hands."

For a moment, no one spoke.

And then, in a barely perceptible whisper, she said, "Thank you. You saved me."

Zabbatini smiled.

"No," he said. "You saved *me*."

It was after midnight when they left the hospital. They drove in Deborah's Jeep Cherokee to Mickey's Pizza Palace, so that Dad could pick up his car, which he had left there. Then they said good-bye. Harry brought his mother back to Encino. Deborah and Max went home.

"Do I have to go to school on Monday?" Max said. It couldn't hurt to ask.

"Yes," Mom said with a sharp edge to her voice. "You do."

"But why?" Max said.

"So that you learn something useful." And under her breath, she added, "So you don't grow up to be a magician."

When Max saw the empty guest room at home, he felt a tinge of sadness. He hoped the old man would recover soon.

But now it was late. Mom tucked Max in and gave him a good-night kiss. "Happy birthday," she said, and turned off the light.

Max fell asleep at once.

ᐧᐧᐧ

When Max went to school on Monday, he felt like the star witness in a mob trial. Suddenly, he was all the rage. Joey Shapiro couldn't wait to hear what had happened with Zabbatini. This was, without a doubt, the coolest birthday party he had ever been to.

Max told him how he got to ride in the ambulance, how he was privy to Zabbatini's fight for life in the operating room. He painted a vivid picture.

"Then what happened?" Joey asked.

"We visited him in his room."

Max told the story of how Zabbatini had saved his grandma's life. Joey was deeply impressed.

During lunch break, Myriam Hyung and about a dozen other kids surrounded him. Max Cohn was a star. At least for one day.

After school, Dad picked him up. They went to Baja Fresh, and Max ordered a cheese quesadilla. Dad took out a pen and paper from his briefcase.

"What are you doing?" Max asked.

"I'm making a list," Dad said.

"Of what?"

"Of all the people who wouldn't be alive if Zabbatini hadn't done what he did."

Besides Max and his dad, there were Grandma, Uncle Bernie, and Max's cousins Esther, Mike, and Lucas.

Dad whistled and leaned back in his plastic chair. "Seven people," he said. "Wow." He gazed at his son.

Max shrugged as he ate a slice of avocado. It was not necessarily a good thing that his stupid cousins were on the list.

"None of us would have ever been born," Dad said. "He stared out the window over Los Feliz Boulevard, with its traffic and cars, and watched the stark clear light of the midday sun reflecting on the windshields outside.

∿

Max was sitting in front of the TV, playing a video game, when the call from the hospital came. Mom picked up the phone. She had come back from a meeting at her attorney's office, unusually tense even by her standards, and had started frantically cleaning the house, a sure sign that she was agitated and uncertain.

The divorce papers were lying on her desk, unsigned as of yet. Deborah felt conflicted. She was unwilling to forgive Harry's affair with the yoga instructor. But she also knew that Max needed his father more than ever. And last Saturday, he had been there for his son, no question about it. She was wondering if their marriage could possibly survive. But the trust between him and her had been irrevocably broken. She needed more time.

"Good news," her attorney had said when he called her that morning. "The judge approved the divorce. I have the papers right here. Now you both need to sign. And then it's over."

And then it's over.

When Deborah hung up the phone, she was deep in thought. That afternoon, she had driven to Woodland Hills, to Mr.

Gutierrez's office. When she came in, Harry was already there. He looked pale.

"Let's roll," Mr. Gutierrez said cheerfully, and clapped his hands.

"Great," Harry said, without much enthusiasm.

Deborah just nodded.

Mr. Gutierrez laid out the papers and held out a pen.

"Who wants to go first?" he asked.

Harry and Deborah looked at each other. Neither of them made a move.

Mr. Gutierrez frowned.

After some awkward stammering, it was decided that Deborah should take the divorce papers with her. She could read them through carefully at home, sign them, and then send them back.

But instead, she was cleaning. She was wiping the windows, wearing yellow rubber gloves, when the phone rang.

When his mother took the call, Max looked up from his video game. A minute or so later, she came into the living room. Max immediately knew that something was up: he could tell by the look on her face. He put down his paddles and watched as she took off her rubber gloves.

"What?" he asked, with a trace of fear in his voice.

"Come here," she said gently.

He came over to her. She hugged him.

"There's something I have to tell you," she said, and even before she began, Max knew what it was.

The Great Zabbatini tremendously enjoyed dying. Dr. Arakelian, who realized the end was near, had generously agreed to keep her patient medicated on morphine during his final hours. There was no point in letting him suffer. His heart was too weak—it could give out at any moment. As soon as the morphine flowed through his veins, his mood improved. He felt a sense of calm and warmth. Like a newborn baby. When the nurse came in to check on him, he thought he was seeing Julia Klein again. His eyes widened in surprise. He feebly raised his hand and gave a short moan. The nurse bent over him, and Zabbatini felt as if it was his Persian princess. His mind tumbled back in time, to the moment when he had bent over her and kissed her mouth. Now it was she who bent over him. He closed his eyes, and her lips touched his, and nothing was ever softer or sweeter.

"I love you," he whispered.

"I'm sorry?" said the nurse. She looked at him. Was he talking about her or someone else? She shook her head. Dying patients said the darnedest things.

In actuality, the patient was already somewhere else by now. It was all so easy. All he had to do was let go.

He could still feel Julia's hand on his old, withered cheek. Her eyes looked deep into his, and she said, "All is forgiven."

So that, he realized, was dying. To forgive life. To forgive the living. No more yesterdays, no more todays, no more tomorrows.

All he heard was silence. All he felt was peace.

Standing next to Julia were his father and mother. And, to his surprise, the Locksmith from upstairs.

His parents had come to say good-bye. All three of them.

Tears welled up in his eyes, and he held out his hand. "You're here . . ." he said.

Laibl, who in death had fully recovered from the wounds of life, took his son's hand into his own, a gesture of tenderness he had rarely afforded him when he was among the living. The Locksmith was looking at him, touched. His mother was smiling at her son. She was humming a song. A simple melody, the same one she had sung to him when he was a newborn in his crib.

Far above in the distant sky
The wind carried a lonely cry
Far above, where eagles fly

And now, at the end of a very long journey, little Moshe Goldenhirsch of Prague, who had crossed an ocean and a century, had finally reached home.

THE WAY THINGS ARE

Moshe Goldenhirsch didn't have any relatives. There were no heirs. His life insurance was barely able to cover the hospital bills and the cost of the funeral. Deborah and Harry decided that it would be the decent thing to do to arrange his funeral.

Mom bought Max a dark suit jacket and insisted he wear it. Max felt ridiculous in that thing. The funeral was held at Forest Lawn. A yellow decal with the word FUNERAL had been placed on the windshield of Mom's car. It was a warm sunny day in Southern California, a harsh contrast to the coldness in Max's heart.

When they reached the shady, treelined cemetery, Max could see that there were very few mourners present. Throughout his life, the Great Zabbatini had collected and discarded friends and lovers with callous ease. There was hardly anyone who remembered him, and even fewer who wished to bid him farewell. Max saw Ronnie, the manager of the King David, and next to him was Luis from the magic shop. Plus a few colleagues and staff members from the Magic Castle who Max didn't know.

Mom parked the car and together they walked to a small non-denominational chapel. Dad and Grandma were already waiting. Dad was dressed in his best suit, and Grandma was wearing her dark blue dress. Max was surprised to see Myriam Hyung and her parents. He was even more surprised that seeing her made him happy.

The ceremony was simple and short. The rabbi was a small Orthodox man with a bushy beard and watery eyes. He shook everyone's hand except Mom's and Grandma's. He was not allowed to touch women. Mom was miffed and withdrew her outstretched hand.

Everyone sat down. The wooden benches were cool and uncomfortable.

"We are here today," the rabbi began, "to bid farewell to. . ." He paused and looked at a piece of paper.

"Goldenhirsch," Dad interjected. "Moses Goldenhirsch."

"Right," the rabbi said. "Moses Goldenhirsch." He murmured a few perfunctory words in Hebrew.

Then, an assistant in a workman's blue overalls wheeled out the coffin, a simple, small pine box on a metal stretcher.

"There he is!" said the rabbi cheerfully, as if a long-awaited guest had finally arrived. Then he loudly proclaimed, "In death, we are all the same. Prince or pauper."

The coffin seemed too small to hold an entire life, Max felt. He was surprised that the Great Zabbatini and all that he ever was could fit into such a small box.

There's not much left at the end, he realized.

The rabbi asked who would push the stretcher outside. Dad looked at Max, and they got up.

They both put their hands on the cool metal and started pushing the coffin out the double doors and onto a tar path leading into the cemetery. It was heavier than Max had expected.

It's hard work, he thought, burying the dead.

An employee in a neon-yellow outfit, like that of a traffic cop, walked slowly and somberly in front of them, guiding the way.

Soon, they reached an empty grave. Next to it was a pile of earth. A huge excavator stood by the gravesite. Two workers were leaning against the giant machine, watching the procedure with disinterest.

When the funeral procession had gathered around, the workers picked up the coffin, using two straps, which they placed underneath the wooden box. They slowly lowered it into the ground, his final resting place.

There goes Zabbatini, Max thought darkly. It was hard for him to say good-bye. Although he had only known the old man for a brief time, it was like saying farewell to an old friend.

When the coffin was in the grave, the workers drew the straps out and rolled them up. The rabbi took out his prayer book and began to chant in Hebrew.

"And so we bid farewell," he finally proclaimed in English, "to Moses Goldenhirsch, a good soul, and a true son of Israel."

Dad took a shovelful of earth and dropped it onto the coffin. It sounded like a gust of rain against a window. Max did the same. Then Mom, then Grandma, and then the others.

The rabbi asked, "Who will say Kaddish?"

Dad cleared his throat and stepped forward. He nodded at the rabbi and wrapped a prayer shawl around his head—the only other time he had ever worn it was at his bar mitzvah, to which Zabbatini of course hadn't come. He began to tentatively sing in Hebrew. Gradually, Dad's voice became stronger, more assured. Then Grandma joined in. Then Mom did. Then Uncle Bernie. Then Aunt Heidi and her kids, his cousins. And at last, Max joined in as well.

When he looked at Mom and Dad he saw, to his surprise, that they were holding hands, something he hadn't seen in many months.

What's going on? he thought.

Mom glanced at him and reached out to him. Max took her hand. On his left side stood Myriam Hyung, who also held out her hand. Max hesitated—Myriam was a girl, after all—but then he touched her hand and held it. The longer he listened to the Hebrew words, the calmer he became. Max hadn't felt this peaceful in a long time. He had no idea what the future held, but he knew now that his parents loved him, and somehow, they were going to get through it all.

He stared into the dirt and darkness of the grave, as if he were waiting for Zabbatini to appear, as if the coffin had been empty all along and the old man's death had been an illusion.

And so their voices rose up together, the voices of the living, who never would have been alive had it not been for Moshe Goldenhirsch and his trick.

When Max looked up and saw the sunlight streaming through

the trees, he understood, with sudden clarity, that he owed this man more than just his life. The Great Zabbatini had given him a glimpse of the wonders and beauty of the world.

This wasn't a trick, Max realized.

It was a miracle.

THE

END

ACKNOWLEDGMENTS

Before you put the book aside, I'd like to offer a few words of gratitude. Most of all, I want to thank *you*, dear reader. You never know what you're going to get when you pick up a book. If you made it this far, I'm hoping it was worth it, and so I wanted to thank you for your trust.

I also would like to thank my parents, who divorced when I was a child, which inspired this story in the first place. They are otherwise wonderful and loving parents, which is a pity, because an unhappy childhood is probably the greatest gift that parents can give their children. (At least if you want to be a writer.) I also want to thank my brothers, Gabriel and Gideon. Just because they're always there for me and because I'm proud of them.

In addition, I'd like to thank the teachers who have inspired me along the way. Especially Mrs. Schorr, my German teacher in Saarbrücken, Germany, who treated her students as if they were her own children, and who showed me that grammar can be fun. At the time, it seemed like a wasted effort. I'd also like to thank Professor Julio Torres for teaching me the categorical imperative, which changed my life, and Professor Rhonda Guess at Los Angeles City College, who was an incredible inspiration in my life, and who taught me so much about journalism and the craft of writing.

I'd like to thank Elke Corsmeyer, a bookstore owner in Gütersloh, Germany, who, by a strange coincidence, came across the original English-language manuscript and submitted it to Diogenes Verlag in Switzerland. Without her help, the manuscript might never have found a home. A great big thank-you to my fearless editor in Berlin, Margaux de Weck, who helped turn the manuscript into an actual book. And my heartfelt thanks to Philipp Keel, the publisher at Diogenes, who wasn't afraid to risk everything for this story, and who took it all the way to America and the rest of the world. And of course, I'd like to thank Marc Koralnik, my agent and my good friend.

I wrote the first draft of this book in Los Angeles in 2007, in about six weeks, working mainly at night and encouraged by my friend Brian Forbes. At the time, I was broke and underemployed, and working on this story kept me sane. And after so many years of polite rejection letters, it's still amazing to me that it was actually published. The fact that you can now hold it in your hands is owed to Judith Curr and the incredible Johanna Castillo at Atria Books. Thank you, Johanna, for your faith in this story, and a great big thank-you to Elaine Colchie for her incredible work editing the final English draft. I'd also like to thank Melanie Iglesias Pérez at Atria for her support.

And of course, I want to thank the magicians: Andrew Goldenhersh in Los Angeles, who permitted me to use his name; Ashley

ACKNOWLEDGMENTS

Springer in Brooklyn, who helped me with my questions; and of course Dr. Oliver Erens in Stuttgart, Germany, who was my advisor in all things magical. He taught me the history of stage magic, and he helped me design the tricks in this book. To that end, I'd also like to point out the incredible book *Hiding the Elephant* by Jim Steinmeyer, which was a great help and inspiration.

And from the bottom of my heart, I'd like to thank my beloved Lily. You are a blessing in my life.

ABOUT THE AUTHOR

Photo © Philipp Rohner / © Diogenes Verlag

Emanuel Bergmann was born in Germany and is a journalist and translator. He has been living in Los Angeles since 1990. A bestseller throughout Europe, *The Trick* is now being published in several countries.

THE TRICK

EMANUEL
BERGMANN

Reading Group Guide

This reading group guide for The Trick *includes an introduction, discussion questions, and ideas for enhancing your book club. The suggested questions are intended to help your reading group find new and interesting angles and topics for your discussion. We hope that these ideas will enrich your conversation and increase your enjoyment of the book.*

INTRODUCTION

When the son of a rabbi walks into the tent of a traveling circus, his life is changed forever. Mesmerized by the Half-Moon Man and his beautiful assistant, he decides to leave home and train as a magician, eventually rising to fame under the stage name the Great Zabbatini. As Europe descends into World War II, Zabbatini is discovered to be a Jew, and his battered trunk full of magic tricks becomes his only hope for survival.

Seventy years later in Los Angeles, ten-year-old Max finds a scratched-up LP that captured Zabbatini performing his greatest illusions. But the track in which Zabbatini performs the spell of eternal love—which Max believes will keep his parents from getting divorced—is damaged beyond repair. Desperate for a solution, Max seeks out the Great Zabbatini. What he finds instead is an elderly, cynical magician in need of redemption who no longer believes in anything.

TOPICS AND QUESTIONS FOR DISCUSSION

1. From the beginning of *The Trick*, Moshe Goldenhirsch's story is woven like a fairy tale—a stark contrast to his reality when Max finds him at the King David Home for the Elderly in Los Angeles. How did this affect your perception of the magician? How did meeting Moshe Goldenhirsch affect Max's belief in the Great Zabbatini?

2. How does Dr. Ginsky's reaction to Rifka reflect the sociopolitical environment of that time period? How did his demeanor change when she mentioned that her husband was Laibl Goldenhirsch? Consider how this scenario might have played out today. How would you have reacted?

3. At the core of *The Trick* are themes of fathers and sons, identity, and coming-of-age. How did Rifka's secret affect Moshe's relationship with Laibl, the Locksmith, and the Half-Moon Man? Compare this to Harry and Max's relationship. How did Moshe and Max's relationship affect each of them?

4. On page 53, "Max realized for the first time that people had wounds you couldn't see." What are the invisible wounds

each of the characters carry with them? (Moshe's parents, Max's parents, the Great Zabbatini, Max's grandmother, etc.) How does it affect their beliefs, the way they see the world, and how they interact with one another?

5. On page 77, Deborah shouts at her son: "I should have had that abortion—then I wouldn't have to deal with any of this!" What do you think of Max's reaction to his mother's outburst? How would you have reacted in that moment?

6. How is grief handled in *The Trick*? How do the characters mourn when Rifka passes away, when Max's grandmother survives the death camp, when Max's parents announce they're getting divorced? How does this parallel the invisible wounds they carry and impact their ability to move on?

7. Moshe has an emotional reaction to seeing the Statue of Liberty when he first arrives in the United States. The Statue of Liberty has become a powerful symbol for incoming humanitarian refugees. How was seeing the Statue of Liberty upon arrival different from the airports that receive them now? What happens when those ports aren't as welcoming as they had hoped?

8. Compare the challenges that young Moshe struggled with in Europe versus the problems Max faces in Los Angeles. Can they be compared? Despite the difference in gravity, do they weigh equally on each boy?

9. Disappearing is a common theme in *The Trick*, whether literally or metaphorically. Discuss its effect in each instance.

10. Max believes with his whole heart that the Great Zabbatini's eternal love spell will keep his parents together, but the magical whimsy of a child can only go so far. What would have actually saved their marriage? What caused Deborah and Harry's relationship to fall apart?

11. Piles of suitcases are often shown in pictures of the Holocaust as a symbol of death. How, in *The Trick*, do they represent life?

12. For Max's grandmother, it's important to share her past and the story of how she survived the Holocaust. Have you heard similar stories from your grandparents? Do you think it's important to preserve our family history and continue to pass it down from generation to generation?

ENHANCE YOUR BOOK CLUB

1. *The Trick* recalls the melancholy humor of Isaac Bashevis Singer's stories and Jonathan Safran Foer's *Everything Is Illuminated*, and the heartbreaking pathos of the film *Life Is Beautiful*. Read those titles and watch the film with your book club for comparison. What are the similar themes that occur? Compare and contrast how each book approaches them.

2. The Great Zabbatini's actions during the war create a ripple effect that trickles down to Max Cohn's very existence. Do you know of any such event in your family history? Follow up on the lives of refugees and survivors that have been mentioned in the news. How have their lives been impacted by an act of kindness of this magnitude? How many more weren't as lucky?

3. To learn more about Emanuel Bergmann, read reviews of *The Trick*, find him on tour, and become a fan of his Simon & Schuster author page at http://www.simonandschuster.com/authors/Emanuel-Bergmann/2115017483.